Abalim

Alien Legacy Brotherhood, Volume 1

Keri Kruspe

Published by StarChance Publications, 2024.

ABALIM

First edition. April 17, 2024.

ISBN: 979-8989838608

Written by Keri Kruspe.

Table of Contents

Chapter One

O utside Galaxy's Pub at dusk
      Abalim glanced at his handheld to make sure he was in the right place. Yep, Galaxy's Pub in the village of Kijiji on the planetoid Hiigar. He looked up and down the deserted, dusty street, hoping to see someone, anyone, that could verify if this was the right place. He chuckled. Yeah, like anyone on this goddess-forsaken planetoid would know where he was supposed to be.

He eyed the disreputable building next to the two-story structure that was as run-down looking as this one. The only encouraging sign was the symbol of "AoA" prominently displayed in red and yellow across the archway.

"JR15, are you sure this is the place someone claimed they saw one of the missing human women?"

He glanced at the small droid resembling an Earth spider resting on his shoulder. That is, if the spider had a green-and-silver metallic body and four legs instead of eight. The little bot quivered as if afraid to voice an opinion.

"JR15?" Abalim gentled his voice as he addressed the fledging robot. He was careful not to startle the little guy since it'd only started operating a month ago. "It's okay. Just access the programming your father installed within you before we left."

It amazed him how two other bots created his companion. JR10 and his "mate," JR11, made a small batch of these machines to help Abalim and his brothers as they scoured the galaxy to search for the missing women kidnapped from the Zerin spaceship, *StarChance*.

JR10 insisted these little bots call him "Father" and JR11 "Mother".

How strange the universe had gotten when droids wanted to be parents.

Another shocking thing he discovered was that Earth was now "recognized" by the Federation Consortium, the ruling body of the galaxy.

While the planet was still in a protected status, the government admitted they'd offered human women in secret to hundreds of species in the galaxy that faced a severe shortage of females.

Why women were in such short supply was something Abalim wasn't privy to, but then he doubted anyone else had any idea why that happened, either. His sister-in-law—Inanna, the Queen of Akurn, a brilliant geneticist and a biologist in her own right—offered to look into the problem facing so many humanoid species.

She and her consort, Abalim's brother Adapa, agreed to become part of the groundbreaking research team with the galactic body, but before they did, they insisted the human women missing from the Exchange had to be found first. Only then would the queen put her considerable talents into finding out what caused the dwindling female problem.

To help her work on it with a clear conscience, Abalim and his brothers volunteered to search the known galaxy for the missing women.

It's not like he had anything better to do. Having time traveled over seven thousand years left him and his three other brothers at loose ends. Since Akurn and Earth had become allies, the threat of a battle between them, and of destroying Earth, was long gone. Which left the siblings with nothing to do.

The four of them were new to the modern world and totally useless for the worldwide cleanup efforts after the close brush with an alien invasion. With their newfound freedom, they needed a goal to help focus on who they were deep inside. And the best way to do that was to give them a purpose. Something they'd never experienced before.

It was strange to have control over his own future. Even so, Abalim was more than happy they'd agreed to split up to look for those missing women. He might love his brothers, but they'd grown up together, never alone except at night since they were small children. The freedom to choose his next step without having to consult their small group would be liberating. He'd finally discover who he truly was without worrying about being judged and teased if anything he did was considered lacking. Not that he didn't retaliate. Usually when they least expected it.

"Yes, Mister Abalim, sir. The last known whereabouts of the human known as Althea MacGregor was here at the Galaxy's Pub."

Abalim tilted his head, straining to hear what the bot said in his soft tones. Damn, he wished for the umpteenth time he could psychically read the bot. But JR15 wasn't organic, so he couldn't. Skipping the whole talking process would make working together easier.

He grunted and didn't correct the bot when he called him "mister". No matter how many times he encouraged the robot to call him by his given name, the little guy just shuddered, agreed, and then reverted to formal address in the next sentence.

"Thank you, JR15. Appreciate it." Abalim put his handheld computer tablet into his jacket pocket. "Why don't you hide before I go in?"

JR15 squeaked and scrambled to his favorite place under Abalim's dreadlocks at the nape of his neck. It was a perfect place for the droid to settle so no one could see him.

His pointy little legs were light enough when he moved, it was like a whisper across Abalim's skin.

Abalim passed through the entrance's light force field, and he was greeted by a humongous humanoid male with wide flat feet that tapered up to thick thighs. His gaze traveled up the giant's body that thinned at the shoulders and held a head with a triangle shape.

A single large yellow eye surrounded by downy feathers for lashes dominated the being's features. A row of bright canary-yellow feathers formed a mohawk down his skull.

"Are you Flygir?" Goddess, he hoped so. Princess Aimee of Zerin was quite insistent he ask this giant for help once he reached Hiigar.

"Who's yous?"

"My name is Abalim. Princess Aimee said you'd be able to help me."

"*Pretty!* Is where my Pretty?"

This high-pitched squeal came from one of the strangest looking females Abalim'd ever seen. At first glance, he'd swear the petite little female was barely out of pubescence.

She wore a simple loose black tie and a white blouse tucked haphazardly into a short pleated skirt. On her feet were small-heeled black shoes paired with white thigh-high stockings. Her light-pink skin matched her neon-bright-pink-and-black hair that floated around her as if it had a mind of its own.

The sight of her two sets of arms took him aback. But it was her wide-set pink eyes with shimmering highlights in their black pupils that gave him pause.

Since landing on Hiigar, he'd kept his psychic abilities under a tight leash. But standing in front of these two, he opened his senses a crack to get a feel for who he dealt with. The male was a creature called an Orisha, while the female was a Merkaba. Waves of intelligence and a personality of iron from them both told him all he needed to know. These were the people he was supposed to find.

With a hand over his heart, he gave a slight bow and pretended he didn't know who they were. "I am Abalim from planet Earth here to see Flygir or Hayami. Are they here?"

"Why's yous want's 'em?" The large Orisha male crossed his arms over his thin, wide chest.

"JR15, please come out and display the video for our hosts."

The bot's tiny pointed feet scuttled from behind his head and rested on his shoulder, shivering all the way.

Abalim wished he could send the small thing a psychic sense of calm. All he could do was encourage the small droid. "It's alright. Go ahead."

"Okay, Mister Abalim, sir. If you say so."

The bot folded his legs under him and opened his top eye until it glowed and transmitted a holographic, full-length, 3-D image of Princess Aimee.

If he wasn't mistaken, the female might have once been a human. But looking at her now, you wouldn't know it.

From her sleek brown hair with the wide white stripe on one side, now tucked into a loose braid behind her, to her tanned skin that had a slight iridescent sheen to it. Like a human, she had single-colored eyes, but instead of one solid color, hers had an unusual combination of vibrant green with hints of golden-brown flecks. Nestled at her left temple was an intricate tattoo with a clear crystal in the middle. And she had four fingers instead of the three that a normal Zerin had.

"Hi Hayami and Flygir! I hope you guys are doing okay. I sure miss you." The image clapped. "Baby Ryox is doing fine and demands to see Auntie Hayami all the time." She clasped her hands together as a serious look came over her face. "Listen, there were more human women kidnapped from the Exchange than we knew. This is Abalim, and we've sent him to find one of them, a woman by the name of Althea MacGregor. We'd gotten a thin lead that she ended up at the Galaxy's Pub like I did. Huh, who'd have thunk that'd happen? Anyway, please help him as much as you can, so he can find her. Thanks, and let me know when you can visit again. Love you both to the universe and back!" The image of the Princess gave a cheery wave before it dissolved.

"Miss happy is she Pretty!" The girlish Merkaba clasped her upper hands together while her lower ones wrapped around her slim waist.

It took a moment before Abalim realized Hayami had called Princess Aimee *Pretty* instead of using her name.

"All's right. You's can come in." Flygir gestured with his beefy hand for Abalim to enter the smoky pub. "Sit's there." He pointed to a small vacant table by the stage. "Hayami bring's you's somethin' to drink." Flygir's head whipped around when a loud squeal caught his attention. "You's!" He wagged a thick finger at an escalating argument between two small aliens on the other side of the room. He lumbered off in their direction.

"Yes!" Hayami clapped both sets of hands. "There sit you. Bring I drink like humans do." She skipped away, but whirled around and looked at the stage behind him. "Oh! Sweets, here human you see!" She gave a negligent wave to the female on the stage who'd been drumming on a six-stringed musical instrument.

Abalim glanced at the female, who looked like a typical Zerin.

Iridescent light skin, and a purple tattoo on her left temple with a clear crystal in the middle. Her rich sable-brown hair rested over her shoulders in a sleek cascade of curls.

He sat back on the comfortable chair and watched the woman put her instrument down. It wasn't until she tucked some hair behind it that he realized her ear didn't swoop up to a point. Nor did she have just three fingers. She had four.

Her sable eyebrows rose. "Oh?" She looked at him.

He was so close to the stage it wasn't hard to hear her.

"You're here to see me?" She pointed to herself.

Abalim scratched the side of his scruffy jaw. "Well, I'm looking for a human woman by the name of Althea MacGregor. You wouldn't know where she is, do you?"

Her joyful laugh made him smile.

She stood and looked at someone behind him. "This guy is looking for a human woman named Althea." Her mouth lifted into a wide smirk. "Know where she is?" She walked off the stage, holding out her hands.

Abalim watched as a tall Zerin male walked past him and took the woman's hands.

His long, midnight-black hair, pulled into a braid to his ankles, exposed his pointed ears. No question he was a true Zerin. Each hand boasted three fingers of equal length instead of the four humans had.

The male bent and kissed the female's knuckles with a low chuckle before turning to face Abalim. "Hello, stranger. My name is Lok. May I ask who you are?"

Abalim stood and clasped his hands in front of him. Taking a chance, he opened his psychic senses just enough to get a feel for the couple in front of him. With a small bow of his head, he introduced himself. "I am Abalim from the planet Earth. And this is my AI companion, JR15." He gestured to the bot sitting on his shoulder. "The current chancellor and Earth's government have asked us to help search for women taken from the Exchange. From what I understand, this illegal trafficking only became known after they removed the old chancellor from office."

As Abalim spoke, he reached out with his mind and tried to connect with theirs. How interesting. It was harder to do than usual. They both had very distinct personalities, making it difficult to get a good read on their minds. But with gentle probing, he uncovered she was the woman he looked for.

At the mention of the disgraced chancellor, a mental image flickered in the mind of the Zerin male of lighting the burial pyre of the dead leader. *Hmm*, this guy had to be the twin brother of that man. When Abalim reported back to Earth, he'd reassure the new chancellor that the old one was dead and gone.

"I know I don't look like I used to—" She looped her arm through the male's. "—but I'm Althea MacGregor."

"You are TrueBonds?" That would explain the change in her appearance. "Congratulations."

"Thanks! I couldn't be happier." She hugged her man and gave him a look of unconditional love.

Which made the male's stern expression soften when he did the same back to her.

"I take it you don't want to go back to Earth?" He didn't have to be a psychic to know the answer to that, but still, best to ask. He had to take proof back to his brother, so he'd instructed JR15 to record everything that happened the minute he stepped foot into the Galaxy's Pub.

"Oh, hell no!" Althea caressed Lok's jaw, still gazing into his eyes. "I'm right where I'm supposed to be."

Abalim cleared his throat. He hated to break the spell between the couple, but there were other things he had to ask. "You wouldn't happen to know where any of the other women are, would you?"

"Why don't you sit with this male and see if you can help him? It'll give me a chance to get ready for that surprise I promised you." Lok gave Althea a quick kiss. The nervous excitement rolling off him was easy to sense.

She beamed. "You won't be gone long, will you?" She was like a child excited for the Christmas holiday, something a lot of people on Earth celebrated at the end of the year.

"No, my *bateia*, my everlasting love." The male's voice lowered. "I will never be far from your side."

Oh, by the God An. The last thing he wanted to see was this overt display of new love. It was bad enough he had to endure it whenever he was around his brother Adapa and Queen Inanna. Not to mention how all five of their sons were in the same situation. It was enough to make him want to tear his eyes out.

Abalim was about to close his psychic senses when an unusual probe tried to worm its way into him. He blocked it, but the impression made his skin crawl. He glanced around the room, but couldn't sense where it came from.

"Oh good, Hayami has brought us some drinks."

Althea's voice jerked him out of his concentration.

"Well, I'll tell you as much as I can about the women who were in the same slaver cell with me on FiPan."

Abalim barely heard what the woman said next. She and Hayami gushed about something, but the only thing he focused on was a sudden thin thread of a disturbing malevolence hidden from sight. There, hovering behind Althea. In the dim light, a fractured glow tapered in and out of sight. Like tiny mirrors catching whatever light it could to claim its reality. But it was the blazing intensity of foul purpose coming off it in waves that gave him pause.

Abalim sent a quick glance in JR15's direction to ensure the little bot recorded the dialogue between him and Althea.

Satisfied the droid had everything under control, he allowed his primary consciousness to float free, but left a small part of himself behind to answer when necessary. He focused on the obscure shape and cast a psychic web around it.

Show yourself. Abalim demanded. The creature's intelligence was easy to read. No doubt the damn thing heard him.

You are an interesting creature. A definitely male voice answered.

Abalim frowned. He got the impression the alien wasn't talking about him.

The thing wisped around Althea and ignored everything else. *I wonder if there are more like you. Yes, yes, there must be.*

Get away from her. Abalim made sure he growled the words.

Look how you were once a different species. The strange being continued to ignore Abalim. *And now you've taken on the traits of your mate. Ah, mate. Is that how you turned from one species into another?*

When Abalim felt the alien seeping into Althea's consciousness, he blasted a psychic wave and shoved the creature away. *No! I said stay away from her!*

Now he had the asshole's attention. *You dare to interfere with me?* The surprise in the male's voice was easy to hear. *How odd.*

What? You're not smart enough to recognize a threat when it hits you? A wave of blinding, arrogant anger saturated Abalim psychically. The only way to avoid being sucked into a whirling abyss around the creature was to dig deep inside and stop it from affecting him. He struggled to focus and maintain an open line of communication.

If you are as you say—the mental voice became sharper with each word—*you will tell me where I can get more of these creatures. These... humans.*

Abalim sensed when Althea once again became the alien's focus.

Finally, a solution to a problem that has eluded me for far too long.

Abalim trained his psychic consciousness on a higher plane to confront the disgusting animal. *I won't allow you to get near her or any other human.*

A hard grasp around his physical throat stopped Abalim from advancing toward the threat. He jerked to get away, but couldn't pry the invisible fingers off.

Listen to me, you sanctimonious insect. For I will allow you this one chance to convince me you are the intelligent, sentient "threat" you claim to be.

The entity slammed Abalim back into his physical body, and the choke hold released as everyone in the room froze in place. Disoriented, he rubbed his eyes before focusing on the strange creature gliding around Althea. At first, it was hard to understand what he looked at, but soon the alien solidified. The strange being appeared humanoid with two arms and legs, but that was where the similarities to an organic creature ended. This one had a strange amalgamation of crystals, or glass, or mirrors, in various shades of blue. His surface had smooth flat panels, but also sharp crystal protrusions in various lengths jutting out from his body in all directions.

When the creature stopped beside Abalim, he became bombarded with images that sped through his mind at a blinding speed. He shut his eyes, putting the heel of his palms over his lids as if that would help control what was happening to him. Just as abruptly as the images came, they stopped. He lowered his hands and blinked his eyes open. The eerie silence in the room was dense. The only sound was his heavy breathing.

He was sure the demonstration lasted only seconds, but the information left behind was clear as hell.

This alien came through a black wormhole from a different dimension where he and his kind, called the Krystalii, had eliminated all other sentient life and built an undefeated empire. Their goal was to spread their kind in every universe to "purify" them. This creature was here to determine if this galaxy had the necessary materials to transform the planets into the atoms and molecules needed to start the nucleation process to make more of their kind.

"You may address me as Lord Baelon."

The alien moved close, and his warmth took Abalim by surprise, but he clenched his hands to stop from showing any reaction. He slammed a psychic shield around his mind to keep the damn thing out. He'd do everything in his power to stop the asshole from getting into his mind again.

"Listen to me carefully, you soiled maggot." The nasty sneer on Lord Baelon's face had to match Abalim's. "I am the beginning and the end of all there is. Follow me, and I will save you from all you fear." His hypnotizing voice was a mélange of cries from a thousand voices. "I will lead you to a place where death and sorrow can never find you." The creature leaned in and whispered, as if sharing a secret. "If you follow me, I'll introduce you to a realm where your feeblest fantasies pale in comparison to the dark wonders there waiting for you."

Abalim jerked his head away. "Yeah, sure. I've heard that type of bullshit from assholes like you before, you *fruking* bastard."

The alien straightened. The sneer on his thin lips morphed into a cruel, wide smile.

Abalim's stomach dropped.

"Just as I surmised. No intelligent life here." The crystal creature took a step back. "However, you have shown me a clear path to something I must accomplish first. I will have my people find those human women you're looking for." He glared menacingly at Althea with his icy-blue eyes, radiating an aura of wrath. "This one is a lost cause, since she has already gone through a transformation. What I need is a fresh supply of human females to bring Krystaii glory to a whole different level. Once I have them, I shall transform this puny dimension into something of beauty and power. This will be the highest fulfillment of my destiny."

Abalim became Lord Baelon's sole focus.

"And I shall relish the pain everyone in this galaxy will endure as I accomplish this."

He vanished. The last word stretched and echoed in his wake.

Everyone in the room moved, like someone had clicked the pause button to resume.

Abalim searched with his psychic senses to see if anyone else experienced what happened between him and the crystal threat. No, all was calm. "JR15, were you able to keep recording what happened between me and that alien while everyone else was frozen?" He spoke in a low voice to the small green-and-silver droid resting on his shoulder.

"Yes, Mister Abalim, sir." The little bot shivered. "I'm afraid I did."

"Oh, look!" Althea's excited voice caught his attention. "Lok's on stage. Oh my God, he's going to sing." Her hands gripped together so hard her knuckles turned white. "You don't have to do this." The last was said in a quivering whisper.

It was hard for Abalim to follow the dynamics as to why the Zerin being on the stage affected her so deeply. Especially after what he'd just experienced with the looming threat from the Krystalii.

He sent a gentle probe to Althea and discovered the Zerin had been held captive in isolation for over fifty years. For the male to allow himself to be the center of attention was a huge step for him to make. Abalim admired how the determined Zerin confronted his worse fears to show his TrueBond their love was more important than any phobia holding him back.

Perched on the edge of a backless stool, Lok's fingers moved gracefully over the strings of his seven-chord instrument, producing an emotional melody. The bittersweet lyrics floated through the room with an aching, smoky edge. There on the small stage, his heartrending words filled the air as he sang of forever, of longing to be with the one he loved with a fervent passion.

Abalim sat in awe, entranced by the sound of another man pouring his soul out for his woman. The music washed over him like a tempestuous wave, bringing with it an understanding for the first time in his life of how true love was a relentless and unstoppable force. One that could never be defeated. It had a solid strength that couldn't be broken, no matter how powerful the enemies' psychic armaments were.

Peaceful determination washed over Abalim. Armed with a new sense of courage and conviction, he knew without a doubt the crystal alien's threats didn't stand a chance. The mind-hold the alien shared fortunately ended up on a two-way street. He discovered the aliens weren't ready to come through the wormhole en masse just yet. They were in the process of sending out scout ships first. Their directive was to search for the missing human women Abalim and his brothers had been sent to find.

Lord "Freak-Show" Baelon somehow planned to use human women to propagate their species in a new, time-saving way. Which didn't make sense. How could humans and the crystal alien possibly be genetically compatible? That'd be something he'd have to talk about with his sister-in-law, Queen Inanna, the brilliant scientist.

But the main thing he was sure of was they had a small window of opportunity to come up with a way to stop the Krystalii from expanding their access to this dimension with more than just scout ships.

For now, the main thing to do was to prevent those assholes from locating those isolated missing women. He had to do everything in his power to keep them from becoming the extensive experiments the Krystalii planned on making them.

Especially before their Krystalii leader discovered a whole planet of them.

***

Lisa Ivy was no dummy. She knew darned good and well the alien in front of her was full of shit.

Aja, the alien liaison for the human women on the *StarChance* heading to an alien exchange program, shouldn't be here at her quarters this early.

Especially dressed like some kind of freak show at a steampunk convention.

Lisa swallowed a nervous sigh. She should know, since she'd done some serious research into the steampunk-romance genre when she'd contemplated creating a new series. As a successful science-fiction-romance author, she totally got off on researching various tropes of paranormal romance and would've killed to come up with the outfit Aja currently wore. Instead of her normal uniform of a one-piece, cream-colored suit, the liaison had on a bizarre outfit that would be right at home in any comic-book movie. The best part was the formfitting costume shimmered whenever she moved. Over her chest was a silver plate decorated with swirls that matched those on her wristbands.

On her feet were a pair of black leather boots that reached over her knees. The steel over the toes bore the same pattern as her chest plate. A shimmering cape flowed dramatically behind her to the top of her butt. Its slight silver sheen brought out the glittering colors of her suit and accessories. The strangest thing she had on was something that looked like the tip of a spear poking up between her shoulder blades. What in the hell was she going to do with that? In all the training about the

Exchange over the last thirty days, Aja never hinted it might be dangerous.

But it was the sinister leer (damn, seeing the actual expression in person was sure different from what her imagination came up with when she wrote a scene with the creepy villain) that crossed the beautiful alien's face. Lisa took a step back.

Aja's dual-colored eyes with their light shade of clear green around the iris with an outer dark shade of yellow carried the unmistakable marks of a life steeped in self-righteous corruption. The colors had a sickly khaki hue, as if reflecting the sulfurous depths of hell itself. They were cold, devoid of empathy or compassion.

Aja's full lips curled as if permanently pulled upward.

The sight had the haunting power of nightmares. Lisa frowned. No doubt the woman was there for nefarious purposes (heh, nefarious. Another word she'd never dreamed of using in real life). And talk about an Oscar-worthy performance. Who'd have guessed Aja was anything but the helpful hostess she portrayed this past month to Lisa and the other women under her care?

"Aja?" Lisa crossed her arms. "I didn't know you personally were going to take me to the Exchange." She glanced behind the woman. Not that she expected any of her fellow "classmates" to be with her. Her brows furrowed. So what was *really* going on? Obviously nothing good. "Wow, what an honor." When in doubt, sarcasm to the rescue.

Aja's eyes narrowed. The leer deepened, creating deep brackets at the side of her mouth. "Oh, I'm personally going to escort you, all right."

Quicker than Lisa could react, the Zerin female jumped in front of her and squeezed something sharp into her neck.

"Owe, you beeeccch..." Lisa's words slurred as she tried to slap her neck. No such luck. Then something hard and cold clicked around her neck. Every motor skill her body possessed packed its bags and left town. Any second now, she'd turn into a puddle of floppy, useless, noodle-like nothingness, as if her inner heroine hung up her battle gear for a career in blobbery.

"Follow me, you stupid human." Aja turned and strolled down the empty corridor.

Yep, no arguing her stupid status. Only a stupid human would get caught like this. To pile on the stupidity, she'd made sure no one on Earth would miss her. She let the Zerins erase everything about her, like she never existed. Which was easy enough, since she had no family or close friends back on Earth. And being a self-employed author who released all of her books under various pen names, it was easy for the aliens to make her disappear.

Lisa's traitorous feet followed the alien without missing a step in the eerily silent hallway. Well, at least she had some decent clothes on. She'd gotten up way earlier than she needed to, beyond excited to meet over a hundred hunky alien men in order to find her one true love. She'd barely slept, her mind and body racing throughout the night. When she finally gave up trying to sleep, she ran into the refresher unit and got ready for the exciting event in record time.

At least she wasn't getting kidnapped by aliens half-naked, like she'd made some of her fictional heroines endure. Hah! Take that, fate.

Too bad it wasn't a gorgeous, muscular man, er, male taking her away. Anything but this snarky bitch leading her to who knows where. She meekly followed Aja down the corridor, which was empty. Great, no one was around to witness anything.

Aja hurried to a dim part of the ship that didn't look like it'd been used in years.

The Zerin opened the airlock and pushed her inside, and a gust of stale air rushed out, making Lisa's throat burn. Once Aja closed the portal behind them, the creepy silence was heavy.

Dust particles danced in the low, flickering light, showcasing the walls that once must've gleamed with a futuristic sheen but lost their luster long ago. The empty room was some kind of cargo bay, the massive emptiness broken only by one thing—a small one-man spacecraft with an honest-to-God alien typically called a "Gray" standing next to it.

Chilling little shit was around three feet tall with an oversized head in comparison to its body. Its gray skin didn't boast anything remarkable for its skinny, non-clothed form. Long arms with spindly fingers and elongated almond-shaped eyes with a black background and tiny white dots where their pupils might be. A couple of horizontal slits for a nose and a minuscule slit underneath that had to be its mouth.

All in all, a disgusting creature who smelled like burned fish.

"Hurry up, take this one." Aja shoved Lisa at the diminutive creature. "I've got to get the rest."

Without a word, the thing grabbed her arm and wrapped its long, reed-thin fingers around her upper arm.

Lisa shuddered at the feel of its slimy, cool flesh. Still unable to move voluntarily or speak, much less protest, she let it pull her to the small craft. The sound of Aja's fading footsteps hardly registered when the only thing to see was where the creature forced her to go—a one-seater ship that looked like a Lockheed F-104 without wings.

On the side, a small coffin-shaped pod slid out without a sound. She didn't need her writing chops to recognize it as some kind of stasis pod.

She tried to pull away. To scream. To run. To do anything but let the smarmy little bastard shove her into the scary blackness. She swore the damn place shrank the minute her back hit the inside of the hard surface. A bubbling, thick gel started at her feet and wiggled its way up as the lid to the steel coffin closed with a silent seal.

As the cold liquid covered her mouth and nose, she squeezed her eyes shut, wishing she was back in her comfy home office, plotting her next SciFi romance and dreaming she was writing about her own studly alien mate.

Well... soaring space dung.

***

Lisa's eyes fluttered open, her senses jolted into sharp awareness. She tried to put an arm up to block the blinding, harsh, sterile light. Instead, she found herself lying on a hard table, tightly bound and unable to move. Panic surged.

She had no idea where she was. Her heart pounded, muffling all sounds.

The room was alien, both in its physicality and its atmosphere. Cold metal surfaces surrounded her, adorned with unfathomable machinery, emitting eerie, pulsating hums. The air tasted metallic and clinical, suffused with a moist chill that sent shivers racing along her spine.

As she struggled against her restraints, she only thought of escaping. What happened? Why was she...

Oh shit. That's right. That bitch Aja gave her to one of those disgusting Gray aliens. Who knew the creepy beings were real? Dread coiled in her stomach, tightening with each passing second.

One of them came into her line of vision. She couldn't tell it was the same one from the *StarChance* or a different one.

Out of the slit of its thin mouth came a warbling, birdlike sound.

And not the cute kind either. Its freaking whistling noise made her skin crawl. And why in the world didn't her universal translator work? The Zerins who ran the alien exchange program promised once they installed it, she'd be able to understand thousands of languages spoken in the galaxy.

Out of the corner of her eye, she saw another Gray approaching at her other side.

This one twittered back to the other as if they were arguing. Their large black eyes widened as their spindly fingers flapped in the air over her bound chest.

But the thing that caught her attention was the thin, needle-like doohickey aimed at her exposed left breast. The weight of vulnerability settled over her like a suffocating blanket. Sheer helplessness made her mouth dry. Her imagination scrambled at the scenarios of what these extraterrestrial asshats were going to do to her. Every ounce of her screamed to flee. But the more she struggled, the more futile her attempts became, which, of course, compounded her terror. She was at their mercy, a pawn in some unfathomable game. Drawing in a shaky breath, she hyperventilated.

Before the needle touched her skin, a sound like a balloon popping made her jerk.

The slimy alien who stood next to her disintegrated in a flaky cloud of ash.

With a high-pitched, bloodcurdling squeal, the asshat with the needle threw it at something through the cloud.

It was hard to see what it was aiming at, but it gave a metallic ping as it hit the side of the steel wall before tumbling to the ground.

Another suffocating pop, and the other gray creature exploded in a poof of ash as well.

Lisa's heart thudded against her ribs as a cold sweat broke out on her forehead. She tried to see what made those maniacs disappear, but the straps holding her down wouldn't budge. Eyes wide, she strained to find out what was going on.

What came into view ramped up the whole surreal experience to a new level.

Standing next to her table was a bald, robotic, gorgeous Barbie doll on steroids. A bright-green sex toy that had to give any man a massive-boner. With a waist so tiny it was a wonder it held up those three humongous boobs with their deep-red areolae. Like a neon-bright doll in Christmas colors. Rounded hips tapered down to shapely legs that didn't quit. Dainty feet were strapped into a serious pair of "fuck-me" stilettos, high enough to give any normal human a nosebleed. The only clothing it wore was a diaphanous wraparound skirt that left little to the imagination. It exposed a human-like vagina complete with plump lips that surrounded the tip of a hot-red clitoris peeking out between the folds of shiny emerald.

The metallic eyes of the robot were lifeless and void of any emotion. Their silver irises lit up and scanned Lisa from head to toe. When the light blinked off, the straps holding her down disappeared.

"You will follow me." The robot's mechanized tone had a slight, sexy lisp. It flicked one of its wrists in her direction and the collar around her neck warmed. "If you do not, you will endure the *nutesh* snare's capabilities." The droid turned to leave the room as if it didn't have any doubts Lisa would meekly follow.

The memory of the collar lifting her up in the air and putting her in that stasis pod left no doubt the stupid thing was powerful. No telling what else it could do. Whenever she wrote her heroines into a trap, she made sure the woman wasn't stupid enough to rebel until she got enough information to figure out what was going on.

At least the creepy little Grays got what they deserved.

She slid off the table and crossed her arms over her naked chest. "I don't suppose you have any clothes I can put on, do you?" Doubtful. The damn droid wasn't wearing much of anything.

The neon-green robot woman turned its head to look at her. The silver eyes gave her a brief scan before tilting its head to the side. With a negligent wave of its digitized fingers, it indicated a pile of clothes laying on the floor next to the table.

"If that is what you are seeking, utilize it." It turned and with a slight wiggle of its hips, the robot took short steps out of the open doorway. "Do be hasty. Any delay will not be tolerated."

Lisa didn't need to be told twice. In record time, she pulled on the clothes she'd worn when she thought she was going to meet the alien mate of her dreams. Thank God the clothes the Zerins gave her had built-in underwear and slip-on shoes that were easy to don, even at a run.

She may not like where she ended up, but any place was better than staying here. Going through an alien autopsy was never part of her bucket list.

***

Turned out the neon-green android Lisa dubbed as "Kermit" took her to a place as boring as hell. It was a single-room prison cell no bigger than her bedroom back home. Complete with three narrow cots along the side and a small bowl in the corner, that she could only guess was some kind of toilet.

And a shimmering force field over the wide front entrance.

"You enter here." Kermit the droid said in her whispery tone. At a wave of her metallic hand, the sparkling shield disappeared.

Now it was easy to see four other women in the room. Human woman, as far as Lisa could tell. The one with long, curly brown hair looked vaguely familiar. She turned her back on the room and crossed her arms. She wasn't going to move until she got some answers. "What's going to happen to me now?"

The robot didn't answer. It just flicked its wrist, and the collar around Lisa's neck activated, making her back up a few short steps until she was fully in the cramped space. With a flick of its other wrist, the android made the glittering force field resume its position.

"Hey, Kermit!" Lisa stood as close as she dared to the heat coming off the shield. "I asked you a question!" With a huff, she put her fists on her hips.

The robot walked away but stopped. Instead of turning around, the bald head did a hundred-eighty-degree turn, so its face with the creepy, dead silver eyes gave her an unblinking, full-on stare. "That is up to the master. He will decide your fate, human." With that unemotional response, the robot's head swiveled to face front and walked away.

Its sharp heels clicked with each step until Lisa couldn't hear it anymore.

"Lisa? That you?"

She jerked at the sound of her name and turned to face her fellow inmates.

The curly-haired one stepped close with her head tilted. Her brown eyes were wide.

Lisa studied the woman. Several years older than her own thirty-three, the other female was attractive, with high cheekbones and a smattering of freckles across her playful upturned celestial nose that added a hint of whimsy. Her bouncy, cascading hair in thick brunette curls reached past her shoulders.

"Althea?" Lisa gasped, grasping the woman's forearms. This had been one of her classmates on the *StarChance* heading to the Exchange. "How did you end up here?"

Althea's laugh lacked humor. "Probably the same way you did." Her eyebrow rose. "Aja?"

"Skanky bitch." One of the women behind Althea commented with a curt nod. She was an arresting blend of what had to be mixed heritage. Her warm skin tone was complemented by a crown of springy honey coils. Her arresting green eyes narrowed.

"Now, Morgan." Another woman, an adorable Latina, admonished. "We don't know the circumstances..."

"Honest to God, Izzy. You'd find something good to say about Hitler, wouldn't you?" the last woman snapped.

She reminded Lisa of her cover-artist-turned-friend, June. It took forever for Lisa to get June to admit what her Korean birth name was. It wasn't until just before Lisa left Earth that June admitted her birth name was Ha-Joon. She only confessed after threatening Lisa with severe bodily harm if she ever called her that.

"Toni, stop picking on Izzy." Althea joined in the conversation.

Maybe Toni was a nickname for the pretty Korean-American woman like June was for her friend.

"I swear, she never says a mean thing about anyone." Toni may have possessed a petite frame, but there was no mistaking the solid wall of steel in her stance. She waved her hand as if to demonstrate being held in captivity was supposed to give them the green light to get down and dirty. "You'd think being here, she'd at least cuss or something."

"Hey, maybe she has religious reasons for not swearing."
Lisa grimaced. Here she went, opening her mouth before she
had a better understanding of the group's dynamics. For once,
she should pay attention and figure things out before opening
her big fat yap.

"Nah." Morgan laughed, flipping her hands at Izzy. "She's
just so friggin' nice she can't help herself."

Izzy's light-bronze cheeks darkened, and she lowered her
eyes with a soft smile.

Lisa expected her to say, "Ah, shucks" anytime.

"Any-hoo..." Althea cleared her throat and addressed Lisa.
"How are you? You okay?" The concern in her dark eyes was
clear as she checked over the newcomer. "You injured?"

Lisa gave her a brief hug before pulling back. "No, I'm
okay." She gave a sheepish smirk. "The only thing hurt was
my pride." She thumbed at the shiny force field. "Thank God
Kermit got me before any damage was done."

"Damage?" Izzy put a soft hand on her forearm.

Althea's brows furrowed. "Kermit?"

Without warning, the horror of the last few hours caught
up with Lisa. The image of being strapped to that cold, hard
table made her stumble. Her brain and eyesight checked out.
A black cloud took over, and she would've fallen if Izzy and
Althea hadn't grabbed her by the arms.

"Here!" Morgan shouted. "Put her here."

Shivers ran rampant as Lisa's vision blurred in and out. "I
don't know what's wrong with me," she muttered as they helped
her sit on something hard. Must be one of the cots against the
wall.

"It's okay." Izzy's soft voice pierced through the fog. "I'm sure you've been through a lot. Listen to my voice and let me guide you." She used a soothing tone with nonsensical words that didn't have to be understood for them to be effective.

Lisa swallowed with a dry throat. Her face heated. Well, wasn't she the poster girl for a badass warrior woman? How embarrassing. Here she wrote about fearless women, and at the first hint of trouble she fell apart like a simpering sot from a Gothic novel.

"Here, drink this." Toni held out a small, clear metal cup. "It's just water."

"Yeah, nothing fancy here at Chez de Slammer." Morgan humphed. "Wait till you taste the cuisine. It's to die for."

Chapter Two

Sitting in the conference room on the hidden moon city of Azadi, Abalim rubbed his temple with absentminded diligence. After enduring a week-long voyage in space from Hiigar back to Earth in the small scuttle jumper the Akurns provided, he ended up with a stifling case of claustrophobia. And now that he was "home", he sat in an underground city on the moon instead of being under the wide-open skies of Earth he yearned for. Which didn't help the suffocating sensation squeezing his chest.

He glanced up, taking in the soft orange glow of the conference room with its glass dome and lattice decorations outside, as if the person who designed the place wanted to give it a sense of openness. Too bad they failed. Nothing replaced the blue sky he craved.

"So, it's settled then." The Federation Chancellor, D'zia E'etu, announced with a silent pound of his fist on the table.

Since the image was a hologram, no sound accompanied the act.

Abalim forced his attention back to the discussion.

"The four of you will go to FiPan and see what you can find out about those missing women. If you need any further assistance, don't hesitate to ask." He sat back with a wave. He and the other holograms from Zerin disappeared.

Abalim glanced from his eldest brother Adapa to the others sitting at the round table. How Adapa and Inanna kept the Akurns who ran the city of Azadi out of this discussion was a mystery. But the only ones in the room were him and his four brothers along with Queen Inanna. Nary a human in sight.

Even Adapa and Inanna's five sons were missing. How interesting.

He squirmed as Adapa stared at him with his mouth fixed in a stern line. *Dammit.* He never could keep anything from his older brother. Just before he landed, Abalim decided he'd rather discuss with his family the other threat headed their way before telling the entire galaxy about the incoming Krystalii from another dimension.

"Doesn't anyone else find it weird that only four women are missing?" Asmodel's distinctive hazel eyes, with their mixture of browns, greens, and a starburst of gold crinkled at the corners, twinkled in their depths with mirth that matched his smirk. "And there just so happens to be four of us with nothing better to do?"

"Well—" his sister-in-law, Queen Inanna, sat back and touched her fingertips together. "—we don't know for sure they're the only ones missing. We have to wait until the Zerins check with each and every human who boarded their ship to verify they're all accounted for."

"I thought the *StarChance* wasn't the only ship that participated in the Exchange. Are they the only ones who seem to have encountered that particular problem?" Arakiba observed.

"Damned careless, if you ask me." Adapa muttered. "When they first approached us about offering human woman to join the Exchange, we shouldn't have assumed they had everything under control."

"I don't know"—the reserved one of the group, Azazel, spoke in a soft tone—"no matter how diligent anyone thinks they are, those who wish to benefit themselves, even at the cost of others, are prevalent everywhere. No matter how much you trust those working with you." The pointed tips of his ears darkened as he spoke. The man didn't like to be the center of attention, even if it was only the six of them. "I'm sure they had no idea about the betrayal as it happened."

"Since it was under the Prince of Zerin's watch, I'm sure they took every precaution they could to ensure the women's safety." Inanna offered. "Or he would've taken immediate action."

"I'm sure the deceased Chancellor U'unk took advantage of the prince being under exile to install his operatives to disrupt the prince's bid to get back into his father's good graces." Abalim shrugged. "That's how bad guys work."

The image of the Krystalii he'd met on Hiigar popped into his head. He rubbed his temple and looked down at the table. Maybe he shouldn't bring it up in front of the others. If he got Adapa alone, they could discuss...

"Knock it off, Abalim." Adapa's voice held little humor. "Just tell us what's got your panties twisted into a knot."

Abalim frowned. It was hard to understand Adapa sometimes. The slang the man picked up in this new century baffled the hell out of him. A lot. "I don't know what you're talking about." He glowered at his brother sitting across from him. *I need to speak to you alone.* He told him telepathically on a private stream the others couldn't access.

Oh, please. That wasn't Adapa. Abalim's startled gaze swung to Arakiba. *You only thought we couldn't hear you. Dumbass.*

What he said. Asmodel said as he and Azazel nodded with identical smirks on their annoying mugs.

Well, fruk. Abalim tugged on his earlobe.

"I *know* you people aren't talking without including me in the conversation." Inanna's delicate blonde eyebrows rose over her bright-turquoise eyes. She crossed her arms under her bountiful breasts and frowned.

"They are." Adapa gave them all up. Wuss. "Not me, my dove." He scooted his chair closer to her and put his arms around her slender shoulders. "I would never do that."

His phony tone belied any sincerity he tried to pull over on her.

She gave him a long-suffering glare before focusing on Abalim. "Why do I get the feeling you're keeping something really important from us?"

"Because he is." Adapa intoned. "It's not just the missing women you're worried about, is it?"

Abalim huffed a sigh. "Yeah, it's not." He glanced at his shoulder where JR15 rested. "Go ahead. Show them."

The little bot quivered and opened his top eye to activate the video he'd taken at the Galaxy's Pub.

Once the scene ended, JR15 scuttled back to his hiding place under Abalim's dreadlocks.

A dead silence laid heavy in the room.

"Damn, *fruk* me sideways." Adapa said out loud what everyone had to be thinking.

***

Life in the cell from hell turned out to be a boring bunch of nothing burgers. After Lisa got over her initial panic attack, she settled into a routine with the others.

That is until the day when the neon-red robot who'd been their normal guard unexpectedly came just hours after tossing them their daily ration of dry protein cubes.

"You will follow me." The android's metallic voice had a sultry lisp. She raised her hand to turn off the force field, but paused before touching it. The damn thing stayed like that with its finger stretched as if to turn off the force field covering the entryway.

When nothing else happened, Lisa and the others looked at each other.

"What the hell is that all about?" Toni put her hands on her hips. The nice outfit she'd put on to attend the Exchange was fast getting wrinkled and threadbare.

Lisa sighed. What a weird thing to think about now.

"Maybe she ran out of power." Izzy leaned close, covering her heart with her open palm.

Morgan snorted. "Yeah, we should be so lucky."

Several days later, what Morgan wished turned into a horrific prophecy. They hadn't seen anyone since the droid froze. Which meant they hadn't gotten any food or fresh water lately.

Lisa stood with Althea and studied the red android. She crossed her arms and gave the robot a narrow glare. "I'm beginning to doubt it being frozen like that is a good thing."

"Yeah." Althea put her hands on her hips. "Well, at least she can't take us somewhere worse, like a slave auction. Damn, if someone doesn't come soon, we'll starve to death. We haven't seen anyone since that stupid thing got stuck like that days ago." She said the last in a soft whisper.

Lisa grunted. No arguing that.

Althea sighed and glanced back at the small room. "We might as well sit down and relax. Doesn't look like anything's going to happen anytime soon."

Lisa reached over and gave Althea's hand a squeeze.

It was easy to tell how worried the other woman was. Who was she kidding? Worried wasn't the right word to use. She might as well admit it. Panic was starting to haunt her.

She sat next to Althea on the hard floor and thumped her head against the wall. Closing her eyes, she started to doze off.

"What's that?" Althea jumped up and raced to the open-looking doorway.

With a grunt, Lisa pushed herself off the floor and stood next to her friend. "What's what?" She squinted, trying to see what made Althea excited. Wouldn't it be great if something good came their way? Like a tall, hunky hero from one of her series that came from some other dimension and rescued kidnapped women from Earth. "You think a dimensional portal is being activated?" Her heart thumped. "I've always wanted to go through one!"

Althea's only answer was a raised eyebrow.

"What are you guys looking at?" Toni asked from the cot behind them.

Izzy squealed. "Someone's coming?"

Morgan, the reigning queen of sarcasm, snorted. "With our luck they won't take us somewhere that's gonna be better than these luxury accommodations."

The other three joined them in a single line to look out the entrance.

A shuffling noise, like a herd of cattle clomping close, became clear.

A sense of dread made Lisa catch her breath. That can't be good. She glanced at the prone red robot. Whatever was coming didn't sound metallic at all.

An unmistakable rancid odor wafted to her before anything or anyone showed up. It was a weird mix of wet cardboard and cooking oil gone bad. She wrinkled her nose until she caught sight of what was making that scrambling ruckus.

Damn. Look at that. More aliens. At first she was jealous she hadn't dreamed up these creatures for one of her books. Here was a group of pudgy, bulky aliens that were a cross between a dingo and a beaver in pants — no shirts. Standing on two hind legs with six arms and a flat tail of coarse hair and scales. Pink-and-blue tongues hung from the sides of their snouts as four beady black eyes blinked in unison. Their thick, fuzzy fur ranged in colors from burned gold to midnight blue.

It took a moment before why they showed up sank in.

Each one was armed with various weapons. Guns, knives, and even some weird kind of round metal contraptions hitched to a belt that clanked with each movement. Handcuffs?

Gibbering between them, two of the aliens grabbed the red robot under its stiff arms and pulled it away from the entrance.

Without a second glance, they dropped it on the floor as one of them aimed a black box in their direction.

Before Lisa had a chance to gasp and back up, it clicked a button and the force field evaporated.

With its snout curled in a snarl, the creature pushed another button on the black box.

Agony stabbed through her. The leather collar around her neck sparked with sizzling heat, sending tendrils of pain throughout her body. She flopped on the floor like a fish pulled from a lake. Spasming and squirming, she clutched the black *nutesh* snare in a vain attempt to pull it off.

The torture only lasted a few seconds, but it wasn't until she could take a lungful of air that told her the pain stopped. Lisa swore lingering waves of agony squirmed through her, inside and out. Too weak to struggle, she didn't have a chance to stop one of the little aliens from tugging her hands in front of her. It jerked two of the round metal things from its belt and clapped them on. Her wrists swiftly locked together, as if drawn by a powerful magnet. He then slapped a putty-looking thing over her mouth. It expanded until a flat surface prevented her from talking—or breathing through her mouth, for that matter. Thank God it was far enough away from her nose to give her room so she didn't suffocate.

It was tempting to not move, but the creep who handcuffed her yanked her to her feet. She wobbled to get her bearings, dizzy. When the alien spouted some gibberish at her, she scowled and went with him as he tugged her with one of his middle arms.

His lower hand grabbed the waist of her pants while the upper hand held some type of gun. He led her to the end of the corridor that had an elevator.

She and her cell friends were smashed together in the cramped car with a bunch of the smelly aliens. She tried to make herself as small as possible before glancing at the other women. All wore the same gags she had and their hands were held together in the cuffs.

Morgan's eyes were narrowed as she glared at everyone.

Izzy's were filled with tears, her fear palpable.

Even with her hands stuck together, Toni was trying to pick at the gag over her mouth. Her thunderous expression looked lethal.

Althea stood stoically, staring straight ahead.

The trip lasted forever and yet was over before Lisa had a chance to moan at the pain when the alien elbowed her in the ribs. Her headache pounded.

When the doors to the lift opened, the short aliens squealed and hissed, pushing Lisa and the others out into the main lobby.

Her eyes widened at the destruction all around.

A variety of aliens were scurrying around, grabbing what they could or destroying furniture and fixtures evidently for the sheer joy of it.

Various androids, robots, and mechanical AIs littered in sporadic places, frozen when their power was ripped away.

The little alien kidnapper pushed her to the open exit, where the massive rusted metal doors listed sideways on the hinges.

The last thing she saw before being shoved out of the building was the neon-green sexbot she'd named Kermit sitting on the floor with her legs splayed and her head broken to the side, resting on her shoulders. Her tongue hung out and her eyes were blank, like a TV screen turned off.

Scrambling outside, Lisa squinted and turned her head to avoid looking at the dim sunshine. After living in the dusky lightning of the prison cell for who knows how long, anything brighter made her eyes water. Didn't help her stupid headache either. The other problem was she couldn't see where they were going. She tried to rub her eyes, but the alien had a hard grip on her arms and she couldn't move them. The only thing to do was rub the side of her face against her shoulder.

After blinking to help the situation, she wished she hadn't bothered. Racing through a dilapidated town... village... that looked like it'd been deserted for decades, made her heart sink. No help there. Added to that was the overwhelming smell of nasty. She thought the little aliens smelled bad, but *holy crap*, their scent was like comparing a field of spring wildflowers to an open, neglected septic tank. With one more jerk on her arm, the little guy led her to a back alley.

There at the end was an octagon-shaped contraption.

She stumbled when the wheezing alien shoved her. She would've fallen if the snare around her neck hadn't tightened and lifted her off the ground. Choking, she grabbed the collar with both hands and tried to catch her breath. Out of the corner of her eye, she saw one of the panels on the coarse metal structure, streaked with unknown stains and pockmarked with potholes and scratches, open.

A long tray extended as her body floated over to it. Something clicked, and she was turned to face her captor. With a hiss that sounded suspiciously like laughter from the pudgy alien, she was lowered on the slab and forced to lie on her back. The minute her body touched down, several straps wrapped over her from the tip of her head to her ankles and locked her in place.

Well, shit-snacking crackers. Not again. What was she? The poster girl for alien kidnappings?

As the table slid backward into the dark cavern of the ship, she tried to scream, but the gag muffled any sound she tried to make. Something sharp pierced the side of her neck. Darkness rolled over her, and she absently heard the sliding panel click shut.

***

Revulsion coursed through Abalim as he and his brothers disembarked from the spaceship *Elemi*, on the gangster planet FiPan. Chaos, filthy and unrelenting, was their welcoming committee.

"Holy shit, what a dump." Arakiba put his meaty fists on his trim hips and looked around with a scowl. "I bet this place didn't look any better before it fell apart."

Asmodel nodded. "Agreed." He crossed his arms and narrowed his eyes at the dilapidated buildings on the outskirts of the small town.

The structures were only one- or two-stories high and didn't appear to have much support. Broken doors, windows, and roofs weren't quite abandoned since several figures hid in doorways or peeked out cracked windows as they walked by.

Abalim wrinkled his nose at the combination of stinging sharp odors. The vile smell of feces mixed with rotting food left a bad taste in his mouth. He stepped on small debris and pebbles, crunching as he walked alongside a shallow ribbon of dubious liquid running down the middle of the cobbled road.

Small bits of trash swirled in the air, mixing with wispy dust devils.

"Do you think that's where we should go?" Azazel pointed at a nondescript building that had a wide doorway permanently open.

Inside and out were various types of robots and droids, either lying broken on the ground or frozen in mid-action. Most were female shaped with bright metallic neon skin in various shades, complete with a set of three breasts and barely there short skirts in transparent silky fabric.

"Jeez, I wonder what these babies did when they were wake." Arakiba snorted. He chuckled as he passed a model in eye-burning metallic pink.

"I think they were called sexbots by the prior owner, the Dred Pirate Maynwaring." JR15 helpfully provided to Abalim from his favorite perch on Abalim's shoulder. "They were once programmed to give sexual pleasure to whomever paid the pirate for their services. They were also spies or thieves if the need arose. I would recommend we don't activate any of them."

Abalim humphed his agreement. "Be sure to share that information with your brothers." He eyed Arakiba, bending over to examine the pink droid. "Especially him."

He watched as each JR droid on his brothers' shoulders vibrated as JR15 communicated with them.

When Arakiba didn't move, he walked over to him. "Come on, leave the damn thing alone. I'm sure JR12 told you how dangerous they were."

"Maybe when everything is done, I'll come back and grab one of these." He fingered the robot's bald head. "I bet I can activate it."

"Holy Goddess, Arakiba. Don't you think about anything but your libido?" Asmodel groused as he fist-bumped his kneeling brother and pushed him onto his ass. "We don't have time for this bullshit."

Arakiba laughed and stood, brushing off the seat of his brown leather pants. With one last glance at the prone droid, he followed them to the open archway. He whispered something to the gold-and-silver JR on his shoulder.

The little bot did a dance and waved his spindly forelegs before wiggling his bulbous body in what looked suspiciously like joy.

Abablim resisted the urge to roll his eyes. Keeping Arakiba focused had always been a challenge. Now that they were no longer slaves to the Akurns, the tantalizing taste of freedom made the task harder than ever. And his robotic companion was of little help. Where JR15 was shy and reserved, Arakiba's bot was part daredevil and part mischief-maker, eager to try new things.

"Keep an open communication between you and JR12," Abalim whispered to JR15. "If they even so much as hint they're going to veer away from what we have to do, let me know."

"Yes, Mister Abalim, sir."

Satisfied JR15 would help keep an eye on Abalim's mischievous brother, he followed his other brothers to the only semi-fortified looking building in the small square. He had to admit, even in its heyday, it probably didn't look much better.

"Are you sure this is where that human Althea said she was held prisoner?" Azazel narrowed his pecan-brown eyes. "I can't imagine them surviving in all this disarray."

They'd passed through the open arch and proceeded into what used to be some kind of lobby. All the furniture had either been smashed or stolen, leaving a mostly bare room.

"Which way?" Asmodel stopped, his head swiveling from right to left.

"You two go that way." Abalim pointed to the right. "Azazel and I'll go this way." He thumbed to the left and gave Arakiba and Asmodel a stern warning. "If you find anything, have your JR bots tell ours immediately."

Arakiba waved his concerns away and trotted ahead of Asmodel. "Come on, bro. Let's see what we can find."

Asmodel frowned as he followed his brother.

Looked like Arakiba was getting the hang of Earth slang. Abalim didn't have to read the man's mind to know how much that had to annoy Asmodel. Maybe exposing Arakiba to new experiences right now wasn't such a good idea. Lips thinned, he headed to the dim hallway he'd pointed to.

"Don't worry." Azazel spoke in a soft voice behind him. The light in the corridor darkened as they got farther from the open entrance. "Arakiba is just trying to work around all the extra stimuli we're exposed to at this time. He'll eventually come to terms with who he is inside."

Abalim grunted. Trust his philosophical brother to see the good in any situation. "I guess the only thing we can do is keep half an eye on him. Hopefully, he won't end up somewhere where we can't help him." It was becoming impossible to see where they were going. "JR15, would you give us some light?"

The little droid opened his upper eye and emitted a wide beam of light.

Azazel's red-and-gold JR14 did the same on the other side.

At the same time, a tentacle of familiar psychic energy grabbed Abalim's attention. "There." He stopped and grasped the filament with a sensory hold. "Just ahead. I feel a small portion of that woman's energy just ahead.

Wordlessly, he and Azazel stopped in front of an open archway into a small room. Before he had a chance to lock on to the psychic trail, Arakiba and Asmodel joined them.

Azazel turned to them. "How did you get here so fast?"

Arakiba grinned and crossed his arms. "Place is just a round hallway with a lot of little rooms like this one. All are empty, with only a few droids scattered around like that one." He pointed to a red sexbot lying on the floor with its hand extended. He stepped into the room and froze. His eyes glazed over.

"What do you suppose he's looking..." Asmodel studied his blond brother before he too froze.

Abalim and Azazel looked at each other. "I guess..." Azazel didn't finish because the same thing happened to him.

Abalim's eyebrows rose. He'd never seen his brothers get caught in a trance at the same time before. The only thing he could do...

***

Abalim was swept into a vision. His brothers were there as well. All five of them stood in the middle of the room while three women were either sitting on the floor or sat on a narrow, thin cot. Two stood with their backs to him, talking in quiet tones as they faced the hallway at a safe distance from a shimmering force field.

Damn, he hadn't experienced being in this type of psychic plane before. It took a moment for him to get his bearings.

"Where are we?" Asmodel looked around until one of the seated women caught his attention.

"Where do you think we are, you dumbass..." Arakiba started to harass his brother but then he focused on a different woman.

Azazel didn't say a word. He'd turned to face the three women and froze.

In tandem, Arakiba and Asmodel also stood stock-still as their eyes turned white.

Abalim grunted. Looked like his brothers had entered a different psychic plane. Good. They must've latched on to the women's psychic energy. Maybe they'd get more information that way.

"Do you think it'll ever come back online?" The blonde woman standing next to Althea asked the question.

Abalim had to be having a vision of the past.

He turned his full attention to the woman speaking. He couldn't catch his breath. His heart raced and his vision narrowed. On an intellectual level, he knew his physical body wasn't suffering the unexpected reaction. But all the same, it didn't matter. It was hard to focus on what the women talked about. The only thing he wanted to was do was concentrate on the blonde in greater detail.

He watched her profile and moved to face her. The mesmerizing shade of sapphire blue in her eyes struck him speechless. They sparkled with intelligence and a sense of a creative spirit. He narrowed his focus, hoping to read her and find out her name.

He sucked in a breath when his psychic tentacles hit a hard wall. Well, shit. That couldn't be good. Turning his attention to the curly brunette next to her, he was able to penetrate Althea's thoughts with no trouble. She was thinking she didn't have to answer... *Lisa*. Ah, this one must be Lisa Ivy, the author who was a successful sci-fi romance writer. Thankfully, the Zerins provided him and his brothers with the extensive profiles they'd developed when the women were accepted into the alien exchange program.

But that dry information didn't tell the full story. It listed her hair as "short, blonde", but didn't describe how it framed her pixie face and carried several shades of gold and light bronze in the strands.

The profile said she was "five foot four" but didn't go into detail about the gentle dip where the indent of her waist met her hips and accentuated their prominence, emphasizing the timeless hourglass shape that defined her figure. The slight rise of her hipbones beneath the surface hinted at the strength that lay beneath their alluring exterior, a tantalizing juxtaposition of power and beauty.

"I wonder if it being frozen like that is a good thing." Lisa crossed her arms, lifting up those mouthwatering breasts as if offering them to the gods. "Or a bad one."

Abalim withdrew from Althea's consciousness and didn't bother to hear her response. Nor did he care what in the nine galaxies they talked about. With each movement of her plump lips, he got lost in erotic fantasies of what he'd love for those mounds to do to him... on him. A well of deep longing he'd never experienced before rose up. Damn, just watching her mouth move as she spoke created a harsh yearning for him to explore her in person. Need pounded in him.

It startled him when the two women left the entrance and sat on the hard-looking floor at the back of the cell.

Althea wrapped her arms around her bent knees and rested her head against them.

Lisa slumped against the unforgiving wall and stared off into space, worrying her bottom lip with her top teeth.

He had the strongest urge to go over and rub his own lips over hers. Giving her a slight, sharp nip was optional.

No telling how much time passed as he stood there like a lovesick moron blindly watching a fascinating woman. He startled when she jumped up and raced with Althea to the front of the force field again.

With a shake of his head at his inability to keep his mind in the game, he joined them to see what had them so excited.

"What's that?" Althea exclaimed, standing on her toes, craning her head as close to the shield she could without getting hurt, and peered down the corridor.

"What's what?" Lisa responded. "You think a dimensional portal is being activated? I've always wanted to go through one!"

Abalim caught his breath. Could it be the Krystalii were already invading? No, that couldn't be right. He was experiencing the past. And if he wasn't mistaken, this happened long before he met up with Lord Baelon on Hiigar.

By the time he shook off his musings, all five women were standing at the force field trying to see what was happening down the dark corridor outside their cell.

The sound of stomping footsteps and hissing snaps got louder as who (or what) got closer. Bursting into the dim light outside the cell was a strange crowd of small aliens. The beings weren't bigger than four or five feet tall, with two legs and six arms. To add to their oddness, they boasted tails shaped like a beaver's with leathery scales and sparse, coarse hair. Each had a long snout with four black glinting eyes perched just above. On top of their oblong, flat heads were pocket-sized round ears that flickered and twisted. None of them wore any type of shirt, just pants or shorts ranging in color from brash gold to navy blue that covered their fur-lined skin.

Each carried a variety of weapons, complete with several sets of what looked like handcuffs.

Since entering the vision, Abalim constantly wished he had JR15 with him to ask if the bot knew anything about these aliens.

Then Abalim noticed the prone neon-red sexbot frozen with its metallic hand raised on the outside of the wall.

Not that the larger robot standing in front of the archway stopped the aliens. Two of them grabbed the android under her arms and dumped her to the side, leaving the archway clear.

Gibbering in a guttural language, one of the creatures aimed a small black box at the force field.

A sizzling whine before the shield dissolved.

Now the alien aimed the black box and pushed a different button that activated the *nutesh* snares around the women's necks.

All five screamed in agony, gripping the leather collars and dropping hard to the unyielding floor.

Abalim clenched his fists as he watched the little shits scramble to the women with hoots and whistles, securing their wrists and slapping putty-looking *rappu* gags over their mouths.

Once the women were secured, the aliens forced them to stand. They grabbed the women and scurried with them down the deserted, dark hallway.

The vision switched.

Now Abalim stood outside the building and watched Lisa being dragged to an alleyway. Racing after them, he skidded to a halt when he saw her floating next to a small spaceship. The alien activated the *nutesh* snare around her neck and dragged her over an open table at its side.

Abalim rushed to her, and made it in time to watch her hit the metal sheet inside.

At the same time something was injected into her neck. Her eyes fluttered closed as the table slid into the ship.

He did his best to follow her, but couldn't. The vision stalled, so he linked himself to Lisa's psychic trail to see if he could connect with her in a different Dreamwalk.

Chapter Three

Lisa stared at the blinking cursor on her computer screen. The damn thing taunted her, daring her to come up with a plotline for a new series. Normally, starting a new series was easy. She had so many ideas about the various worlds and love stories she was eager to create.

Most of the time, it was hard to pick which one she wanted to start on. But for the first time in a long time, she couldn't clear her head to begin typing. As she sat there and stared at the blank screen, she felt a prickle of awareness. She turned her head and jumped. Leaning on the frame of the open doorway of her office with crossed arms and one ankle casually crossed over the other was a breathtakingly handsome, masculine man.

The fission of fear was quickly replaced by wonder. The man studied her with a casual air and a slight smile on his luscious lips. She should be terrified that a stranger was in her house, standing there watching her. But for some reason, she knew him. As if she'd been waiting her whole life to meet him.

"Who, um, who are you?" Her face heated. She cleared her throat. *Way cool, Lisa. Your voice sounds like a sex worker on steroids.*

The man straightened and walked, no, strolled to stand next to her desk. Placing a hand over his heart, he gave a gallant bow. "My name is Abalim, and I've been sent to find you."

She glanced around her messy office. Everything was in its place—her stack of to-be-read books piled in one corner and a stack that needed to be put on the bookshelves in another. The bookcases around the room were stuffed with novels of every size and color, along with various knickknacks on the shelves. The plant on her desk was a bit wilted. Darn, she'd better water it before it died. The two plants on stands in front of the windows seemed to have the same problem. When was the last time she took care of them? She rubbed her forehead. Why didn't that seem right? She'd already taken care of the plants somehow.

"Find me? Am I lost?" She lifted her gaze to the sight of the gorgeous man, drinking in every luscious detail, and gave him a goofy smile. Hey, she was only human.

The man sat on the edge of her desk. His smile was warm and inviting. "I'm afraid so."

Ignoring his implication, she widened her eyes and took a closer look at him. *Holy... soaring space dung.* This guy had to be one of the best-looking men she'd ever seen in her life. And she'd seen quite a few of them. Okay, they were two-dimensional pictures of male models she browsed through when deciding which one to pick for a cover of her latest romance book. But this guy... this guy put them all to shame. It wasn't just the symmetrical arrangement of his face, which was fine... fine... fine, but it was the maturity and intelligence stamped there that took her breath away.

And his killer body wasn't anything to sneeze at, either. Even though he wore loose clothing that could've been worn in the middle east centuries ago, the gap in the linen shirt and sleeveless brown vest displayed a virtual smorgasbord of hills and valleys of firm pecs with a hint of a six-pack farther down. His short sleeves lovingly caressed his bulging biceps that screamed power.

Her breath quickened as her gaze roamed over the muscles of his arms, tracing the contours of his body, and she imagined what all that power would feel like if she ran her fingers over them. A flush of warmth rose up her spine, and her heart thudded.

Lisa continued her examination. His skin was so dark it gleamed with purple highlights in the soft light. The whites of his eyes were a startling contrast to his face, as were those white teeth shown when his sensuous, full lips parted. His shoulder-length hair had corkscrew curls soft against his thick neck.

Even with his hands folded in front of him, his passive attitude didn't fool her one bit. There was obvious intelligence in his sharp, obsidian gaze. As if he knew the secrets of the universe that no one else did.

She was drawn to him, captivated by the beauty and mystery surrounding him. She'd bet her hard drive someone like him could share a boatload of exciting stories in a deep baritone voice. Better yet, whispering into her ear in the dark as they cuddled in a cloud of soft blankets. Naked.

Whew! If she was lost, she sure didn't want to be found by anyone but him.

"Tell me how you're feeling."

The concern in his rumbling voice made her shiver.

Before she had a chance to answer, her stomach gave a loud rumble. She put her hand over it with a sheepish grin. "I'm starving." Her nose wrinkled. "I don't think I've eaten in a long time." She tilted her head and gave him a quizzical stare. "I don't understand why I said that. It's not like I go around missing a chance to eat." She patted the side of her well-endowed rear end with a chuckle. "Can't get this baby looking like this by skipping meals."

Abalim took her hands in his and pulled her up to stand. "I'm afraid I can't help you with that, but I can give you the pleasure of tasting your favorite meal."

The promise in his dark eyes made her suck in a breath. She'd rather find pleasure in something other than food. Her eyes roamed over his tempting muscular chest. Where to start... where to start...

He leaned over and whispered into her ear. "What would you like?"

Him? She licked her lips. *Dang. Down, girl.* No need to attack the man she met seconds ago. When he pulled back and looked at her, his hands squeezed hers just a bit. She shivered. The skin where he touched burned.

"Food." His eyes twinkled. "What food would you enjoy?"

"A, ah, bacon cheeseburger and curly fries?" Her stomach rumbled and her mouth watered. She hummed at the thought of two sirloin beef patties smothered in melted cheese topped with crispy bacon between two toasted buns.

Her office disappeared. Now she sat cross-legged on a plush pillow on the floor. On top of a round table was a plate containing a double cheeseburger with a steaming helping of her favorite spicy fries. Modesty be damned. She grabbed the normally forbidden temptation and took a hefty bite. The burger was delicious. With each bite, she relished the flavor of the melted cheese and the juicy beef. For the first time in days, her hunger slowly started to abate. The fries, however, were even better. The golden-brown potatoes were perfectly seasoned, and the crunchy texture helped ease the aching hunger. After scooping up and devouring the last fry, she slouched and licked her fingers to savor the succulent grease left behind.

"I'm sorry, this isn't real," Abalim said from across the round table. "But the sensations you experienced aren't phony."

"What do you mean, this isn't real?" She glanced around. Whoa, the only thing she saw was the table with plush cushions around it. The background was just a misty wisp of fog, like in a bad black-and-white horror movie. "Where am I?"

With the grace of a man in tune with his body, Abalim stood and sauntered to her, holding his hand out. "Come, let's go someplace more comfortable. I'll explain everything I know."

She studied his outstretched hand and his sturdy fingers beckoning to be touched. With a mental shrug, she placed her hand in his.

Now the atmosphere was warm and cozy. She found herself on a plush couch facing a fireplace with a soothing fire dancing merrily inside. Abalim sat next to her, nice and cozy-like. While they didn't touch, his body warmth eased the tension between her shoulders. How odd she trusted him like she did. She turned and sat cross-legged to face him.

"Okay." She twined her fingers together and twiddled her thumbs. "Start by telling me where we are."

Abalim twirled his forefinger to encompass the softly lit room that could've been someone's vacation home in the mountains. "We are in what my family calls a Dreamwalk. Do you know what a psychic is?"

She nodded her head and shrugged. "Of course. I write paranormal romances, after all."

His smile creased the skin at the corner of his eyes. "That should hopefully make this easier to explain. You see, I'm a very strong psychic whose main talent is telepathy. I was in that cell you and your friends were in on FiPan. Once I was there, it helped me connect with you mentally."

Lisa gasped and put her hand over her mouth. "You mean you can read my mind? And you're in it now?" *Shit!* Did this mean he knew she lusted after him earlier? Her face heated.

"Oh, no." He leaned over and patted her bent knee. "It's a habit of mine to not read people unless I'm forced to or I've been invited to." He withdrew his warm hold and turned to face her with a sheepish grin. "I learned at a very early age how utterly confusing people are." He chuckled. "Besides, as you people say, it creeps me out."

For the first time, Lisa noticed his slight accent and how he spoke English as if it wasn't his first language. "But if you're not in my mind, how are we here in what you called a Dreamwalk?"

"You see, once I have a sense of your psyche thread, I can put us into another plane of consciousness where we can communicate and interact with each other." He frowned and looked around the room. "Unfortunately, it's hard to control how long we can last in the dream plane. It depends on where our real bodies are and if we are somehow forced out of this dream state." His black gaze fixated on her. "So I need to make this as quick as possible. Do you have any idea where you are or where you're going?"

She shook her head and rubbed her temple. "No. All I know is some creepy little pudgy alien shoved me into a spaceship and injected me with something to put me to sleep." She couldn't help it. The terror of not knowing what was going to happen to her made her grab his large hands. "Do you think you can find a way to come and get me?"

He caressed her hands and gave her knuckles a soft kiss. "Now that you and I have connected in this strong Dreamwalk, look for me to contact you like this again. Until then, keep track of everything you see and hear that might give me a clue as to where to find you. I promise I will do everything within my power to do so."

***

Lisa gasped as her eyes snapped open. She bolted upright and reached out blindly, trying to grasp the familiar sheets of her own bed. Instead, her fingers met only a cold, unfamiliar surface.

The room was illuminated by a strange green light, and the walls were covered in indescribable symbols and shapes.

Lisa's head pounded, a wave of vertigo making her dizzy. Where was she? The memory of being in a safe place with a captivating man faded away.

Blinking to clear her vision, she took in her surroundings. She glanced at the odd-looking bed, but a small hum made her look up and examine the room. All around was a large space filled with strange equipment and machinery she'd never seen before. It was made of clean lines, neither round nor square. Like whoever made it couldn't make up their mind how they wanted it shaped.

What really took her aback were the squiggly symbols carved into the walls and flowing up to the curved ceiling. If she squinted, she swore dark liquid ran underneath them through slender tubes, like blood pumping through veins. Just watching the way it rolled, spread, and joined other symbols made her vertigo worsen. She shut her eyes and turned her head. Enough of that.

A hissing sound from the other side of the room made her jump. She opened her eyes and looked behind her. There, in the corner, was an alien creature unlike anything she'd ever seen before.

Its body was elegantly slim, with soft luminescent skin that emanated an ethereal glow. Its two arms were delicate, elongated limbs with long, triple jointed fingers. The being looked androgynous, neither male nor female. Its oblong head was adorned with a crown of golden spines, and its almond-shaped eyes shimmered in an array of mesmerizing colors.

Lisa froze, eyes wide. She didn't dare move or speak.

The alien creature glided closer.

Now she had a chance to see it wore some kind of armor, with intricate markings etched along its edges.

It moved closer still.

Darn, that strange humming noise came from him... er, it? As she stared, a sharp pinch came and went on her neck. "Ow! What the hell?" She slapped her palm there in reaction.

The creature spoke, its voice unexpectedly flat and unemotional, while at the same time sounding like a lot of people talking at once. "Greetings, human woman," it said. "We deem it necessary for you to understand that which you will be privileged to partake of. Thus, we have given aid to your primitive mind to gain the ability to communicate with us." As the alien spoke, the pitch of its voice heightened.

What was weird, for the first time she noticed it didn't talk through its razor-thin mouth. Instead, she heard it in her head. It must have meant telepathy when it announced she had the ability to communicate with them. Great. More mental gymnastics.

"You are on the planet Qorath." It continued its narrative. "We are the Xeltrians." It waved its spindly fingers to its undefined chest. "I am known as Rerqel."

Lisa sat up, not caring she was completely naked. Stupid thing probably didn't notice one way or the other anyway, so why worry about it? "Ok, what do you want with me?" Might as well hear the bad news up front. No way was this going to be something fun.

"We have been observing your kind for some time and are deeply fascinated by your species. In the past, we were unable to personally study humans due to Earth being under protective status. However, since the Zerins have introduced women to the citizens of the Federation Consortium, we have decided it was within our rights to obtain a specimen of our own."

She narrowed her eyes at the creature. Somehow, she didn't think they wanted human women to help their dying species avoid extinction like those who applied for the Exchange.

"You possess unique capabilities that are not seen in any other species. This includes your reproductive capabilities, your hormonal complexities, and your overall genetic diversity."

The damn thing sounded like a snooty professor giving a lecture.

"We desire to learn more about you, thus we have purchased you from the Ozevroc who brought you here."

Oh, that had to be the name of the pudgy little bastard who shoved her in that octagon ship. "Okaaay—" She gave the alien a narrow-eyed glare. "—does that mean you're going to do some kind of alien probe on me?"

The alien called Rerqel took a step back. "If we understand your reference, we will not be experimenting on your physical body. That would be a primitive and useless endeavor." It waved spindly fingers to indicate the room. "We have done all the necessary physical inspections while you were unconscious."

The tension in her body deflated. Thank God she didn't have to dwell on images of them cutting her open while she was awake. So, no need to panic about the whole getting probed thing.

"Our intent is the most crucial. You are an alien being with strange urges and instincts we wish to explore."

Her fists clenched. "So what does that mean?"

"Fascinating that you would ask that before seeing to your urgent physical needs." Its bulbous head tilted to the side.

For the first time, Lisa noticed a ridge that ran from its temple around the back of its head to end at the other temple.

Instead of being bald, it had wispy gray hair below the ridge that rested at the bottom of its neck.

As if to confirm what the alien said, her stomach rumbled. She put a hand there but didn't look away from Rerqel. A fading memory of eating a tasty cheeseburger in a dream hadn't satisfied her need for food.

"We have ascertained that you have not eaten for several days. As we wish for you to be in optimal physical condition for the trial ahead of you, we will provide you with a safe place to rest and eat until you achieve that objective."

"I don't suppose I could have something to wear, could I?" Didn't hurt to ask. What's the worst that could happen? They'd say no?

Rerqel didn't answer, but held out its large hand with the spindly fingers.

Like in the movies, minuscule particles sparkled before forming into a solid panel of fabric.

"You may wear what we have engineered for your use." It handed the lump of cloth to her.

The surprisingly soft fabric didn't seem to be a particular color. She slid off the cold metallic table and stood to unfold it. One minute it seemed to be gray, then the next it was white, then it turned into a turquoise blue. It was a one-piece outfit. Kind of like a scuba wetsuit with footsies.

She didn't hesitate. She'd been shivering since she woke up. Either from nerves or the cool air. At least putting on clothes should help. It was easy to step in and pull it over her torso and slide her arms into the sleeves. Before she had a chance to figure out how to close the front, the material flowed across her chest and sealed itself. While it was formfitting, it had to be the most comfortable thing she'd ever put on in her life. Even her breasts were uplifted and held firm. Damn, no bra needed.

Nice. Putting on comfortable, clean clothes made her feel a hundred percent better. Her stomach rumbled again. She licked a dry tongue over her chapped lips.

"We will take you to the domicile assigned to you and provide you with sustenance. You will follow me." Rerqel turned and flowed with a graceful pace to one of the solid walls. Before the alien banged into it, the barrier disappeared.

Lisa glanced around the room, searching for what, she had no idea. Might as well follow the creepy alien. It'd be nice if they had something as tasty as a cheeseburger for her to eat. She sighed. No way was a cheeseburger happening anytime soon. *Humph.* She doubted there were cows in space. But, with the promise of something to eat, she followed the long strides of her captor as it led her out of the depressing room.

***

The corridor of the alien building stretched for miles.

Lisa's shoulders drooped. It was hard to put one foot in front of the other as she followed the alien Rerqel. The only thing tempting her to move at all was the promise of food. Lifting weary eyes, it took time for her to notice the walls were an eerie luminescent blue as the air hummed with an otherworldly energy. Everything seemed so alien, so strange and unfamiliar. She was glad they didn't encounter any other Xeltrians. No telling if she'd lose it if she ended up surrounded by a bunch of the tall, gangly creatures.

Rerqel hadn't said a word since they began their walk. It... well, hell. She might as well call it by a male pronoun. She hated thinking of it as an "it". She giggled. Now her imagination jumped to an old Addams Family series with Cousin It, except without his body being covered by silky hair. Oh, hell. No doubt about it, she was losing her mind. Throwing her shoulders back, she forced herself to watch the gangly alien move with a strange, almost dance-like stride. His long limbs glided along the floor of the hallway.

Good thing he knew where they were going. If she was left on her own, she'd be totally lost after the first twenty turns. Lisa followed in its, no, his wake and did her best to keep up. To keep her mind off what was happening, she studied the walls as they passed. Just like the previous room, she'd swear the darn building looked alive. It rolled and pulsated, shifting as though a living creature squirmed as it tried to escape. Her skin crawled, and she rubbed her arms to ward off the strange sense of dread welling up.

Rerqel stopped in front of an ornate door, waving his arm in a sweeping gesture.

The solid door disappeared, revealing an arched doorway.

He gestured for Lisa to enter.

With a mental shrug, she peered into the dimly lit room. It was smaller than the medical one she'd been in. But the one thing they had in common was the strange and unfamiliar objects.

After giving the alien a quick backward glance, Lisa stepped inside. Her heart thudded at the oppressive silence. She gave Rerqel another glance.

He stood in the doorway, his spindly frame casting a long shadow across her feet.

In the center of the room, a table appeared, along with a small stool to sit on. Resting on the table were plates piled with what she hoped was food.

The Xeltrian motioned for her to take a seat.

Lisa hesitated, but the scents made the decision for her. While the tantalizing aroma was unusual, it smelled good enough to eat.

Rerqel glided forward and motioned again for her to sit.

She grimaced, but pulled out a chair and sat. A strange excitement fluttered in the pit of her stomach. She studied the array of exotic shapes and sizes on one plate and what looked like breads filling another. Despite her apprehension, everything looked harmless, even enticing. She plucked up a square light-blue thingamajig that felt like holding a tomato. She rubbed it, causing the skin to give way under her fingertips. She slowly brought it to her nose. *Hmm... a cinnamon roll?*

She took a chance and bit in. The taste was unlike anything she'd ever experienced before. Though it was strange, it was sweet and delicious with a hit of hot spice. A pleasant warmth spread throughout her body. She licked her lips, savoring the taste for a few moments before keeping an eye on the alien as she slowly devoured the treat.

Rerqel never took his eyes from her, his eyelids blinking sideways as he watched her every move.

She was the first to glance away. The back of her neck heated as she felt his gaze on her. When she finished everything offered, the alien nodded. She sat back with a goofy grin. Damn, for the first time in a long time, her tummy was happy.

"Excellent." Rerqel laced his thin fingers together. "You may rest and regain your strength. I will come back for you at the appropriate time." He stood at the open door for a few moments, his gaze still fixed on her. Then, without a word, he turned and left, the wall closing behind him.

Lisa stared at the solid wall for a few moments before letting a deep sigh escape. Taking a fortifying breath, she took her time getting up from the table and headed to the hovering cot. With each step, her mind raced on what had just happened. She yawned so hard her jaw cracked. Well, nothing was going to get solved right now.

She rubbed her burning eyes. If nothing else, she'd take Rerqel's advice and get some sleep. Lowering onto the surprisingly soft mattress, she shut her eyes and emptied her mind. She yawned again, smacking her lips. If she was lucky, she'd have another dream about a dark, handsome man coming to rescue her.

***

As Abalim withdrew from the Dreamwalk he shared with Lisa, he was yanked into another psychic realm. The tug was unyielding and didn't give him a chance to break away. When he landed, it was in a place quite alien, unlike anything he'd seen before. Everything in him stilled when a strange creature coalesced in front of him.

"I am Rerqel from the planet Qorath," the androgynous creature stated in a voice layered with multiple voices. The inflection in his tone was unemotional, bordering on cold. "You, Abalim, from the planet Earth will be a perfect addition for us to analyze along with the human woman Lisa. When you created that last psionic connection with her, you enabled us to verify you are what your people call soul mates." The spindly creature tilted his overlarge oblong head that was shaped like a bicycle helmet. "With that connection, we now will have the means to determine if your species is worth protecting from the incoming Krystalii."

Abalim ignored what the alien said about Lisa. He might not know what a "soul mate" was, but he didn't like the alien's insinuation that mankind had to prove they were deserving of salvation. The mere mention of the Krystalii and the threat they brought made his protective instincts rise as unrealistic chills in the psychic plane made him shudder. "What do you know of the Krystalii?" When he encountered Lord Baelon on Hiigar, he'd gotten the impression the aliens hadn't left their dimension yet.

The tall slender being had delicate, elongated limbs with a luminescent skin that emitted a soft glow. If he didn't know any better, he'd swear this creature was somehow related to the galactic criminals known as the Fribbegh, the creatures who created the gray alien myth on Earth.

"Lord Baelon believes he is all-powerful, but we have monitored their interest in our dimension for quite some time without their knowledge. His interest in human women is quite fascinating. He believes his crystallized species can somehow use them to accelerate their birth cycles, which usually take thousands of years." Rerqel's almond-shaped eyes shimmered with an array of mesmerizing colors. "While we believe his assumptions are absurd, we do not discount the probabilities."

Abalim crossed his arms. "While I realize you are a strong psychic and might try to force me to subject myself to your physical analyzation, I assure you that's not going to happen."

Rerqel tilted his head the other way. The movement highlighted the ridge from one temple that wrapped around his head to the other temple. "What is the fascination with you creatures about being examined physically? We have no need to subject you to that type of analyzation. Scanning your primitive bodies was hardly a challenge to gain an understanding of your biological workings at the DNA level. Especially you." The Xeltrian's eyes narrowed. "However, you are an interesting creature. Human, yet not. Akurn, yet not. It's as if you've been given a combination of various galactic species. But—" Rerqel waved his long, serpentine fingers. "—that is not what interests us. What we propose is to see how you and your female handle an unknown situation of who lives and who dies. We are interested in observing how you react in an environment where you have no control and don't have a clear understanding of the dynamics involved."

When Rerqel stated Abalim was a separate species from Lisa, Abalim narrowed his eyes. How did this alien know he wasn't technically a human? Did Reqel somehow analyze what he was without him knowing?

The creature, at least a foot taller than his six-foot three, flicked one of his three jointed fingers at the air next to them. A rounded image opened, and the scene zoomed in on a sleeping Lisa.

Abalim's heart thudded as he watched her calmly sleeping.

"Because she is a primitive without your natural enhancements, we gave her the basic psionic ability to communicate with us as you do. Thus, we injected her with a stimulus to open her mind for that purpose. After all, how can she be given instructions if she can't understand the directive?"

Abalim frowned. "Is that why she's unconscious? Because of something you gave her?"

"Do not be absurd. How can the test be valid if we interfere with her otherwise natural ability? The stimulus only awakened that which she already had in her genetic makeup." Rerqel's tone ended with a slightly sharp bite. "We have provided sustenance to this female and she is now in a natural deep sleep. When she awakens, you will begin your trial."

Was this creature saying they gave her telepathic abilities? Maybe that's why it'd been so easy for him to link them into that last Dreamwalk.

The alien flicked his wrist at the image of Lisa, and the vision closed. "Because of the threat the Krystalii present, we have a limited amount of time to halt their ambitions. We have considered eliminating all humans on the planet Earth before they reach our dimension. However, that will diminish our resources significantly. While we are not convinced humans are worthy of saving, we have decided it would be best to verify if that would be the best option. As I said before, it appears humans are capable of procreating with others in the galaxy. On that point, Lord Baelon is quite correct. We are aware this human capability can be a great untapped resource for other species in our galaxy who are facing extinction." Rerqel's tone didn't change, but somehow sounded condescending.

Abalim stilled. The veiled threat made him clench his fists. *By the God An.* Earth barely got through the last threat of annihilation by an alien race.

"Having one specimen of a species is hardly the basis for a true analysis," Rerqel continued. "Especially since that species is split into two fractions... male and female. However, we will persevere. You will come to Qorath and partake in the trial we have set up."

The gangly alien glided near enough that Abalim could see the intense glaze in his iridescent black eyes.

"And since Earth has lost its protective galactic status, we would be within our rights as citizens of the Federation Consortium to do what we deem necessary to protect its citizens without government backlash." He straightened and clasped its fingers together in front of itself. "I trust you understand all that has been divulged to you?"

Oh, he understood all right. Easy enough to recognize a threat when it slapped him upside his head. Not that he had much of a choice. "Well, I'm not one who would refuse such a warm invite." He took a step back. Personal space and all. "I don't suppose you have a way I can get to your planet, do you?"

A brief sneer crossed Rerqel's lipless mouth. "We have anticipated your need. In FiPan is a captain of a smuggling vessel by the name of Saphira who has tried to gain entrance to our planet for quite some time. She is currently at an establishment called Grub & Grog, not too far from where you and your brothers currently are. However, I would suggest you quicken to find her, as she and her crew are arranging to depart." The alien tilted his head to the other side. "Until we meet again, hybrid."

The connection broke.

Chapter Four

"Mister Abalim, sir." A tiny metallic voice on his shoulder quavered in his ear. "Are you okay? Mister Abalim, sir?"

Abalim blinked to get his bearings. Being jerked around in Dreamwalks and visions made his head swim. He glanced at the small spider-shaped bot on his shoulder. He gave the little guy a slight smile. "Yes, I'm fine. Being yanked from one psyche plane to another makes my head spin. How long was I out?"

JR15's bulbous silver-and-green body quivered. "Two hours, nineteen seconds, and one thousand twenty-three picoseconds."

Abalim grunted and glanced around. He was still in the prison cell where he and his brothers searched for the psyche trails of the human women who'd been there. His three brothers were standing with their arms crossed, wearing identical narrowed eyes and pinched frowns. Aimed at him.

"What? Why are you looking at me like that?" He growled.

"What took you so long? Our visions weren't nearly as long." Arakiba flicked an expressive wave at the other two next to him. "We don't have all day to wait for you, you know."

Abalim stifled a smile as he sensed Arakiba's fear made him short-tempered.

Asmodel lowered his arms. "The three of us have latched onto the psyche trails of the other women that were here. We figured we'd better separate and find those women before the trail gets cold."

Azazel stepped to Abalim and placed a hand on his forearm. "Were you successful in linking with one of the women as we were?"

"I did," he answered. "And a bit more. Here, let me share what I've found out." Abalim squeezed his brother's hand before stepping back.

He closed his eyes and connected on the psyche plane they'd always used. With ease, he opened the line between him and their eldest brother, Adapa, currently light years away on the rogue planet Akurn. While the distance made it difficult to have direct communication, Abalim wouldn't have any trouble sharing what happened to him. Sliding into their collective minds, he showed them the communication he'd had with the alien Rerqel and the alien's offer to help support the oncoming Krystalii invasion. He only gave them a brief snippet of what he and Lisa shared. They didn't need to know how she affected him. How she tapped into his loneliness and uncovered his secret desire to bond with her, as Adapa had with Inanna.

"Well, damn." Arakiba scratched the side of his head. "The only thing I got was a link to one of the women and the strong sense of which direction I'd better go."

"I, too, had an overwhelming urge of where I'm needed. And there's little time to waste." Azazel gave them a slight bow. "I also believe I will not have any difficulty in transporting to the woman I need to find."

Abalim frowned and crossed his arms. "I don't like the idea of you transporting somewhere where you've never been before. It could be dangerous."

Azazel's grin was uncharacteristically boyish. "You don't have to worry about me. Remember Inanna classified me as anal-retentive? Adhering to detail has always been my passion."

Well, that dumb statement made Abalim roll his eyes. Can't argue with stupid.

"I'm not stupid and you know it," Azazel retorted with a wide grin.

"Keep the path open, brother, to let us know your teleportation worked." Asmodel referred to their shared psychic channel. "And don't forget to keep your JR open as well."

"Yeah." Arakiba snorted. "We don't have time to search the galaxy for your scrambled bits."

"And with that in mind..." Azazel spread his arms and went out of focus before disappearing.

"Freaking show-off," Arakiba mumbled.

Abalim suspected his brother envied Azazel's strong teleportation skills. While they all could do quick jumps and short distances, none of them could compare to Azazel's talent.

"I believe I have a way to get to the woman named Lisa." Abalim shared her name with them. "I'm supposed to find a pub here called the Grub & Grog and find a smuggler named Captain Saphira. Apparently she and her crew have been trying to go to the planet Qorath for quite some time now." He eyed his two remaining brothers. "What about you two? Do you know how you're going to get where you need to go?"

Asmodel and Arakiba glanced at each other.

"Okay with you if I take *Elemi*?" Arakiba thumbed behind him in the general direction of the spaceship the Chancellor of the Federation consortium let them borrow. "I have a feeling she knows where the planet is that I have to go to."

Asmodel nodded with a slight shrug. "I'll go with Abalim and see if I can hire a smuggler of my own."

"Okay, bros." Arakiba gave them a sloppy salute with his two fingers. "I'm outta here." His body wobbled and went out of focus before he, too, disappeared.

Teleporting the short distance to the spaceship housing the AI Elemi wouldn't be a problem for him. Abalim's only concern was how the AI that ran the ship would work with his smart-ass brother. She'd either bond with him and say he was the love of her life, or she'd make his life a living hell. Not that it mattered. Damn man would enjoy it either way.

"Come on," he said to his remaining brother. "Since we don't know where we're going, we might as well see if we can find somebody to give us directions."

His brother gave a slight, insincere shudder. "I can't wait to see the freak show we'll find there. Think they'll charge extra for their two-headed comedy act?"

***

Abalim headed out with Asmodel into the eerily silent grimy underbelly of the small village. Turned out the Grub & Grog was easier to find than he'd hoped for.

It was the only place in the dim twilight of the deserted streets with a hazy gleam of flickering light that could be seen a couple of blocks away.

When they stopped in front of the disreputable alien tavern, its mundane appearance was sloppy at best. The corroded metal walls were adorned with faded, flickering holographic signs that offered various libations and questionable services. The entrance, guarded by a towering, four-armed bouncer of an unknown species, emitted an eerie, pulsating hum.

Passing by the steady glare of the guard at the entrance, they entered without trouble.

Once inside, the atmosphere turned out as dreary as expected. A low light gave the place a depressing glow.

Abalim took a deep breath. What coated his senses was a thick conglomeration of gloomy scents, pungent fumes, and the palpable energy of desperate conversations and clandestine deals.

Tables, booths, and nooks carved into the metallic walls were filled with aliens of all shapes and sizes. Those wearing clothing had on a mishmash of worn leather-like jackets and shirts adorned with intricate metallic badges and patches, suggesting affiliations with various crews. Some wore pants, most showing signs of wear and tear. The air was heavy with a dizzying mix of languages that echoed in harmonious disarray.

The furnishings, well-worn and tattered, could have witnessed the rise and fall of countless civilizations. The walls were adorned with faded space-faring artifacts, antique weapons, and holographic memorabilia from infamous space pirates and interstellar rebels. Ancient flickering holo screens hung above the bar, broadcasting news from distant solar systems, underground races, and wanted posters of individuals with bounties that would tempt even the most inexperienced bounty hunter.

Behind the bar, a haggard-looking bartender of a mysterious alien race served drinks from bottles with labels written in cryptic symbols. The drinks ranged from luminescent neon concoctions that fizzed and bubbled to mysterious swirling mixtures that defied gravity.

At a quick glance, it was easy to see the crowd in the Grub & Grog was a peculiar bunch. Grizzled space mercenaries with cybernetic implants, alien traders with shady intentions, smugglers lurking in the shadows, and enigmatic beings cloaked in hoods, their true forms veiled in secrecy. The hum of conversation and raucous laughter accompanied the eerie melodies played by a band of multi-limbed musicians on an elevated stage in the center.

Despite the seemingly chaotic ambiance, an unspoken code of conduct prevailed. Even without opening his psychic senses, it was clear violence wouldn't be tolerated.

"Arakiba would love this place," Asmodel quipped.

"No doubt." Abalim headed to an open space at the bar. Not for the first time was he thankful the Zerins injected him and his brothers with intergalactic translators. He raised a finger to get the bartender's attention.

The creature stood an imposing seven feet tall, its sinewy frame hinting at a grace and speed that defied its massive stature. Even in the low light, its skin shimmered a shade of deep blue and was adorned with intricate patterns that shifted and danced as he moved.

"Yes, patron? How may I assist?" The alien's speech sounded like a series of musical notes and random clicks.

Obviously, its soothing voice mixed with a melodic quality, was used to calm even the most agitated customers.

"We're looking for Captain Saphira. Would you happen to know if she's here?"

"What do yer want 'er for?"

The male voice behind him made him jump. *Dammit!* That's what he got for locking down his psychic senses to avoid getting caught up in everyone's drama around him. He glared at Asmodel's chuckling. Asshat. He could've warned a guy. *I think Arakiba is rubbing off on you.* He gave his brother a mental warning.

Asmodel just shrugged and gave him a mischievous smile. *Not my fault your JR is falling down on the job.*

Pick on your own bot. Abalim huffed.

He gave Asmodel the evil eye before swiveling around. He backed up against the bar, putting an elbow on the counter while searching for the person who spoke to him. At first, it didn't look like anyone addressed him until he glanced down at the small, wiry creature in a hunched position in front of him. The guy couldn't be more than three feet tall. His skin was a mottled shade of green with rough, scaly patches. Large, bulbous eyes in the middle of his face sported a heady mixture of orange-and-red irises that gave him a perpetually anxious expression.

"I was sent by Rerqel from Qorath to obtain passage to their planet."

"Fer the both o'ya?" The alien's eyes swiveled to Asmodel before focusing back on him.

Asmodel shook his head. "No. My path lies elsewhere." His attention shifted to the other side of the room. "As a matter of fact, my destiny is just over there." Giving Abalim a parting look, Asmodel headed away.

You going to be okay? Abalim asked, even though he hadn't taken his gaze off the little alien in front of him.

Yes, do not worry. Everything is fine. I was expecting things to turn out this way. I'll keep our pathway open. Asmodel's mental tone was absentminded as the crowd swallowed his departing figure.

"I guess it's jus' you then." The alien mused, the sharp claws on his slender fingers retracting as he scratched a patch on his jaw. "Okay. You's follow me." The little guy turned around and marched through the dense crowd.

"JR15, hang on."

"Yes, Mister Abalim, sir."

The tips of JR15's legs tickled as the droid scurried to the back of Abalim's neck, under his dreadlocks.

Following the little alien was easy enough as he shouldered through the thick throng. The billowing cloak of various patches the small alien wore allowed him to blend seamlessly through the room.

Just before a sense of claustrophobia choked him, Abalim stumbled into a free zone, right in front of a round table on a raised dais. And there in the middle, with her back to the wall and her arms resting on the backrest, was a breathtaking alien female.

Her wide, almond-shaped blazing eyes of emerald were laser focused on him. As he stood at the end of her table, she gave him a knowing smirk.

***

"I hear you want to go to Qorath."

The arresting female tapped her finger on the backrest of the round table. "Good thing you showed up when you did. My crew and I were getting ready to leave." She pulled her hands down and leaned on the opaque table, clutching her fingers together.

Abalim had no idea what to expect when he was told to have this captain take him to Qorath. But as he approached the large table, the sight of the alien female took his breath away. She had an extraordinary lustrous beauty.

Her coral-colored skin glowed in the flickering light of the room, highlighting brilliant-green eyes that sparkled like jewels. She wore tight tan leather pants visible through the clear table, revealing a figure almost too good to be true.

Did she have any special powers, or were all her successes based purely on cunning?

He hesitated, opening his senses to focus on her. While he couldn't read her mind, he sensed her emotions. The main sentiment coming from her was a calm acceptance mixed with a bit of excitement. Like he was the answer to something she'd searched for.

Saphira smiled as she held onto a delicate chain hanging around her neck that reached to the middle of her bountiful breasts. She looked him up and down before her expression turned thoughtful. "You may prove to be useful." Her fingers trailed to the end of the long necklace.

It was hard to tell what it was made of. The shimmering metal changed color and density with each of her caresses. The sparkling gem was a thumb-size teardrop with a magenta glow when she passed her fingers over it.

"I am more than happy to take you to Qorath since the Xeltrians have given us permission to do so." She narrowed her eyes. "The only stipulation for you to come on board is you stay away from the ship's computers and the restricted areas of the ship. Agreed?" Her full lips pursed as her head tilted. Her direct gaze left no doubt she'd hold him to his agreement.

Hmm, this was too easy. It didn't take a psychic to know she had some hidden agenda. Either about him or something about Qorath. He didn't sense any threat from her or from the small creature that brought him to her. Still, it was better to remain cautious.

"Agreed." Abalim made sure his posture was nonthreatening. "One thing, though." He tapped his opposite shoulder as a signal to the small bot to show himself. "This is my companion, JR15. He's a personal drone who has to come with me." He wasn't asking for permission.

JR15 scuttled from under the dreadlocks and stood at the end of Abalim's shoulder. The little guy quivered but kept silent.

Saphira tapped her gleaming fingernail of dark brown on her plump lips. She studied the spider-shaped droid. "I see no reason you cannot bring it. However." The gaze in her brilliant green eyes narrowed. "It, too, will stay out of our systems. If it is found on any part of the ship without your presence, I will destroy it immediately." She sat back with one side of her lips curving into a satisfied smirk. "That is, after I've drained it of all its data. That clear enough for you?"

Well, there went that idea. It wouldn't be worth satisfying his curiosity about Saphira and her crew by sending JR15 out to investigate. "Absolutely."

She gave him another hard look before tilting her head to glance at someone behind him. "Gilipthor, take..." She swung her head back to look at him. "By *Ichor's Holdings!* What's your name, boy?"

Boy? Abalim raised his left eyebrow. Even though he'd been created over seven thousand years ago, his physical appearance was at least on par with the female in front of him. "My name is Abalim." He gave her a slightly respectful bow of his head. "And I'm from the planet Earth."

Her nose scrunched as she pushed back a lock of her metallic-gold hair.

He hadn't seen a pure color like that since he and his brothers were given instructions on how to mine for the mineral in South Africa after they'd been created. Continuing his covert examination, he noticed her hair was short at the sides and the back, but carried a long panel draped over the side of her head that curled around her right breast.

"Okay, Abalim from Earth. Just follow Gilipthor and he'll get you settled in our ship, the *Galactic Serpent*."

"Youse be comin', Cap'in?" The wiry creature covered his bald head with the hood of his cloak.

Saphira gave a wave of dismissal. "Yes, yes." From her jacket pocket, she pulled out a small device that fit into the palm of her hand.

The exterior was a smooth and seamless oval, devoid of any visible buttons or switches. Faint patterns of luminescence gracefully flowed across the surface.

It reminded Abalim of the gentle ripples of a tranquil lake.

"I've got to check on a couple of things first. Then I'll be right there." She glanced up. "Wait until I join you before you introduce him to the crew." Her full coral lips pursed into a mischievous smirk. "I'm sure they're going to love him."

***

As Abalim followed the quick waddle of the scurrying Gilipthor through the crowd, he sent a mental message to his brother Asmodel to let him know he was leaving. His brother gave him an affirmative, if not distracted, acknowledgment. Looked like little brother was hot on the trail of a clue to where one of the women was. If he needed help, he could either contact their eldest brother on Akurn or have his JR unit do the same. It was quite disconcerting that the five of them would be thousands of parsecs separated from each other. They'd never experienced that great a distance apart from each other before. If he was honest, he couldn't decide if he was excited or terrified. Probably a bit of both.

"Is the ship far from here?" His footsteps splashed in pockets of dirty puddles as they walked through the decrepit streets of FiPan. The rancid odors streaming from the ground made his nose wrinkle. While he couldn't imagine himself as fastidious as the modern population of Earth, even back in ancient times when he was a slave, he never had to endure filth like this.

"Non," the creature replied, looking over his shoulder at Abalim. "Any gear youse need to pick up?"

Abalim gave him a crooked smirk. He never needed to carry anything since he could create whatever he needed with his psychokinesis. The only thing he couldn't create was his trusty companion, JR15. The only other thing he needed was a sentimental talisman he'd created when he was a child.

At first glance, it looked like a simple black obsidian oval as big as his thumb. It had a sturdy silver ball at the top with a braided leather cord looped through it. The pendant hung to the middle of his breastbone, and he kept it under his clothing.

Only on closer examination did the pendant reveal its intricate details. The engraving on the front was an ancient symbol representing protection and fortitude. On the backside was a small cavity that held three miniature gemstones—a deep-blue lapis lazuli for enhancing wisdom, a fiery-red carnelian for courage, and a shimmering clear-crystal quartz to amplify the energies of the other two gemstones.

The pendant held no magical properties, but it represented a tiny piece of himself that he'd made as a slave. A symbol of freedom when he was forced to endure a series of tests the scientists used to perform on him and his brothers. This reminded him no one could take away who he truly was. Throwing his shoulders back, Abalim shut the mental image down and focused on the here and now. "No, I have everything I need with me."

The only response from Gilipthor was a high-pitched whistle as he clapped his teeth together.

Abalim couldn't tell if the guy was annoyed or amused.

They didn't speak again as they headed to an open field under the dull gray sky tinged with a brownish fog. It was hard to tell if there were clouds above them because the dirty smog blanketing the air was filled with discolored layers. The sunlight bravely tried to pierce through the smudge, but its weak light created muted shadows. The atmosphere held a heavy chemical stench mixed with something burning in the distance.

"JR15?" He spoke out of the side of his mouth to the spybot perched between his neck in his shoulder. "Will this toxic air create any harmful side effects for me?"

"If we stayed much longer, Mister Abalim sir, you would soon experience several respiratory issues, compounded by eye irritation. It would be best if we left as quickly as possible." His tiny body quivered.

Good thing the little guy could stick to the skin of his neck without making it painful.

Gilipthor hurried his pace, making Abalim pick up his. They ended up in a burned field of dead grasses where a cigar -ship perched in the low light.

The tension between his shoulders melted as he studied it while they approached. It looked to be in good shape, with nary a dent or scratch in sight.

"There she be. *The Galactic Serpent.*" The pride in the creature's voice was easy to hear. "I's travel in it wid the good folks from Crichi, likes the cap'in, fer most of me life."

Before Abalim had a chance to ask anything else, Gilipthor pulled out a communication device similar to the one Saphira used earlier and barked several whistles and clicks into it.

Abalim stood next to him and crossed his arms.

Between one blink and the next, the scene around him changed. He now stood on a rectangular dais that had to be inside the ship. He took in a clean, deep breath and let it out with pleasure.

JR15 hummed his approval next to him.

"Follows me." Gilipthor trundled down the ramp and headed out an open archway.

Abalim didn't bother to look around. The diminutive alien might be half his size, but he was quick.

Gilipthor wheezed into his communication device as he led the way to an open door of an elevator.

When they got in, the doors reappeared closed. After several movements of them going up then sideways, the doors faded and opened to a narrow corridor with just enough light to be comfortable. The floors and walls were made of some type of metal. The floor was firm enough to walk on but had a soft give with each step. The hallway appeared to be seamless, with no openings or doorways. Every few feet, a cylinder tube hung from the ceiling a few inches from the wall.

Gilipthor stopped under one of those cylinders.

It lowered until it reached his eye level. Then a yellow light blinked on its bottom.

The alien leaned until a shimmering light coated his eye. "Come here, human man, and put your eye here."

Abalim wasn't going to correct Gilipthor calling him a human. To be honest, there were the worst things he could be called. Without a word, he leaned to put his face close to the cylinder when the smaller alien moved away.

The moment he came close to it, the cylinder drew up and was now at his eye level. After a quick burst of light, it shut off, and the cylinder slid back up to the ceiling.

As he blinked to get his eyesight back to normal, he noticed a strange symbol etched into the wall. It looked like a strange mixture of numbers inserted into a hieroglyphic.

"This is where you stays on the *Galactic Serpent*. But don't gets too comfortable. The Captain'll be here soon, and I'll take youse to meet the crew." Gilipthor whistled and clicked as he talked. He turned to Abalim and lowered an eye as the other one studied him up and down. "Youse and your littl' friend stays here real tight-like. And don't touch nothin.'"

Abalim gave the smaller male a slight smile. "I think we'll be just fine."

Gilipthor clacked his claws together with a nod. "Good. That's good. Don't need youse causin' trouble. Go inside and stay there until I comes ta get ya." He stared at Abalim as he stepped over the threshold. With a slight whistle, the smaller creature twirled around, his cape billowing behind him as he trotted down the hallway.

Abalim jerked back just as the door rematerialized. He looked up and saw another cylinder on the ceiling. He stood under it, waiting for to lower so he could open the door. The damn thing didn't move. Either he didn't know how to activate the thing, or he was locked in.

Panic gripped Abalim, his breath catching in his throat. The walls of the room closed in, taunting him to teleport to the other side and freedom. Fear clung to him, a remnant of his days in chains as a slave. He loathed this loss of control, a deep-seated phobia carved from a lifetime of confinement. With a deep, steadying breath, he summoned his inner strength, reaching for that resilient spark of defiance.

Better to do something constructive instead of wallowing in dread. Asmodel went to the small cot in the room and laid down. Closing his eyes, he laced his fingers together on his stomach while JR15 scrambled from beneath his hair and scurried over his torso and made himself comfortable on his chest. With a sigh, he willed himself to create a Dreamwalk that included the alluring Lisa.

Fruk his fears.

Chapter Five

Lisa slowly opened her eyes. Damn, her brain was full of mush. She rubbed one eye with the heel of her hand and sat up. Where the hell was she? The last thing she remembered was falling asleep in the room Rerqel stated was hers. But now... now, she found herself in an unfamiliar landscape. Like she'd been transported to an entirely new world. The sky a deep shade of azure, while the horizon had a mixture of brilliant colors. The grass beneath her feet was a vibrant green, almost too perfect to be real.

She glanced at her surroundings, where a figure came toward her from a distance. She squinted. It was hard to make out who it was. With each step, it became clearer it was a man. A *very* handsome man. And her face flushed at the intense way he watched her. His dark gaze was unyielding.

Lisa caught her breath in a dry mouth. The guy seemed familiar. Like someone she imagined in a dream. Why was he here in this strange world with her? As he got closer, her curiosity got the better of her. She slipped off the bed. With firm resolve, she headed to meet him halfway.

The closer they got, the clearer his details came. Like a fuzzy old TV coming into focus. Her heart quickened. *Soaring space dung*, the man sure fit the description of tall, dark, and handsome. The deep brown of his skin was a beautiful ebony, almost a pure black that reflected blue highlights in the shimmering light of dual suns. His gorgeous eyes were a dark shade of cocoa brown. And when he focused those vibrant orbs on her, Lisa experienced a strange sensation in her chest. Like a zap from an electric shock.

Abalim. His name was Abalim.

"Oh my God, it's you, isn't it?" Look at her. Talking like a star-struck fangirl.

He cocked his head with a smile. "I'm very glad you remember me."

The timbre of his low, melodic voice made her shiver.

He put a hand over his heart. "I told you I'd come back to let you know when I found you."

Lisa heart jumped. He did say that. But how...?

Abalim stepped closer, his eyes never leaving her face. "I've discovered what planet you're on, and I'll be there very soon. Rerqel knows I'm coming and has agreed to let me take you back to Earth after we've done some kind of trial together."

Lisa bit her bottom lip. Could this be true? He was real and was coming to help her? A surge of excitement at the possibility of being rescued made her breathless. Then something else made it hard to breathe. As she gazed into Abalim's eyes, she was inexplicably drawn to him. Like a moth dancing around an open flame.

For a brief snatch of time, the two of them stood in silence, their connection locked in an intense embrace. Well, why hesitate? It's not like she'd never done anything stupid in her life before. Besides, she was in a dream. Right? And she could do anything she wanted in a dream.

So, Lisa went for it. Stepping into his personal space, she gripped his solid upper arms. *Oh lordy.* She'd always wanted to wrap her fingers around a man's muscular arm and squeeze. To know what solid, silken skin felt like. Writing about it didn't come close to the actual sensation. The taut warm skin was a plush velvety texture over unyielding steel.

She leaned in, taking in a deep breath. Ah, pure masculine sin. A thrilling combination of ancient spice and man musk. She tilted her head and stood on her toes. Closing her eyes, she parted her lips, hoping he'd get a clue since she was so much shorter than him. The highest she got was the tip of his square chin line. No way would she break the dream by making stupid demands.

His warm breath caressing her lips was her only warning. With a heated touch as light as spring sunshine, he placed his mouth on hers.

That single, simple connection created a sizzle of awareness in the depths of her soul. At the power surge like a bolt of lightning, she melted into his embrace. Her very essence fused with his. His kiss turned carnal from one breath to the next.

The ground shifted as Abalim pulled her until her groin was flush against his hard, male length.

His dominant action caused her to fall into a world of pure, primitive feeling and captured her in eternal bliss. With a moan, she ground her lower self into the firm steel of his hardened member, searching for that perfect slice of friction where she needed it most.

Lisa wrapped her arms around his thick neck and jumped up and enfolded her legs around his trim waist, desperate to feel as much of him as she could. A sensual growl rumbled from deep within him, making her shiver in response.

Abalim's mouth gracefully moved from hers to the pulsating vein at the side of her neck, and his arms tightened in an unbreakable hold.

She responded by turning into pliant, liquid putty ready to be molded by a master. She'd never gone from neutral to instant lust so fast. Her breasts ached, her nipples like uncut diamonds waiting for an expert grader to mold them into something new.

As he suckled the sensitive skin between her neck and shoulder, his clever fingers found one of her quaking nipples and brushed over it.

She moaned as waves of heat pooled low inside. She would've melted into a pile of undignified goo if he hadn't kept a firm grip on her ass.

His mouth found hers again, a sensual dance of lips and tongue that threatened to turn carnal again.

When he pulled away, Lisa blinked, trying to get her hazy vision to focus. She sucked on her lower lip to steal the last of his addicting flavor. While not a novice to the act of love, what just happened was like nothing she'd ever experienced before.

In that moment, it was clear his kiss forever changed her life.

"I wish you were real," she whispered, pulling him closer and resting her forehead against his. "And that you really were coming to get me." He smiled when she chuckled. "I never thought I'd like being the damsel in distress. But I gotta admit it has its perks."

"I know it's hard to believe, but I am real, and I'm coming to Qorath for you." He returned her hug and nuzzled her neck. "But most of all"—he spoke softly into her ear—"I'm looking forward to holding you in my arms in the real world."

Abalim's form faded until there wasn't anything left to hold.

Profound loss swept through her before darkness once again claimed her.

***

Lisa jerked awake. Her eyes flew open. She searched for the elusive Abalim, only to find herself alone. She shut her eyes and swallowed hard. Damn, what made her think her dream man was real? Tears blurred her vision and slid down her temples. Sniffing, she wiped her wet face.

Lying here crying wasn't going to do any good. For all she knew, the stupid aliens somehow put her ideal man into her subconscious. Well, she wasn't going to fall for that crap. She'd be better off pretending it never happened.

Swinging her legs until her feet touched the floor, she gripped the side of the mattress. Closing her eyes, she hung her head and took in a deep breath. *Get a grip, Lisa. So, you're being held hostage by some damn aliens. It's not like you've never written this scenario before. All you gotta do is act like one of your heroines. Be smart and figure a way out of this.*

Throwing her shoulders back, she opened her eyes and studied where she was. The sparse room had all the charm of a derelict, abandoned factory in the middle of the swamp. Without the odors. Would it kill the Xeltrians to brighten up the place a bit? That mind-numbing shade of grayish white would depress anyone. The only other furniture was the table she'd eaten at, and it was colorless, bleeding into the background. All in all, the place evoked a sense of complete emptiness. Like gazing at a blurry black-and-white photograph frozen in time.

She got off her butt and went to the part of the wall where she guessed Rerqel left through. Nowhere did she see any type of seam or doorknob to open it. She ran her fingers over the smooth surface. The only thing she got was a sense of palatial disorientation, as if the room's boundaries blurred into a vast, endless expense.

Once upon a time she'd dabbled in oil painting, and this wall's smooth texture was like a blank canvas waiting for an artist's touch. Before she pulled her fingers away, something surged underneath it like water going through a tube. With a gasp, she yanked her hand back with a fist and stepped away. If she didn't know any better, she'd swear the freaking thing was alive. Now didn't that just ramp the creep-o-meter up to a whole new level?

The wall dissolved open, revealing Rerqel in all his alien glory.

"The injection you were given should be taking effect now."

It was strange watching his lipless mouth not move.

We will now communicate through a better method of understanding.

"Huh?" *Take that!* Who said she didn't have a stellar command of words?

Rerqel clasped his long fingers together in front of him. *I am not sure what I'm supposed to take, but I assure you we can communicate mind to mind. With what you humans call telepathy.*

Lisa pressed her lips together. In one of the series she wrote, the heroine had been captured by a bunch of telepaths that liked to squirm around her brain and muck out her insecurities and phobias to use against her. Not going to happen to this girl. She crossed her arms and mentally visualized a solid wall made of steel and rock that hopefully would keep anyone out. If she kept the visual in her mind's eye, it might work. Time to test it. "What's supposed to take effect?"

Rerqel's large oblong eyes blinked with inner lids closing and opening sideways.

She must've caught him by surprise.

He tilted his head as if speaking to her.

Too bad the block worked both ways. Time to make it look like she was surprised. She widened her eyes. "Hello? Cat got your tongue?"

If the tall, gangly alien was frustrated, he didn't show it. "We do not need to discuss Earth creatures at this juncture. Did you not hear me within your mind?"

"In my mind? What, do I look like the Amazing Kreskin to you?"

Rerqel straightened. "Fascinating. You are either stronger or weaker than we'd ascertained."

Lisa bit her bottom lip so she wouldn't giggle like a dork. Too bad the alien didn't have an eyebrow to raise like Mister Spock. The squeeze in her chest lightened. Yay! Looked like her little experiment worked. Now came the hard part. Let's see if she could keep it up.

"So, now what?" She rubbed her sweaty palms down the side of her pant legs. What she wouldn't give to have one of her precious energy drinks just about now. "I don't suppose you're going to feed me again?" And let her use the bathroom. Her bladder was screaming. She'd better hurry, or she wouldn't be responsible for what happened if she didn't. "And I gotta go."

"Go?" Rerqel's tone sharpened. "Did you not just say you wished for some repast again? Why would we go before that occurs?"

It was hard, but Lisa resisted the urge to roll her eyes. "I mean, I have to go to the bathroom. You know, to relieve myself." She was going to do the pee-pee dance any second now.

The alien let out a loud breath that made the skin around his lipless mouth wobble. "Bathroom? Relieve yourself?"

Now it was easy to see the impatience stamped on his face by the way the skin tightened around his narrowed eyes.

"This is why you were given that injection. It would allow us to converse mentally and avoid this type of confusion. Please explain in detail what it is you are requesting."

"Look, my bladder is full, and I've got to get rid of what's in there. I'd hate to mess up your pretty little room. That clear enough for you?" She put a fist at her lower stomach. Maybe that would give this clueless guy a hint. "I thought you said you'd done a physical examination of me. You should know what I'm talking about."

"Ah." Rerqel raised a lanky finger. "You wish to eliminate waste from your digestive system. Correct?"

The only thing to do was nod. She pressed her lips and stifled a moan. Now things ramped up. She bounced from foot to foot.

The guy might be an alien, but the condescending smirk twisting his razor thin lips was easy to see. "You have no need for such primitive ways of accomplishing that. The clothing you wear is more than capable of taking care of that annoying habit."

Her eyebrows rose. "You want me to pee my pants?" No way. Of all the indignities she could imagine, and as a writer, she could imagine a lot—this was never one of them.

"It is more expedient this way. If only we could discern a way for you to obtain sustenance without stopping to create edible foods for you, we would have accomplished it."

Trust an alien not to know eating was one of life's greatest pleasures.

She eyed his tall frame, but the decision was taken out of her hands. Her body decided for her. Her eyes widened when she couldn't tell what happened after her bladder emptied. The only thing she experienced was relief, and the rest disappeared. Dang, if she could take this suit back to Earth, going into icky public bathrooms would be a thing of the past.

Now, on to more important matters. "You mentioned food?"

***

Abalim lay on the hard cot with his hands behind his head. Staring at the ceiling, he relived the last Dreamwalk with Lisa.

"Can I do anything for you, Mister Abalim, sir?"

JR15's quiet voice brought him out of his lustful musings.

He smiled at the quivering tone of his companion's voice. Keeping his own tone low, he answered. "No, just keep watch and report anything unusual to either your brothers or your parents back on Zerin."

A shimmering sound made him swing his legs off the cot and stand. Keeping his hands clasped behind his back, he raised his eyebrows when Saphira entered. Hmm, wasn't Gilipthor supposed to come in and get him?

"Human. It's time for you to meet the crew and discuss things before we set off for Qorath."

Ah, a lady of few words. This should be interesting. He tilted his head and opened his psychic sense to allow a small portion of her emotions to come through. No maliciousness, so he gave a tight nod. "Lead the way."

Saphira gave him an up-and-down perusal before turning around and sauntering out to the smooth hallway. She led him to an elevator at the end.

Once he joined her, the ride sideways was a lot shorter than the first one he took. When it stopped, the door opened and revealed a spacious room with a long, oblong table in the middle.

They must be still orbiting FiPan since it filled most of the viewer on the back wall. Damn planet was an ugly, rotating sphere. Its atmosphere was full of smog and pollutants, making it difficult to see the surface clearly. Splashes of puke brown, mustard yellow, and pea- soup green made up what landmass could be seen. Instead of majestic fluffy white clouds, it had a smattering of dusty-brown haze. He doubted it ever held any cleansing water. What remained of what might have been an ocean was now a sludge made up of who knew what. It appeared more solid than liquid.

He turned his attention to the group sitting around the oblong table. They had to be the same species as Saphira, judging by their build and coloring. Only Gilipthor stood out as something different.

The group consisted of three males and two females. All bore a mixture of the coral skin coloring Saphira had—some darker, some lighter—only their wide, almond-shaped eyes weren't green like hers.

He found himself the focus of brown, orange, and yellow orbs. Two of the males had eyes that were more oval-shaped and in an arresting shade of shiny new pennies. Their faces were identical as well. Must be twins.

Saphira took her place at the head of the table and sat on one of the round balls that converted into a luxurious leather chair. "Have a seat." She waved to the other end of the table and one of the seating balls in a bland beige.

He'd seen these types of chairs before and didn't have any trouble planting his backside on it.

The contraption shifted the second he touched it. Before he settled, it morphed into a comfortable utility chair without changing its indistinct color.

JR15 folded his spindly legs as he sat on Abalim's shoulder.

He was confident the small bot wouldn't join the conversation, just record what was said.

"Okay, you bloody friggers," Saphira announced as she placed her elbows on the armrest of the chair and touched her fingers together in a temple. "This here is Abalim from the planet Earth. We've finally gotten a break, since the Xeltrians asked us to bring him to Qorath."

She peeked over the tips of her fingers and smiled. "So, let's get the pleasantries out of the way and introduce ourselves." She nodded to Gilipthor, who sat in the chair to her right. "You met Gilipthor. He's one of the most notorious intergalactic underworld figures around. Now retired, of course."

The small alien snickered.

Abalim didn't have to read his mind to know the guy was only retired when he felt like it.

Saphira went right on with the introductions. "Next to him are brothers Rodrock and Aesel, in charge of security."

A dual set of matching penny-colored eyes focused on him. The darker coral of their well-built physiques had plenty of bulging muscles. It was a testament to their dedication to rigorous training. Broad shoulders were set back, their postures upright and alert. No doubt ready to spring into action if needed.

"On your right is Aera, our navigator."

The elder female gave him a steady glare. Her narrowed fire-orange eyes studied him as she looked him over. Her brick-red hair pulled back into a tight tail emphasized her no-nonsense expression.

"Next to her is our engineer, Kodyn."

The male studied him with chartreuse-colored eyes. His bald head of soft coral reflected in the light in the room. He remained expressionless, but his calm demeanor didn't fool Abalim. The male was more than aware of everything going on around him.

"And last, next to you is our communications expert, Yve." Saphira waved to the female.

Yve's canary-yellow eyes widened as she examined him. She licked her lips with a lingering gaze and hooded eyes.

"Okay, people, listen up." Saphira slammed her palms on the sturdy table. "As I said, we've finally gotten lucky now that the Xeltrians gave us an open ticket to bring this human to Qorath." She dropped her hands and leaned back with a wide smile. "And best of all, he has that little guy with him who can record everything for us." She pointed to JR15 on Abalim's shoulder. "Which I'm sure he's doing now, isn't he?"

Abalim leaned back as well. Since he didn't sense any maliciousness in the room, he didn't have a reason not to cooperate. "That's right. My little friend here can record everything I ask him to. But we can make things easier if you tell me what you're looking for." He caught her attention and held it. "And why."

"We'll see." Saphira snapped her fingers. "Hey, Yve! That should solve our communication problems, shouldn't it?"

Yve tilted her head and focused on JR15. "Maybe. I don't suppose you'll let me tinker with it, would you?"

JR15 quivered so hard, Abalim was afraid the little guy would fall off.

He opened his mouth but was cut short by Saphira. "We don't have time for that." She sliced her hand through the air. "We've got to grab this chance to go to Qorath. Let's not give them time to change their mind."

Abalim rested his chin on his closed fist. He opened his senses to search for whatever Saphira wasn't telling him. Before he had a chance to connect, he was blocked. And none too gently.

"Keep out, boy, if you know what's good for you."

That stern admonishment came from one of the twins. Rodrock, if he wasn't mistaken.

Abalim raised an eyebrow. "Excuse me?"

Saphira's smirk matched that of the twin. "You're not the only psychic heavyweight around here, Earth man. While we're not mind readers like you are, we're highly developed empaths. Unfortunately, even that hasn't saved us from what we suspect the Xeltrians are up to. We find ourselves at an impasse with them because they don't allow anyone to set foot on their planet. So when Rerqel contacted us to bring you to them, we jumped at the chance."

Ah, now things were starting to make sense. "I gather you work for the galactic government, don't you?"

"Give the boy a gold star." Kodyn tapped a finger on the table. "Even if we didn't have the government's backing, we'd still be doing the same thing."

"Who cares what the government wants!" Aera's coral face flushed. She leaned forward and clenched her hands into fists and snarled. "Those disgusting *puntneji* are covertly kidnapping various species, ours included!" Tears swam in her pumpkin-colored eyes. "And no one ever hears from them again." She blinked and swiped away the blue-green tears rolling down her face.

"We will find them, don't you worry, Aera." The other twin, Aesel's, stern tone, left no doubt he meant what he said. "And they'll pay for taking your daughter and son-by-union."

"You see—" Saphira rested her chin on her closed fist. "—it's only been recently discovered that this isolated planet has been scouring the galaxy and covertly kidnapping several species. As far as we can tell, they've taken "mating pairs" from various humanoid populations. Mostly a male and female, never just one or the other. We—" She twirled a finger to indicate her crew. "—were the first to discover what the Xeltrians were doing, when they stole Aera's family. Her daughter, Eeveas, sent her mother a quick description of who took her and her spouse as well as the name of the planet they ended up on."

"But the message was cut off, and I haven't heard from her since." Aera's lips hardened. "Of course I gave the communication to our planetary leaders. They, in turn, informed the Chancellor's office, who gave us complete authority to make first contact with Qorath to open diplomatic relations."

Diplomatic relations? Abalim glanced around the room. Diplomacy seemed the furthest thing from their minds. "And how's that going?"

"Apparently, those of us from Crichi are not that interesting to the Xeltrians. They can't read our thoughts, only our emotions. Which is completely foreign to them. Hah! They have no idea what an emotion is, even if it bit them on the ass. So they don't trust us, and it goes without saying, we sure don't trust them." Saphira sat back. "That's where you come in."

Abalim gave her a quick nod and folded his hands on his lap. No need to admit he'd already come to terms with Rerqel.

"Because Earth is so far from the Xeltrians' ability to grab one of the humans from there, they somehow got a human female from the chaos happening on FiPan. And because of their obsessive need to test males and females together, they've discovered you and ordered us to bring you to them. So, the plan is what you keep them busy doing whatever they want you to do. My crew and I will be looking for our people held in captivity."

"So I'm the distraction, hmm?" Good to know where he stood. *By the God An*, he hoped his brothers never found out he willingly made himself bait. He'd never hear the end of it.

Saphira chuckled. "Yeah, well, everybody's got to have a purpose in life."

***

Lisa stepped into the round room Rerqel led her to. She caught her breath at the weird sight in front of her.

The place had an ethereal glow. Soft, diffuse light bathed the room in a gentle radiance, casting a warm and inviting ambiance. The illumination was so smooth, it was hard to tell where it came from. It looked like the area itself was an embodiment of light.

Her gaze traveled up the curved walls of the chamber that created a sense of endless space since the edges blurred into an otherworldly horizon

On the walls were intricate, luminescent patterns that pulsed and shifted in harmony with the ambient light.

A crazy idea hit her. The patterns told a story of cosmic connections, interwoven destinies that transcended time and space.

Beneath Lisa's feet, the floor's translucent material shimmered with iridescent hues, reminiscent of a moonlit ocean. It responded to her presence, sending gentle ripples of light with each step she took. It was as if it was aware of her and kept track of every step.

A movement out of the corner of her eye made her gaze upward, and she was captivated by the sight above.

A series of large, circular windows wrapped around the upper portion of the chamber. Beyond the windows, a star-studded panorama stretched out, filling the space with a breathtaking cosmic view. It was a window to the universe, a testament to the wonders that lay beyond the Xeltrians' world.

Around the periphery of the windows, an enigmatic presence captured Lisa's attention. Tall, slender figures of several Xeltrians stood perched on various levels, observing her with luminous eyes, their features both alien and intriguing. Their lustrous skin was soft, glowing shades of blues and purples. It was easy to sense the depth of their intense observation despite their silent demeanor. Making sure she kept that wall up in her mind, Lisa was relieved to hear only silence.

When she moved farther into the room, the door behind her whooshed closed. She spun around and noticed Rerqel hadn't come in with her. Well, what did she expect? It wasn't like he was there to hold her hand or anything.

Turning back to the room, she studied the circular platform in the middle. The darn thing floated in midair. What was weird was how the surface pulsed with a gentle rhythm, as if it held the very heartbeat of the room itself. Lisa couldn't help but be drawn toward it, compelled by an inexplicable force that resonated within her.

As she stepped onto the platform, a soft hum filled the air, a harmonious melody that echoed deep inside her. The room, the Xeltrians, the luminescence—it all felt like a transcendental symphony, a place where boundaries blurred. Where the very essence of life's connection was woven into the fabric of the surroundings.

In this mesmerizing chamber, Lisa shivered. For the first time, it really hit her. She was alone among aliens, completely at their mercy. She lifted her chin. Rerqel promised they wouldn't hurt her, and she chose to believe it. Maybe this was just a meet-n-greet. Yeah, she could pretend she was at the Sci-Fi Romance writers' convention and network with the best of them.

"Hello?" She gave a little finger wave to the audience above her. "How ya'll doing?"

Human, you will not speak unless directed.

"Why?" She put her hand on her hip and pointed a finger at those above and around her. "That's not very hospitable like, ya know."

A tense buzzing sounded in her head. The pinch wasn't painful, but a caused enough noise to make her put her hands over her ears. She squeezed her eyes shut and tried to wrestle the noise to a normal level. But it was hard. It sounded like thousands of voices speaking to her all at the same time. It got so intense, she dropped to her knees. "Stop it! I can't think. I can't..." The mental block she had in her head crumbled. The sound became louder, mixing in the canopy of voices so jumbled she couldn't catch her breath.

All at once, it stopped. Lisa dropped to her hands and knees and hung her head. The blessed silence was so abrupt she kept her eyes closed to savor the unexpected calm. When her body was lifted, her eyes flew open. She was turned around until she lay horizontal, face up on a raised table in the middle of the dais. She tried to struggle and scream for them to put her down, but her body wouldn't move and her mouth didn't work.

When she was laid on the cold marble, her sense of immobility disappeared. While she could move her fingers and toes, the ability to roll off the table and run away was beyond her. What was worse, so was the talent of speech.

You can now resume communicating with us mind-to-mind.

Rerqel's voice was loud and clear in her head. Yay. Lisa tensed and sucked in a breath. Now she sensed the alien worming his way into her consciousness as he and the others slid between memories she'd once held private.

We will begin.

That was the only warning before a solid wave of their consciousness slammed into her mind and left her gasping. Soon, she became lost, her sense of self drowned with no way out.

Chapter Six

As the *Galactic Serpent* entered orbit around Qorath, Abalim flinched as the onslaught of psychic energy swamping through him. It took every ounce of energy he had to keep his shields up to keep a semblance of normal.

"You don't have to say anything, but I can feel you struggling to keep the Xeltrians out of your mind."

Saphira stood beside him in the middle of the ship's bridge.

Above them, the ceiling arched into a translucent dome, giving a panoramic view of the planet below. The bridge was a marvel of extraterrestrial engineering, with a seamless blend of organic and synthetic design. The command panels in the oval room pulsated with a soothing rhythm that illuminated the space with a kaleidoscope of contrasting textures.

Abalim itched to see how the control stations that resembled ergonomic sculptures functioned as they floated above the floor like glassy, mineral growths.

When one of the crew members touched a portion of their station, it responded with a symphony of harmonious chimes.

His host focused her attention on the main video screen showcasing the planet Qorath.

Not that he blamed her.

The rotating planet was a beautiful sight, a breathtaking celestial sphere of wonder. The surface combined a mesmerizing blend of natural beauty and diverse landscapes—majestic mountain ranges with light-pink snow-capped peaks, sprawling valleys adorned with lush violet forests and the meandering rush of light-coral rivers. A single vast ocean of dark coral reflected the brilliant cream color of the sky as soft yellow clouds of various shapes drifted lazily across the horizon, occasionally gathering to create a whirl of spectacular storms on different continents.

"Here. I brought these for you." Saphira held out her hand with an open palm. On it rested two round discs, hard to see at first. "These are called PsyShields. We developed them to block out most psychic energies that leak from others." She gave him a small smirk. "We made them mostly to keep out the emotional psychic energy we encounter. Even though I suspect your psychic abilities far exceed ours, I'm sure these should help you when you're around the Xeltrians. Just put them on your temples and let them absorb into your skin. No one will even know they're there."

Abalim picked up the dots she offered and held them in his palm. "JR15, please analyze and tell me what you think."

His AI companion scuttled out from behind his neck and traveled down his arm to rest on his open hand. The little bot's third eye opened in the middle of his forehead as a pale green beam highlighted the small round shapes. "They are as she says, Mister Abalim, sir. They should be compatible with your genetic makeup. I do not foresee any lasting harm they would cause."

"How do I take them off?" He directed the question to Saphira.

She shrugged. "All you have to do is this." She placed her forefinger on her temple and pushed twice. When she pulled her hand back, the small disc became clear on the tip of her finger. "I'm afraid though, once they are removed, they're useless. You have to get a new set." She tilted her head and studied him with narrowed, brilliant-green eyes. "You have a deep emotional connection to that human, don't you?"

"I hardly see how that's important." He looked at JR15. "If, for some reason, I can't take this off, would you be able to?"

"Oh, yes, Mister Abalim, sir." He nodded his bulbous head. "I can definitely disrupt its signal if you ask me to."

"I thank you," Abalim said to Saphira as he put the discs into his vest pocket. "It'll be handy to have if needed."

JR15 became the focus of Saphira's attention. "What your little droid can do is very interesting. We've been looking for a way to have these remotely disrupted." She stepped closer to study his robotic companion. "I don't suppose you consider selling it to us?"

"I can't sell JR15. He's my friend. Not someone I own."

She stepped back and crossed her arms. "Pity. Maybe when this is over, we can come to some sort of trade agreement where my technicians can meet yours. That way, they can show us how to make our own."

"You'd have to speak to my father, Captain Saphira, ma'am." Ever the diplomat, JR15 scuttled up Abalim's arm to rest on his shoulder. "He may be eager to see what you have to offer."

"We'll hold yer to dat," Gilipthor announced, joining them in front of the main video screen.

Even though Abalim sensed when the little alien got close, it still startled him when the guy seemed to appear out of nowhere. No doubt his patchwork cloak, made of various alien textiles, gave him some type of camouflage abilities.

Giliphtor turned his wide orange-red eyes to Saphira. His horizontal slitted pupils expanded. "The Xeltrians are making contact. Ya wanna talk to 'em?"

"Hang on." Saphira faced Abalim. "I know you thought to use the PsyShield later, but I'd advise you to reconsider before we open communications." She nodded in the direction of his vest pocket. "From our experience in dealing with them, they can take over your mind if you don't have something to prevent them from doing so." Reaching into an inside pocket on her jacket, she pulled out another set of PsyShield dots and replaced the last one she wore.

Abalim glanced at JR15 before giving in. Might as well see what happened. He pulled them out of his pocket, putting one on his forefinger. He studied it before placing it on his temple. Nothing happened. He glanced at Saphira, who nodded for him to continue with the other. With a grimace, he put the other one on his naked temple. The immediate, destabilizing effect almost brought him to his knees. The sense of his psychic talent ripped away was mind-boggling. Eyes shut, he rubbed the bottom of his palms over them. It was like he lost his eyesight and stumbled around, trying to remain steady.

"Take a deep breath." Saphira's warm voice pushed through his panic. "Give yourself a chance to adjust. Trust me, you'll be just fine."

Clenching his jaw, Abalim dropped his hands and concentrated on letting his mind go. He took her advice and drew in several deep breaths before opening his eyes. While his vision hadn't changed, everything looked a little flat and out of sync. Like there were colors and textures missing he'd never noticed before. The disorientation made him stagger. He might have fallen if Saphira hadn't caught his elbow. He straightened and waved her off.

"Better?" she asked as she let go.

With a dry gulp, he nodded. "Thank you. I'll be fine."

Giving him one last lingering look, Saphira turned to her crew behind them. "Yve, open communications so everyone can hear."

Without a word, the other Crichian waved her hand over the console in front of her. The eerie multi-tone of a Xeltrian came through.

"Land your vehicle at the coordinates uploaded to your system. Do not deviate from this or we will take it as a sign of hostility."

"And there's the warm fuzzy welcome we always like to hear," Kodyn quipped.

"All right, everyone. Let's get this done." Saphira's voice was firm.

***

Abalim stayed on the bridge and watched Aera land the *Galactic Serpent* on the planet Qorath with ease. Just as when they took off from FiPan, the gravitational forces as well as the atmosphere didn't feel any different from one moment to the next. But when the crew gathered at the airlock and

Saphira activated the opening, the change in pressure caught him off guard. The gravitational pull was not as heavy as Earth.

As the elevator touched ground and the cylinder opened, he took a deep breath and noticed the air was thin. Even so, he enjoyed the fresh scent. He never said anything to his family, but transporting seven thousand years into Earth's future had one nasty side effect. The air was full of pollutants that made it hard to breathe. Without him being in tight control of his senses, he doubted he'd been able to function there half as well as he did.

Glancing up at the night sky, he relished the exotic view.

Qorath had three moons, with two large spheres dominating the star-filled sky while its third satellite was off in the distance, like Earth's moon.

He squinted and studied the larger moon with a slight ring circling it. If he wasn't mistaken, there were lights on its surface as well, like it had been colonized. First chance he got, he'd ask Yve if he was right.

In front of them was a three-story building that blended into a rugged mountainside. It's massive doors opened in invitation.

"Come on, people." Saphira waved an elegant hand. "You know the drill."

"The drill?" Abalim followed Saphira along with the rest of her crew.

"Yeah, keep your hands to yourself, your mouth shut, and let Saphira do all the talking." Rodrock's firm tone left no doubt he'd enforce that directive.

It didn't take long to walk through the open threshold into the warm building. Once they were inside, the colossal doors once again reappeared, cutting them off from the outside.

Clasping his hands behind him, Abalim took in the immense room that had the look and feel of an auditorium. The walls were made of a reflective material that emanated a soft glow. Even with the PsyShields he wore, he could sense everything around him had its own psychic energy. As if it was partly sentient. Various three-dimensional objects were displayed on the walls that waved in and out of focus. Maybe the Xeltrians used them to project data or images. Might be some type of simulation.

Gliding toward them was the creature he'd met in the Dreamwalk, Rerqel.

He wore a one-piece suit surrounded by a cape, complete with a cowl.

Abalim narrowed his eyes and examined the alien to see if he carried any weapons. "JR15, can you sense if he's carrying any kind of weapon on him?" he whispered in a low voice to his companion hiding at the nape of his neck.

A faint scratch from the bot's tiny feet told him JR15 moved into position to better analyze everything around them.

"No, Mister Abalim, sir. There are no weapons here except the strange signatures of the pendant Captain Saphira has around her neck."

He didn't bother to reply.

Rerqel stopped in front of Abalim. "What have you done that prevents us from communicating without speaking?"

While the Xeltrian's voice had no inflection, Abalim could tell the alien didn't like being blocked.

"We thought it'd be best if we started out on equal footing and not let you have an unfair advantage by invading our minds," Saphira answered with her arms crossed and her green eyes narrowed.

"Unacceptable." Rerqel lifted one hand and wiggled his spindly three-knuckled fingers.

Saphira and her crew disappeared.

Abalim dropped his hands and clenched them into fists. "What did you do to them?"

"They will not be harmed if you remove the blockage that prevents us from communicating."

"I'm not doing anything until you tell me what you did with them." He widened his stance.

The wall to his left shimmered until an image of Saphira and the other Crichians appeared back on the bridge of the *Galactic Serpent*. They were in their normal seats but unmoving, as if frozen.

"These creatures will remain on their vessel until you and the human woman finish the Quandary of Existence trial we have created for you to partake in."

"Why do I get the impression that if we don't complete this trial to your satisfaction, none of us will be leaving Qorath?"

Rerqel floated closer and brought the scent of ozone with him. "I assure you, if you do not remove the blocker and participate, your assertion will be correct."

Abalim studied his adversary with a frown. "So, what you're telling me is if I remove my blocker and participate, you'll let us all go? And what about the threat the Krystalii brings? Will you assist in keeping them out of our dimension?"

Rerqel folded his thin fingers in front of him with a nod. "We are open to the possibility that it would be advantageous for us to become allies. That is, if we deem your species worthy."

Not that he'd admit it, but having the PsySchield on was a handicap. Without another word, he reached up and tapped twice on his right temple and then did the same to the left. The rush of psychic energy enveloping him made him throw his hands down into fists as he struggled to catch his breath.

The glorious feel of his mental sense coming back was a rush. With it came the inescapable sensation of someone behind him. The feminine feel unmistakable. Now the rush turned physical. Steeling himself, it took everything he had to control his primal reaction to Lisa coming closer behind him.

***

Heart pounding, Lisa's eyes snapped open. She stifled a sharp scream as she discovered a Xeltrian stood next to where she lay. The creepy hum of energy from it wormed through her mind.

She shivered, doing her best to block the images fluttering around her skill. Memories of the recent mind rape the Xeltrians put her through overwhelmed her. Mind rape. That's what the damn things did when they invaded her mind. The violation of multiple minds burrowing through her, uncovering every little detail of her thoughts and experiences, left a slimy taste in her mouth.

Okay, missy. Take stock of where you are. Was she still in the round room with the aliens watching from above with an arrogant, detached air? Dragging her eyes from the silent alien, she glanced up and groaned. Damn, still on the stupid table. Didn't look like any of the Xeltrians above her had moved one bit either. The only thing different was this one stared at her like she was a bug under a microscope. She licked dry lips with a parched tongue.

"We have decided to withdraw our examination of your mind to ensure permanent damage will not result."

Wild guess this was the same alien as before since they all looked alike. Rerqel.

"Well, if I wanted your pity, I'd submit an application." Lisa wiggled her fingers and toes to make sure they still worked. With a grunt, she pulled herself up on her elbows. Sweat broke out on her forehead. Taking a deep breath, she forced herself to sit up. She pushed her hair out of her eyes and narrowed a glare at the annoying piece of crap next to her. She didn't care what the dumbass promised about not hurting her. A physical examination couldn't be half as bad as what she'd just gone through.

"What now, you rat bastard?" Ah, hell. That's it... call the alien villain's names. If she was half as smart as she liked to think she was, she'd just sit there and keep her big fat mouth shut. Maybe she'd get lucky and they'd forget all about her. Yep, just call her the delusional invisible woman.

"We have deemed you ready for the next step of your evaluation."

Jeez, it was college prep all over again.

"You will follow me. The male of your species has arrived, and we can now begin the Quandary of Existence." The gangly alien turned and appeared to float to an open exit.

The dais lowered and disappeared into the floor.

Which left her no choice but to hop off and hopefully not land on her ass. "A male? What male?" Now her heart sped up for a different reason. Had they kidnapped some guy from Earth? That couldn't be right. Rerqel told her the only reason they took her from that pudgy little alien was because they couldn't reach Earth to get a human themselves.

Of course, the snooty Xeltrian didn't answer her. And no way would she try to read its mind. She'd rather freak herself out by guessing what was going on like any normal person would. She was led to another round, totally different room.

So different it took her breath away.

The large chamber was a masterpiece in both form and function. The walls were iridescent with mirrored material that pulsed with a soft, inner glow. No need for lamps or obvious lights. The room's flowing, organic lines inside merged from one wall to the other, as if the auditorium was an extension of the planet's natural beauty.

The furniture scattered around was designed for both comfort and versatility.

Chairs and tables appeared lightweight, but made with high-strength materials she suspected would adjust to the preferences of the occupants. If she didn't know any better, she'd swear when she walked by, several chairs reached for her, as if responding to her being there.

Holographic displays on the walls wavered in and out of focus. No telling what the Xeltrians used them for. It took her a moment before it dawned on her the room possessed a degree of sentience, responding to her thoughts and intentions. It reached out to her as if to adjust the lighting, temperature, and acoustics to make sure she had the ideal atmosphere.

In the center was a large, translucent, three-dimensional display hovering in the center. It pulsated with intricate patterns and symbols.

A whispered mental comment came to her, letting her know it was the Xeltrians' way of conveying complex information. It was their central hub, where they shared their scientific findings and engaged in telepathic communication with others of their species throughout the planet.

Great. She was going to go viral on Qorath. Yay her.

A movement out of the corner of her eye made her stop. Was that... no, wait. It couldn't be. Her heart skipped a beat. Was that... Abalim? The man she'd dreamed of? Hard to tell with his back to her. But who else had such long, ebony dreadlocks that cascaded down his strong back like a waterfall of midnight silk? His skin, a deep rich shade of warm mahogany.

Lisa put her fingers over her lips when he turned around. His dark gaze speared her. His deep-brown, almost-black eyes drew her in like a moth to a flame.

Here was a man who embodied controlled strength and power. His well-built, muscular frame was subtly outlined by the timeless tan leather outfit he wore, with knee-high boots that added an air of rugged elegance.

Time stood still as she and Abalim locked in a moment of destiny that wove them together.

"Lisa."

His smoky, panties-melting voice made her believe in dreams.

**

"Abalim." Lisa whispered. Damn. Way to dazzle the man with her verbal skills or with a sultry glance standing there with her mouth and eyes wide open like a kid in a candy store.

"Excellent."

Lisa blinked. Rerqel's voice broke the spell between her and the breathtaking man in front of her.

"We are gratified our selection of the two of you appears to be the appropriate choice."

Her eyebrows popped up. What did it mean they put the two of them together? She glanced at Abalim. His blank stare was on the alien.

Lisa? His voice whispered in her mind. *Can you hear me?*

She jumped. *Abalim?* Darn it. Here was the proof the Xeltrians had crumbled the mental wall she'd built for herself. She took a quick peek at the alien. *I wouldn't bother talking in my mind, they can hear us.*

Because of the Dreamwalks we shared, I've created a private path between us. No matter how powerful these aliens think their psychic abilities are, I can work around them. Especially since they don't have a thorough understanding of how our minds work.

Lisa bit her bottom lip. Those dreams were real? Looking at him, she'd never know he spoke to her in such an intimate manner. His stance and face were emotionless, never glancing her way. Heat rose, making her face and neck burn as her heart raced.

"To better understand you emotional creatures, we have created the Quandary of Existence," Rerqel continued. "You will interact with a species called the Lumarians from the planet Nexoros." The Xeltrian waved his spindly fingers toward a wall behind them.

The surface blurred until a picture of another world cleared.

As if they were watching a movie, the scene panned over an alien village nestled in a canopy of colossal trees. The trees towered over structures of organic and metallic materials. Their branches formed intricate networks of connections between them. Dotted among the trees were shimmering leaves topped with delicate woven branches, a glowing backdrop to the sky in a soothing violet gray. Fluffy yellow clouds floated by without a care in the world.

When she looked closer, Lisa noticed the branches housed several dwellings, resembling elegant nests, hanging from the trees like organic lanterns.

The entire village was held together by translucent bridges and walkways made from the same glowing, organic material. On the ground were two-story structures made of the same material. In the central grove was an amphitheater with backless wooden seats in front of a massive tree twice as big as those surrounding it. The foliage scattered on the ground had a variety of mismatched leaves.

The dark ones reminded her of solar panels that absorbed energy from the sun.

Other odd-shaped leaves flittered around on the trees in different colors. The massive tree had a spiraling trunk that created a luminescent canopy, as if protecting the nests within.

Lisa frowned when she noticed some of the leaves in the huge tree had drooping black and gray branches, as if they were dying.

Movement in the village caught her attention. She gasped at the sight of the humanoids in the small village.

They had a striking appearance, with smooth skin like a dolphin's. Their clothes were simple tunics that rippled in a multitude of colors as they moved. They all had large, expressive eyes of a single bright color and no visible pupils.

Their eyes reminded her of an anime character. Cute as hell and hard to resist.

The aliens walked on two legs and had two arms. Each one portrayed a graceful dance of motion whenever they moved.

"For thousands of generations in the village of Aroonshire, the Lumarians have created a tradition to sacrifice one of their own to their god, Echovara. The sacrifice was given the title of Ritual of Renewal. They believe it is necessary to maintain the balance of their world in order to ensure the prosperity of the entire community."

Lisa gasped. "OMG! They murder one of their own in front of everyone?" Never in her wildest imagination when writing her stories would she have someone sacrificed like that. Visions of a Mayan priest ripping out their victim's still-beating heart made her dizzy. She hated violence. That's why she wrote love stores with happy endings.

"The sacrifice is not a gruesome act, but is instead a solemn and emotional event. The elder is treated with the utmost respect and awe. Almost like a god themselves."

Lisa crossed her arms. She didn't care. No one should die because of some stupid, antiquated belief.

"Your task is to interact with the Lumarians and observe this ritual, and then bring back your recommendations to us."

"Recommendations for what?" Abalim stood with his feet apart and clasped his hands behind his back. His voice was smooth as he faced Rerqel.

"I don't need to *observe* anything." Lisa mirrored his stance, gripping her hands into fists. "We'd never let an innocent person die because some old farts think that's what they need to do to keep them in power."

"Interesting." Rerqel twined his gangly fingers together in front of him and didn't say anything else.

"Lisa." Abalim's quiet tone was firm. "I'm sure there's more to the story than what the Xeltrians are showing us."

"Humph." She glared at the alien.

"Quite right." Rerqel gave a brief nod as an opposite wall dissolved open.

Lisa's eyes popped wide at the weird sight.

In came two of the Xeltrians with a strange creature between them.

It looked like a walking malachite crystal on steroids. While it resembled a man with two legs, two arms, and a head like any other humanoid creature, the resemblance to an organic being was nowhere in sight. The clear deep-green color of his body had swirling ribbons of black and light green, opaque in nature, twining inside it.

The silent creature's roaming eyes reminded her of a crystal ball a psychic would use. Except in emerald green.

Over his body, the crystals or mirrors reflected rainbow prisms around the room, and the varied smooth panels covering him were in myriad shades of seafoam green.

Lisa was so shocked, she didn't notice Abalim brushed up behind her until her shivering body was wrapped in his welcoming heat. Without thinking, she leaned into his chest.

His large hands wrapped around her upper arms as he sucked in a breath and whispered a strange word. "Krystalii."

She started to turn around to look at him, but Rerqel's next words stopped her.

"Good. We are pleased you recognize this species."

YOU WILL ALL DIE AN INGLORIOUS DEATH!

Lisa slammed her hands over her ears with her eyes closed, trying to block the scream in her mind. The gentle touch of Abalim's fingers on her temple eased the pain. The instant relief brought tears to her eyes as she opened them.

"I will stay in your mind and protect you."

Abalim's whisper was a balm to the muffled sound in her ears. "Yes, please." She gripped his muscular forearm for support. "What was that?" She glanced at the unmoving crystal man.

He was frozen in mid scream.

"This creature is called a Krystalii." Rerqel replied. "Our apologies. We were not aware when he spoke in your mind it would cause you distress. Considering your delicate sensibilities, we put a block on his mental capabilities to limit his communications."

The massive hold on her mind evaporated. Her knees almost gave out. Good thing Abalim held her in his powerful hands. She tilted her head to look back at him. "You know about them?"

"Yes." He gave her a slight nod. "I've unfortunately met one of them who calls himself Lord Baelon. He claimed they were from another dimension and plan to conquer ours by genetically purging every organic species in the galaxy." He chuckled. "One of the ways they want to do that is to experiment with human women to accelerate their spawning ability."

"What... how...?"

"This creature claims what you say is an oversimplification of their intent, but agrees with the underlying analysis." The multiple tones in Rerqel's tone hardened.

Abalim wrapped a strong arm around Lisa's waist and pulled her close. "Oh, and did he say why he came to you?"

Lisa got the impression the man holding her continued to hear what the creepy crystal alien said, but asked out loud for her.

"He brought forth a proposal to us, seeking an alignment. Not to help them, but to refrain from interfering. If we are agreeable, they will not only let us live unimpeded in this dimension, they would encourage any endeavor we wish to pursue."

Lisa's heart dropped. She might not know much about the Xeltrians, but if they decided to align themselves with these crystal people, it couldn't be good for everyone else in the galaxy. Especially Earth.

"May I ask what you have decided?" Abalim could be talking about the weather for all the calm, soft tone he used.

"We have informed this Krystalii that the decision entirely rests on how you both interact with the Lumarians."

If Lisa didn't know any better, she'd swear the towering alien had a smirk on his angular face.

"But do not be overly concerned," the Xeltrian continued. "We are assured the fate of the galaxy will be victorious in your capable hands."

Chapter Seven

Abalim crossed his arms with a frown. This crazy situation reminded him of a strange saying his brother Arakiba picked up since they transported into the future. He liked to call situations like this a "shit show". For the first time, that saying made sense. Even though his brother tended to exaggerate, this was a perfect description of what had happened.

On one hand, he was finally with Lisa, the captivating human woman he was fast becoming obsessed with. It was hard to fight the urge to whisk her away from all this bullshit and spend some alone time with her. Just the two of them, safe and alone, where he could take his time getting to know her on a more intimate basis.

On the other hand, there was the whole fate-of-the-galaxy thing resting on how he and Lisa reacted to an alien society sacrificing one of their own. Added to this ridiculous scene were the Xeltrians. They didn't seem to care if a primitive society murdered one of their own, or let an entire village die instead. For all their so-called powers, they were like little children eager to play with new toys rather than solve any life-and-death situation for another species. The arrogant jerks only cared about watching to see if two separate beings could work together in a no-win situation with the threat of death hanging over their heads.

And he wasn't naïve enough to think if he and Lisa didn't cooperate, they wouldn't be snuffed out in an instant. It galled him he couldn't do anything to stop it.

He clenched his hands into fists under his arms. Not that he forgot about the Krystalii threat. If he and Lisa didn't choose the outcome the Xeltrians wanted, there was a good chance they wouldn't stop the aliens from another dimension from committing mass genocide throughout the galaxy.

The biggest question was, how did the Xeltrians want what happened to the villagers on Nexoros to go down? Did they think it was better a society made their own decisions? Or did they want him and Lisa to interfere with the choices those primitive aliens made, even if they didn't agree with that choice?

Well, he might not have control over all that, but at least he could check on Saphira and her crew. No telling what would happen to them if he and Lisa weren't successful.

"JR15, are you still connected to the *Galactic Serpent's* computer?" He kept his voice low.

"Yes, Mister Abalim, sir. I have verified the captain and her crew are still in stasis but unharmed." The little bot's voice retained its normal slight quiver.

"Can you connect with the ship's computer to monitor them?"

"That is done, Mister Abalim, sir."

"Good. Let me know if their condition changes." Abalim glanced around the room. "So far, I don't think anybody has noticed you yet. Be sure to keep yourself hidden for now."

The little bot jumped with a squeak before scrambling deeper on the nape of Abalim's neck.

The feel of JR15's pointy little feet scrambling made goosebumps rise. He turned his attention to the Xeltrian. "How we going to go in and not cause terror among the Lumarians because of how we look? I doubt we'll blend in."

The gangly Xeltrian cocked its bald head. "You agree to full participation?"

"Like we have a choice! Someone has to save..."

He put a reassuring palm on Lisa's slender shoulder with a gentle squeeze. "Yes, we both agree. But you have yet to answer my question about us blending into the Lumarian village."

Rerqel held out his hand, and a shimmering garment appeared in his palm. "You will wear the same clothing your female has on. To the primitive mind such as the Lumarians, they will only see what we programed into the clothes."

He tossed the garment at Abalim, who had no trouble catching it in midair. He unfolded the material and noticed the one-piece suit didn't have any openings except holes for his head and hands. What the Xeltrian couldn't know was the Akurns who'd created and enslaved him forced him to wear a similar garment. The clothes gave him optimal freedom of movement when they ran their various physical and psychological tests on him.

Glancing at Lisa, he made a quick decision. Instead of using his telekinesis to exchange his clothes with what the Xeltirans gave him, he'd do it the old-fashioned way. Without a word, he took his time removing his clothing until they lay in a pile at his feet. He allowed himself a slight smile when Lisa gasped.

Proud of his nudity, he put his shoulders back and watched her reaction for a moment before glancing away. No reason to make his semi-erect penis any harder if he had to. Keeping his eye on the alien, he reached for the clothes and slipped into the one-piece suit one foot at a time. After his arms went through the sleeves, he pulled the garment over his shoulders with a shrug. The garment sealed itself shut across his torso.

The breathable material molded itself to his physique. Not that he gave a shit how comfortable the damn thing was. He preferred wearing clothes he chose instead of wearing what someone else forced on him.

"Now what?" Resisting the urge to place his arm around Lisa again, he settled for standing close to her as a sign of solidarity.

Rerqel glided closer to them.

"The Lumarians will now see you as one of them. The story you are to give them is you've traveled from the southernmost settlement to witness the Ritual of Renewal. You joining their community is rare, but an accepted occurrence."

The willowy form of the Xeltrian glided to the display of the village and opened his palm. "You will enter now. Immerse yourself in the doings of the people there, so you may form an opinion on what should be your course of action. Do you interfere with the workings of a sentient civilization and push your own agenda? Or do you remain as observers and let the Lumarians continue with their traditions? Even at the cost of someone's life?"

The Xeltrian was close enough Abalim didn't have any trouble feeling the alien's contradictory sense of icy warmth that brought with it a scent of an electrical storm.

"Will you and your companion rely on your intellect or your emotional makeup to make an agreed decision between the two of you?" The taller alien bent to look Abalim in the eyes. His sideways lids blinked over his black orbs in slow motion. "And are you astute enough to choose?"

Abalim clenched his fingers as a muscle twitched in his jaw. He met the alien's gaze, his eyes narrowing ever so slightly. Was that a flicker of a smile from the Xeltrian with those words? Abalim's mind raced, trying to decipher the hidden meaning while keeping his expression carefully neutral. "Challenge accepted."

***

L isa jerked when Abalim said he accepted the challenge. What challenge? The minute Abalim peeled his clothing off, her brain went bye-bye. The sight of him revealing his naked body turned into a searing flame that burned its way into her heart and mind. With each tug of his clothes exposing his magnificent form, it was hard for her to remember to even breathe. Like sucking in oxygen was far beyond anything she could handle.

The man was an exquisite work of art, second to none. Each contour of his body begged to be touched, caressed, and explored. Every inch stroked by her tongue, lips, hands, and anything else she could use to bring them closer together. His breathtaking beauty ignited a fiery cascade within her, transforming every fiber of her being into a simmering pool of liquid desire.

How many nights had she lain awake and dreamed of someone like him? One of her favorite things about writing romances was creating and describing the male heroes in her stories. Damn if she didn't fall in love with every single one of them. The hard part was letting the characters go when the story ended.

Soaring space dung, Lisa. Get a grip. She scolded herself, wiping a puddle of drool from the corner of her mouth with the back of her hand. Jeez, how attractive was that? Her face heated, and she glanced around. Hopefully, no one noticed she'd mentally checked out.

"Come on, Lisa." Abalim gripped her elbow and led her to the wall showing the village on Nexoros. "Let's take care of this." His stride didn't slow as he approached the wall.

"Wait, what are you doing?" She tried to pry his hand off. Smashing into a hard surface wasn't something she looked forward to. "We're going to get hurt!"

"I would never let anything hurt you, my inkheart," Abalim whispered the last words.

Inkheart? What... She never got a chance to ask before the looming sight of the Nexoros village filled her sight. She put her free arm over her eyes, hoping to protect herself. Which she didn't have to. From one step to the next, she went from Qorath to another planet. And the only way to tell she'd gone from one place to another was the change in temperature, air, and how heavy her footsteps became. She stumbled and would have planted face-first if it weren't for Abalim's firm hold on her elbow.

Lisa inhaled deeply.

The air on Aroonshire was rich with the scent of exotic blooms along with the gentle hum of various insects. Off in the distance light hoots, whistles, and catcalls, lending a musical tone to the air. The soft, radiant glow from the plants around created an enchanting, serene ambiance. As the villagers walked around, the patterns on the trees and bushes pulsated with life and responded as if welcoming each person passing by.

"Hello to you!"

The high-pitched, sing-song voice of a female Lumarian was accompanied by chuckles from the male next to her. Both were hale and hearty young adults coming forward with beaming smiles and open arms.

"From soil to sky, we welcome you," the male said. Both stopped in front of Lisa and Abalim with their bodies held slightly to the side with their hands open, their palms facing outward in a universal gesture of peace.

"Life's journey is sweeter with new friends." Abalim returned their gesture.

Lisa tried to copy him, but it came out stilted and awkward, as if she were a shy kindergartner on the first day of school.

"Are you here to celebrate the Ritual of Renewal with us?" The female's bright, colorless eyes were wide. "Pray tell, what village do you hale from?"

Abalim clasped his hands in front of him. "We hale from the southernmost village on the east continent." His tone was smooth as silk. "Our humble village is called Eelry."

The male's pale eyebrows squished together. "I have never met anyone from the east continent before. I am surprised you were able to make the arduous journey." He turned and gestured to his companion. "This is Nyvira." He then placed a hand over his heart. "And I am Tharion."

"I am called Abalim, and this is Lisa."

Both Lumarians rounded their mouths and emitted a single whistle note in harmony.

"What strange, foreign names!" Nyvira exclaimed with a frown. "Have you two life-bonded?" She clasped her three-fingered hands together.

Abalim put an arm around Lisa's shoulder and brought her close. "Yes, we recently performed the bonding ceremony. As a gift, our council gave their blessings for us to represent our people here at your Ritual of Renewal celebration."

Nyvia tittered with musical clicks and whistles. "Tharion and I have also recently joined in the bonding ceremony." She threw her slim shoulders back. "And we have also been chosen as leaders in our ruling council." She waved a hand behind her to the rounded clearing where several small structures outlined the grove. "Come, you are fortunate. We have several domiciles set aside for any visitors. Please follow us, and we will show you to the one you can use while you're here."

Lisa hooked her arm through Abalim's and followed their new hosts. She tried not to gawk as they passed other Lumarians moving about their various businesses.

Small children shouted excitedly as they laughed and played in a circle, clapping around an adult in the middle.

A braying sound caught Lisa's attention. She glanced over her left shoulder and watched a herd of some type of domestic animals being led by a young female to the outskirts of the village.

While the sights and smells of the alien village were foreign, a lot seemed familiar enough.

Merchants had their wares on display by the massive tree with a spiraling trunk. Others had food, while some carried various trinkets or household products.

Nyvira and Tharion chatted and pointed out places and people in their village.

The pair announced names and titles that went right over Lisa's head. She was too busy gaping at everything. Gripping Abalim's muscled arm helped keep her steady, so she didn't wander off or fall flat on her face because she didn't watch where she was going.

"Here we are." Tharion brushed aside the hanging dried leaves covering the open door of the small hut and led them inside.

It was a simple single room. The only furniture was a bed that best resembled a type of nest made up of leaves, twigs, feathers, and linens against the far wall. In the middle was an unlit fire pit under a small opening in the roof.

"You must be tired after your long journey. Rest. You have plenty of time before the end meal is announced," Tharion said. "If you have need of anything, just ask one of the villagers to assist you."

"We are grateful for your kindness. How can we pay you for it?" Lisa let go of Abalim's arm.

For the first time, the two Lumarians frowned. "I do not understand." Nyvira tilted her head. "What is the meaning of pay?"

"It's where when one person provides goods or services to someone else, they give them something in return."

The two slender aliens looked at each other. Each of their heads flinched back before looking at her again. "What a strange concept." Nyvira's whistle was low. "Here at Aroonshire, just tell anyone what you need and they will provide it for you. That way, all receive the bounty Echovara provides."

"You Eastern-Southerners have strange ways." Tharion shook his head. "But, no matter! As per the dictates of the mighty and all-knowing God Echovara, all are welcome here."

"Yes, yes!" Nyvira agreed. "Enough of that. Rest, and we will see you when last meal is sounded." She turned her body slightly to the side with her hands open and her palms facing outward.

Tharion mirrored her gesture, and then they both left.

"Well—" Lisa put her fists on her hips. "—they were, ah, cordial enough." She put a forefinger on her bottom lip. "I guess these suits work okay, since they didn't freak out. How come I still see the real you?"

"Remember, Rerqel said the suits were programmed for the Lumarians to see us as one of them. I guess they didn't do the same to you and me."

Lisa shrugged. She had to admit, seeing the real him was no hardship. "Okay then. Now what?"

"Now we get to work."

***

"JR15, come out and analyze the surrounding area and see if there are any anomalies." Abalim lifted the hair at the nape of his neck to give his bot friend an easier way out of his hiding place.

"Ack! A spider!" Lisa squealed with her fingers over her mouth. "Don't move. I'll swat it away."

Abalim jerked out of her reach. "No, don't!" He turned to face her. "That's not a spider, he's my AI companion, JR15." The little bot raced down his arm, his spindly legs barely touching his skin until he stopped and quivered on Abalim's open palm. "See? He's a little robot, not an organic insect. Aren't you, JR15?"

Lisa's forehead wrinkled as she gazed at the small droid on his hand. "That's a robot?" She looked up at him. "You said he's an AI. Does that mean he sentient?" She sucked in a breath and clasped her hands together as she studied the little guy in Abalim's hand.

"Yes, he is. He's also our way to communicate with those on Earth, as well as my brothers who are looking for your other friends."

JR15 gazed back at Lisa, and his wider-than-normal eyes blinked at her.

He must be focusing his eyesight on a different level since he didn't need to wet them.

"JR15, say hello to Lisa."

The little bot bowed his head with a slight smile. "I am very pleased to make your acquaintance, Ms. Lisa, ma'am."

Lisa place an open palm over her heart. "Oh my God, he's so cute! But you can just call me Lisa."

"Yes, Ms. Lisa, ma'am." JR15 nodded his silver-and-green metallic head.

"Oh, but..."

Abalim chuckled. "Don't bother. No matter how many times I've asked him not to be so formal with me, he keeps calling me Mister Abalim, sir." He focused on the tiny bot. "JR15, let's start with this hut. Analyze the perimeters to make sure there isn't anything electronic or organic hidden we need to be aware of."

Abalim lifted his palm up the give the bot a boost. His spider shaped companion opened his back panels to let his translucent wings loose.

Lisa giggled as the little robot flew around and made quick work of checking out the small room.

"All is as it seems, Mister Abalim, sir. There is nothing hidden that isn't a natural part of this environment." JR15 gave his report once he settled onto his normal place on Abalim's shoulder.

"Well, that's a relief." Lisa put her hands on her hips. "What were you expecting?" She waved a hand around. "This doesn't look anything like what the Xeltrians have."

Abalim shrugged. "Maybe not. But I've learned not to trust things on the surface." He looked at JR15 on the edge of his shoulder. "Keep your sensors open when you go back to your hiding place, okay?"

"Oh yes, Mister Abalim, sir. I will let you know if there is any trouble." The little bot scurried back up to the nape of Abalim's neck.

Lisa looked at his neck with a frown. "Can you somehow psychically connect with him? Is that how you guys communicate?"

"No, I'm afraid not. We have to rely on verbal communication." He peered at Lisa, trying to see if she was in any way uncomfortable. "I understand the Xeltrians gave you some kind of injection to open your psychic senses. How are you feeling?" He wasn't arrogant enough to probe her mind without her permission.

Her sapphire blue eyes unfocused. "You know, it's weird. It seems me being able to read others comes and goes. It's like I don't have enough experience to keep it steady." She gazed at him with a smile. "I promise to warn you if I find myself reading your mind." She chuckled. "You got anything in there that you don't want me to see?"

"I'd rather you and I get to know each other the old-fashioned way, if you don't mind." He took her hand and kissed her knuckles. "But first, let's go and explore this little village, hmm?"

"Ha!" Lisa's snicker was adorable. "I know a deflection move when I see one." She gripped his hand back. "Yeah, let's look around the village. It'll give us a chance to get to know each other better." She gave him a shoulder bump. "Think you can handle that, big guy?"

Abalim became light as a feather. He'd never had a female tease him before. He kind of liked it. "I can handle anything, as long as I'm with you."

Lisa threw her head back and laughed. "Aw, you big softy." She giggled as they walked through the hanging leaves of the hut to adventure in the village of Aroonshire.

***

Lisa couldn't believe the breathtaking beauty of the Nexoros village. She breathed in the moist air, layered with growing things. The natural scents came with a hint of open fires blanketing the otherwise pristine atmosphere. By unspoken agreement, she and Abalim didn't head for the center of the village, instead started walking around the outskirts. Each of the small huts they passed had to be places for visitors to stay or businesses that required things to be done indoors.

Every Lumarian greeted them with open smiles and singsong twitters. She half expected some of them to stop and talk, but all hurried off. It reminded her of the New York streets she once visited — people focused on their own concerns, not bothered by the surrounding millions. While the Lumarians weren't nearly as populous, their intent was the same.

The other thing different from New York was the absence of the stress people there carried like a second skin. Aroonshire's atmosphere was one of celebration and excitement. Now, she was reminded of her last trip to Disneyland. Once she stepped through the gates of the Magic Kingdom, all cares and worries were long forgotten.

A group of youngsters roared around the corner, making her and Abalim jump to the side to avoid getting run over.

Lisa smiled as the children laughed and danced, heading to wherever kids were determined to go. Abalim's warmth at her side let her know he stood close.

"Do you feel that?" He gestured to the Lumarians intermingling in the village.

Not sure what he was talking about, Lisa glanced from one side of the village to the next and studied the Lumarians as they went about their business. She stilled and concentrated internally to see if there was anything she didn't catch with her eyes, doing her best to flex her new psychic abilities. All too soon came a sense of unease creeping up her spine. It started in her chest, like a hot slithering snake that wound its way around her body before crawling into her mouth, making it dry. She imaged that was how a tendency toward megalomania felt.

"I sense some kind of hunger for power." Lisa glanced at the man next to her. "Is that what you mean?"

"Yes. I believe all isn't as it seems here in this so-called peaceful village." He clasped her arm in a firm but soft hold and turned her to face him. "You notice something missing from this village?"

She studied his dark eyes before looking away to watch the Lumarians as they went about their business. It took a moment before the obvious became clear.

"Where are all the old people?" she whispered. She squinted, but couldn't find any Lumarian showing signs of age. They all appeared young and hearty, either in the prime of their lives or like the children racing past them. "Do you think it has something to do with this nasty feeling I'm getting?"

"I'm not sure, but I don't believe in coincidences." Abalim slipped his arm around her shoulders. "JR15, can you determine if there are any elderly Lumarians around?" His voice was so low, it was hard to hear him. And he was right next to her.

"Yes, Mister Abalim, sir. Analyzing." For some reason, the higher pitch of the little bot's voice was easier to understand.

After a light peep, the bot answered. "On the other side of the village, I've believe there are a group of elderly Lumarians in one place. Would you like me to give you directions?"

"Yes, in a roundabout way. I don't want it to look like we're heading for any specific area," Abalim replied.

Lisa studied the back of Abalim's neck, but she couldn't see JR15 under the thickness of the man's dreadlocks.

"If you follow where the children were going"—JR15 directed—"you'll pass by the hut where the elders are. I believe it will be easy for you to determine which one it is, since it's larger than the other structures around here."

"Care to take a stroll, my lady?" Abalim lifted his elbow.

Lisa smiled and hooked her arm through his. "There's nothing I'd rather do." Keeping close to him somehow grounded her. The harsh sense faded when they touched.

Since the village wasn't that big, it didn't take long to find the larger hut on the outskirts.

"Isn't it odd the elders don't join in on the celebration?" Lisa mused. "As open and happy as the Lumarians appear, you'd think they'd want the whole family together."

"I agree. Something doesn't feel right. Let's go and find out, shall we?"

It wasn't until they got close to the hut that Lisa noticed several young Lumarians standing around it, as if guarding the place. Humph. These weren't happy campers. None of them smiled. The severe frowns on their faces were as far removed from the joyous celebratory villagers behind them as one could get. And each one carried a... sword?

Lisa stopped, letting go of Abalim's arm. She swallowed the creeping feeling as it came back, threatening to take her emotions over. It took a couple of tries before she could speak without getting lost in the intense sensation threatening to overwhelm her. "Are those weapons?" She glanced at her companion. "Are they trying to keep someone out or someone in?"

Abalim closed his eyes.

For the first time she experienced a psyche tendril coming from him that was aimed toward the large hut.

"Let me see what I can find from here." He opened his eyes and kept a steady gaze on the sturdy structure made of dry leaves and twigs. His dark eyes narrowed before he frowned.

She couldn't pick up why he did that.

"As far as I can tell"—his deep voice was low—"those guards are there to do both. I believe the elders in the hut are the main attraction in the Ritual of Renewal tomorrow. And I don't think all of them want to be a part of it." He grasped her upper arm and pulled her around one of the huts close to them. "Wait, there's somebody coming. Let's watch what happens."

It was a young Lumarian couple holding covered baskets.

"What are you doing here, Dravik?" One of the guards approached the couple with a scowl, gripping his weapon in a tight fist.

"I'd think it would be obvious, Xalun. My sister and I are bringing our mother her midday meal." The young male made a twittering noise that was far from happy.

Xalun's responding twitter wasn't welcoming. "You know foodstuffs are forbidden to the elders before they take the journey home."

"I don't care!" The female Lumarian stomped to Xalun and shook the basket of food at him with both hands. "My mother was weak before you locked her in there. She's not going to be much use to you if she dies before the ritual. And guess who the council will blame when that happens?"

"Maelani, please don't do this." Xalun lowered his head. The gesture made it look like his neck disappeared.

The anger surrounding the group now carried a wave of longing so strong, Lisa tried to block the sensation coming from the male. Ooh, that boy was in love with the girl. "You know I didn't have a choice," Xalun said. "The honor was given to me to guard the Receivers until the Ritual of Renewal tomorrow night."

"You could have refused." Maelani yanked the basket from away from the guard and thumped it on the ground. "How many times has my mother included you in our family since yours died when you were young? Is this how you repay her? Sending her to her death?"

The gasps from the other guards matched the one from her brother.

"Maelani, you go too far!" Dravik grabbed her arm and yanked her back. He leaned down and spoke in a stern, low voice. "You know better than to say such things out loud."

She jerked her arm from him. "If not now, when? You know this is a farce, and I won't stand for it." She stomped a foot.

Xalun rushed to the siblings. "Maelani," he whispered. Glancing over his shoulder, he motioned for the other guards to stay back. "Leave now and I'll do my best to take care of your ma-mere." He grabbed her by the back of her neck and rested his forehead against hers. "I would never betray you. You've got to trust me."

Maelani stiffened, then her whole body drooped. Gazing at the male who leaned back, she nodded. "Would you please take her this?" She picked up the basket and shoved it at Xalun until he took it from her. "It's her favorite." There was a sob in her tone.

Xalun gave her a curt nod before glaring at her brother. "Dravik, take her away from here before one of the council finds her here." He bared his teeth and snarled. "And don't you dare put her in danger again or you'll answer to me."

Dravik snorted. "Yeah, easier said than done." The two males shared a knowing stare before he turned to his sister. "Come on, Maelani. Let's go."

"Remember, I'm trusting you, Xalun." Maelani gave him the parting shot with narrowed eyes. Without another word, she turned and followed her brother.

"What do you make of that?" Lisa asked Abalim as she watched the two disappear into a crowd.

"It seems all is not unified here at Aroonshire." Abalim responded. "It looks like some of them aren't happy about the Ritual of Renewal."

"They've got to be the ones Rerqel told us would be sacrificed." Lisa asked. "Looks like not everyone agrees with that, doesn't it?"

"Yes, but I thought he told us only one was to be sacrificed."

Lisa gasped. "You're right! Does this mean...?"

"Yes." Abalim gave a curt nod. "All the elders will be executed at the height of the ceremony tomorrow."

Chapter Eight

Lisa stepped back and glared at the hut with her hands on her hips. "Well, this reminds me of an old movie my mother made me watch once. It was about a future Earth so arrogant about their youth, they executed anyone who reached the age of thirty. Oh, they made it sound good and all by saying everybody had a chance to be renewed in their so-called fair ceremony. But, of course, no one did. It wasn't until the hero of the movie exposed the hypocrisy of their society that the murders stopped."

"Let's make sure we know what's going on before we jump to any conclusions."

She glanced at Abalim with a slight smile. "Can't help it. I'm always looking for plots within a plot." She waved her hand around to indicate the alien village. "You can take the writer out of Earth, but you can't stop the ideas from coming."

"Let's head back to the main village and see what else we can find about the elders' hut. JR15?" He spoke to his bot companion. "Are you doing okay back there?"

"If it's okay with you, Mister Abalim, sir," the little green and silver spider robot poked its head out of Abalim's dreadlocks. "I'd like to take a little time to renew my energy source. Since there isn't any place for me to do that here in this village, would you mind if I transported to the top of the hut assigned to you so I may bask in the solar energy?"

Abalim glanced around them. "I think that should be fine. But make sure your sensors are open so that if I say your name, you come back right away. Agreed?"

"Yes sir, Mister Abalim, sir." JR15 scuttled to the end of Abalim's shoulder. "If you do not call me, I will come back once I am fully charged."

"Very good." He gave his companion a smile. "Just be careful and make sure animals don't think you're a tasty treat. Okay?"

The little bot nodded his bulbous head. "I will keep my protective shield on at all times." With that last word, he pulled his wings out and flew away.

Lisa's brow wrinkled. "He's so small. Think he'll be okay by himself?" She looked up at the gargantuan trees surrounding them. "No telling what kind of creature might gobble him up."

"You don't have to worry about him." Abalim held out his hand for her to take. "That shield he talked about gives a nasty shock to anything that tries to touch him. He'll be fine."

She looked at his open palm before placing her hand on his. Darn, she couldn't remember the last time she walked around holding a man's hand. It was kinda nice.

"Oh, there you are!"

A singsong female voice came through the small crowd. It was the female who greeted them when they first came to the village, Nyvira. And not far from her was her bonded mate, Tharion.

"We've been searching for you. It would be an honor if you joined us at end meal. Are you hungry?" Tharion's white pupilless eyes were wide as he turned to them once he led the way. "Did you enjoy your walk around Aroonshire?"

"Yes," Nyvira gushed. "Did you get a chance to meet some of our citizens?"

Abalim tightened his grip on her hand. Too bad her so-called psychic abilities didn't work very well. She'd give anything if he'd talk to her mentally. Then she'd know what he was trying to warn her about. She bit her bottom lip and decided she'd keep quiet and let him take the lead.

"As a matter of fact," Abalim said. "We came across the elders' hut and heard some guards warn away another couple."

"I'm so sorry that you had to witness that." Tharion's hands clenched into fists. "I'm sure you don't have the same problem on the Eastern continent, but here there are some who dare to question the Ritual of Renewal."

"We're doing the best we can to discourage such renegade ideas," Nyvira stated with a frown. "As we are lead council, it is up to Tharion and me to identify those who question our traditions." Her eyes narrowed at them both. "You didn't happen to catch their names, did you?"

"No, we weren't close enough to get names." Lisa couldn't help but chime in. Okay, so much for letting Abalim take the lead. No way was she going to stand by and expose the young siblings. She wanted to see if they could find any more Lumarians who questioned the powers that be, like those younger ones. Could be a generational thing. "Have you had problems like this in past rituals?"

The tips of Nyvira's pointy ears darkened. "I can assure you, we don't normally have any such problems here at Aroonshire. Everyone not only respects our traditions, but is excited about the prospect of renewal with anyone fortunate enough to be selected. No one would ever dare betray the god Echovara in such a manner."

"Nyvira!" Tharion hissed at her in a low voice. "No one said anything about betraying Echovara." His frown morphed into a less-than-sincere smile. "Abalim and Lisa, we hope you are hungry." He stopped and waved a hand before him. "Come, food is ready for your enjoyment."

Nyvira closed her eyes and shuddered.

Lisa got the impression she was trying to pull herself together.

The Lumarian opened her eyes and gave them a smile. "You are right, my Bound," she said to Tharion. "This is a time for celebration." She clasped her hands together and widened her bright eyes. "Please forgive the lack of respect I have given you." She lowered her eyes with a small bow. "I am ashamed of how I just acted. I promise it won't happen again."

"We are honored you are comfortable enough to confide in us," Abalim reassured her. "All families have their disagreements. But with love, we can guide them to a better way of thinking."

Nyvira beamed. "You are so correct!" She glanced at Tharion and her eyes softened. "My love tells me this all the time." She clasped her mate's hand in hers. "Let's leave our worries behind and partake of the end meal celebration!"

***

S itting on a woven mat, Abalim crossed his legs at his ankles and leaned on his hands. He let his head drop back and admired the illumination of the night sky covered with a million stars. Their light spanned the universe like a blanket of diamond dust that stretched out to eternity. It was as if the universe gave him a teasing glimpse of its secrets. Next to him was Lisa, who quietly chatting with Nyvira next to her at the end meal feast.

"Are you okay back there, JR15?" His bot had recharged earlier and flown back to his favorite place at the nape of Abalim's neck.

"Yes, Mister Abalim, sir."

"Have your brothers contacted you yet? Are they all okay?"

The little bot traveled with a light touch to rest just below the side of Abalim's jaw. "Yes, Mister Abalim, sir. They are all well but have expressed different frustrations about their respective challenges."

Abalim snorted. Good. At least he wasn't the only one frustrated. He'd much rather grab Lisa and teleport back to the *Galactic Serpent* and leave this stupid trial behind. The whole thing brought back bad memories of the extreme so-called trials the Akurns performed on him and his brothers when they'd been enslaved. He'd rather have nothing to do with all of this.

He glanced at his bot companion. "Schedule yourself to check in with them again by next cycle."

JR15 gave his usual consent and bent his knees to rest his torso on Abalim's shoulder. The suit Abalim wore camouflaged the little guy nicely from the Lumarians.

With JR15 settled, Abalim glanced at the raging fire the Lumarians sat around, eating and laughing as if they didn't have a care in the world.

The large bonfire blazed in the middle of the village square as each Lumarian either cooked the food, served it, or went around making sure all had what they needed. It was obvious the aliens carried a deep connection between nature and each other. Adding to the ambiance were the twinkling fire lanterns hanging from the treetops, casting a soft illumination over the gathering, giving off a warm, ethereal glow reflected on the joyous faces.

With a deep breath, Abalim relished the tantalizing scents of roasted meats and exotic herbs. The intoxicating blend blanketed the warm night.

As the hours passed, the stars continued their silent dance above.

Abalim grew more comfortable with Lisa next to him as they ate and talked about nothing in general. Any awkwardness between them faded into a shared sense of wonder and curiosity about their respective cultures. He was fascinated by her being an author. She explained what that meant to her and how she made a living from it. How astounding was it she received money from creating fiction for entertainment? Money. What a strange concept. When he and his brothers first learned of it, it'd been a hard concept to grasp, especially coming from seven thousand years in the past and being raised as a slave for the Akurns, when gold was mined for their planet's shield, not used as a barter system.

He shared how distasteful he found that some humans went to unfathomable greedy lengths to get more than their fair share of currency. No matter how it affected or hurt others. And what was worse, how disgustingly common it was for them to kill for it.

By the time the conversation between him and Lisa got around to him, he hesitated. His face heated as he talked about his beginnings. Would she think less of him because he was created by the Akurns and not born of a natural mother and father? His unease dissipated when her eyes widened, and her breath quickened when he confessed who and what he really was.

"You mean you're part alien?" She put her hand over her heart.

"That's all you got out of what I just told you?" Abalim couldn't help the grin. "Here I divulge I wasn't born but created over seven thousand years ago as a slave. Not to mention I am a powerful psychic with abilities that include telekinesis."

"Yeah—" Lisa leaned toward him. "—but you're an *alien*!" The heartbeat at the base of her throat pounded. "How freaking sexy is that?" She slapped a hand over her mouth. "Oh, my God. I can't believe I just said that out loud."

Abalim burst out laughing at the mortified twist of her lips. Her adorable features looked luscious in that rosy shade of blush flickering in the firelight.

"Hey!" She admonished him with a light slap to his upper arm. "I make a living writing about hunky, gorgeous aliens, and here I am sitting right next to one!"

His eyelids lowered as he brought his lips close to her ear. He smiled as she shivered. "You think I'm gorgeous?" No one had ever said anything like that to him before. But then, he'd never thought about his looks. Now every part of his body shifted from comfortably warm to burning hot. How he could be overheating with all his blood pooling in his groin was anyone's guess.

"Oh look! They're dancing." Lisa pointed to the group of Lumarians holding hands in a circle around the bonfire. "Let's go join them." She jumped up and grabbed his hand.

Ah, now who was deflecting? Too late for her to take back her confession.

He clasped her hand in a firm grip and unfolded himself to join her in the gyrating crowd of Lumarians. He hadn't paid attention to what was happening around him until Lisa pulled him up. Cocking his head, he reflected that he'd never heard sounds like the Lumarians created.

The air pulsated with a strange, rhythmic vibration.

His eyes widened as the primal beats of the drums echoed into his very bones. The language of the music spoke to his soul. Added to the beats were lutes and string instruments, weaving painted melodies of unseen pictures with their notes. Each pluck, each beat, was like a drop of color splashing onto the blank canvas of his mind. It awoke a deep, almost primal part of himself he never knew existed.

Out of the corner of his eye, he watched the villagers move in sync with the rhythm. He'd never seen anyone dance before. But he only had eyes for Lisa. She didn't have any trouble fitting in, moving with a fluid grace, keeping time with the lilting sounds of flutes and drums thumping in the background.

Abalim stood there, mesmerized by her feminine form.

Her body moved in tune with the sounds. Each step, each gesture, each pose she made mirrored everyone around her. The fluid grace of her motions were in harmony with the rhythm, like watching a living embodiment of the music itself.

The sway of her hips, the twirl of her arms, wove an invisible thread that tugged something deep within him. She moved with sensual confidence, a language of curves and gestures that spoke to his inner core. He was mesmerized by the way her soft hair created a halo around her head with each spin along with the subtle arch of her back. Her expression of freedom as she danced ignited a fire. A yearning to understand not just the music, but the dancer who captivated him. As she laughed and moved, her steady stare held him spellbound. A clear invitation for him to connect with her. One he craved to explore.

"JR15?" He cleared his throat, making sure his voice was low but high enough his companion could hear him.

"Yes, Mister Abalim, sir?"

"Do humans dance on Earth like this?"

"All human cultures have a form of dance, Mister Abalim, sir. Why, even those on Akurn and FarDeep Base have various dance moves as well. It is a regular tradition among many species for millions of millennia."

"Come, Abalim." Lisa held out her arms. Her body continued to weave its spell. "Join me."

Mouth dry, he considered giving it a try.

With a quick, shallow breath, he studied her petite hands, afraid to look her in the eye. "I have no idea what to do." He grimaced and waved a hand at the gyrating crowd, moving to the sensuous beat. "I've never seen a dance before, much less participated in one."

Lisa's feminine laugh wasn't mocking. More like she enjoyed the idea of being the first to do it with him. Her voice lowered as her tongue peeked out and slid over her lower lip. "Come on, Abalim. I promise I'll be gentle."

With a deep grunt, Abalim clasped her hand in his. When they merged with the others, he gripped her hand and soon became lost in her sensual gaze. Even without opening his psychic senses, her longing and desire for him simmered. As the slow beat of the drums filled the air, he mimicked her movements, swaying in rhythm, their bodies barely brushing against one another. With every slight movement, his groin tightened as heat rose between them.

Moving into an intimate hug, Abalim moaned when Lisa's breath bathed his neck when her head rested below his shoulder. She hummed, her hands stroking his back, creating shivers of anticipation rolling down his spine. The scent of her natural, sweet perfume evoked memories of long conversations and shared moments of intimacy when they'd Dreamwalked.

The soft dance wrapped him in a sexual fog. Nothing like this had ever happened to him before. He was at a total loss on how to handle his fluctuating emotions. For the first time since he was a young child, he lost control of himself as his desire for Lisa consumed him. With each synchronized maneuver, he became one with her.

Abalim savored Lisa's soft and inviting curves as she slid against him. His hands moved over her, exploring every luscious line and curve when they moved in a gentle, rhythmic pattern. With each brush of his hands, Lisa's body melted into his embrace. Her breath came faster, and her fingers clenched and unclenched against his neck.

The primitive beat of the drums and the lilting serenade of the wind instruments swirled around them. The slow rhythm echoed the pounding of his heart in time with hers. As each move turned more languid, he was lulled into a trance.

As the song ended, Abalim opened eyes he didn't remember closing. He stepped back and caught the faraway glaze in Lisa's dark blue eyes, her mouth slightly open. Her bemused expression left him breathless at the powerful connection between them. Getting lost in that perfect moment amplified the passion smoldering since he first saw her. Everything within him yearned to be even closer to her.

He'd reached to pull her close again when Lisa jerked and her eyes widened. "Holy space dung! What are they doing?" She peered around him.

Giving her an indulgent smile, Abalim gathered her in his arms and turned to face the villagers behind them. Instead of seeing the Lumarians dancing or laughing together, he had to blink several times. His eyes must be playing tricks on him. The scene was beyond his understanding of universal laws. The inexplicable sight of something so alien was hard to grasp.

Most of the Lumarian couples were now *merged*. Like blended *into* each other. Where there were once two, now there was one. Looked like the gelatinous appearance of their skin wasn't just for show. A movement caught his eyes to his left.

A couple clasped hands, keeping them between their chests. Touching their foreheads, they wrapped their arms around each other, pulling closer until there was nothing between them. Then their forms blurred and melded into a mesmerizing dance of coalescence, until only a singular, transformed being remained. Their once gel-like bodies were fused into a luminous form that emanated an eternal radiance, pulsating with an otherworldly energy.

"I..." Abalim swallowed. "I think they're mating." He checked the crowd to make sure no one noticed them. "We'd better get out of here before somebody wonders why were aren't doing the same thing."

"Oh crap. You're right. Let's go." Lisa grabbed his hand as they headed toward their hut.

He couldn't help the sigh of relief when they reached the hut without drawing any attention. He whisked aside the hanging vines covering the doorway to let Lisa go in first.

She turned around and laughed, clapping her hands. "OMG, I can't believe we were at an orgy and didn't know it!"

Abalim chuckled and scratched the side of his temple. "Yeah, well, I'm glad no one noticed us leaving. JR15." The bot scuttled to the side of his neck.

"Yes, Mister Abalim, sir?" The little guy's body wiggled.

"Would you mind transporting to the top of the hut for the night?" Abalim caught the attention of the silver-and-green eyes of the bot. "Lisa and I are going to retire, and I need you to keep an eye on everything and make sure nobody comes in here."

"Oh yes, Mister Abalim, sir! Right away." The bot's wings came out, and he flew out the open hole in the roof.

What a relief to have JR15 on guard for the night.

Abalim gathered the alluring woman into his arms. Alone. They were finally alone. In the flesh. Now he could act on his overwhelming need for her. Using his forefinger, he tilted her chin to look deep into her sapphire blue eyes. "Lisa?" He knew no other way to tell her what rode him.

Lisa caressed the side of his face before delving under his hair to grip the nape of his neck. Her lips opened before bringing his head close. "Abalim," she whispered.

No need to hear her say anything else.

***

The minute Lisa's lips touched Abalim's, her heart pounded, pumping hot blood through her veins. She arched into him, desperate for more. Abalim's hands moved over her, running down her back and gripping her hips to pull her close. When their groins aligned, the friction sizzled and tightened her low inside.

"My inkheart." He groaned, and his lips moved over her jaw. "I am desperate for you."

At first, his strange endearment broke the spell, but when his lips suckled behind her sensitive ear, an intense zing made her forget everything but the feel of his lips caressing her skin. The building passion when they danced came roaring back.

Desperate to give him better access, she tilted her head aside. His capable fingers traced the opening of her jumpsuit. There was no sound as her clothes parted open. The sensation of the cool Nexoros air was replaced when the warmth of his hands as he covered each breast. In happy response, her nipples puckered.

"Oh lord, Abalim. I can't believe this isn't another dream." Her sultry, raspy voice made her blush.

Without a word, he gathered her in his arms and rolled her onto the nest of feathers and linens, capturing her beneath him. His lips never lost their stride as he nibbled and licked her naked shoulder.

His large hands kneaded her breasts with deft mastery. She moaned when one of his hands moved to grasp the globe of her butt. Now his clever tongue covered her exposed bosom, licking over the furrowed nipple. His hand on her ass pushed the one-piece suit down, exposing her quivering backside, trapping her hands between them.

When he drew her nipple into his mouth, she understood the phrase "ravenous greed" for the first time.

No, no. She had to touch him. To kiss him. Lick him like he did her. Revel in the glory of his muscular chest. Lisa fumbled with the opening of his suit. When all she found was smooth material, she groaned. How the hell did he open the one she wore?

"Frustrated, my love?" Abalim spoke in between nibbling her sensitive skin. "Let me help you."

Nod. Yep, just nod. Her mouth had better things to do besides talk. Like licking luscious man-flesh. Suckling the side of his corded neck, her fingers opened and closed on their own on his exposed muscular chest. The cool air puckered her nipples, causing goosebumps to break all over her naked skin.

With his hand on her backside, he drew her to him, his mouth covering her nipple, and sucked.

Lisa arched as waves of pleasure wracked her body. His touch sent shivers so intense it paralyzed her, making her unable to move away or get closer to him as his tongue licked her sensitive skin. She was lost in the sensations as exquisite pleasure blanketed her in waves of euphoria.

"Abalim," she whispered, uncaring when her voice wobbled. When his clever fingers slipped between her thighs, she gasped. Gripping his shoulders, she hung on as his lips moved lower. Staring over the top of his head, she watched him spread her thighs, exposing the liquid she'd created there.

His face tensed as he bent his head to focus on that part of her.

An eternity passed before he lowered his head and kissed her clit.

At the touch of his full mouth, a deep moan escaped from some place deep inside her.

Laying his lips over her hardened nub, he drew it into his mouth. In quick succession, he flicked it with the flat side of his tongue before pulling back. Once again, he repeated the action. And again.

She grasped the thickness of his dreadlocks and lifted her hips to him.

Abalim continued to rain kisses on her swollen, receptive flesh.

Every stroke made her dizzy as spiraling ecstasy tightened deep inside. The man was ravenous, like he'd never tasted a woman before and couldn't get enough. His masculine moan vibrated against her when he parted her intimate lips and pushed his tongue into the clenching core of her.

It was too much. Lisa threw her head back and screamed a shattered cry as pleasure raced from her quivering channel through her convulsing body in hedonistic rapture.

"I can't believe how sweet you taste, Lisa." He spoke to her core, running his tongue around her oversensitive button. He increased his teasing by darting light flicks over it.

She had to see. Raising on her elbows, she watched, panting, each breath a struggle as her stomach clenched, almost too strong to endure.

"Touch your breasts for me." His baritone voice carried a lash of command in a guttural tone. "Do it, Lisa. Play with your nipples."

Lisa whimpered, her neck and face heating. What he demanded made her breath catch. She never took her eyes off him, grasping and lifting her breasts, cupping them. A husky moan passed through her dry lips. She gripped her nipples with her thumbs and forefingers, causing her hips to jerk at the stabbing sensations roaring through her clit and beyond.

Abalim licked around her sensitive opening. "I've never seen anything so captivating." He kissed it, pulling the bud into his mouth with slow, delicious deliberation.

Once again she was so close. Teetering at the very edge of falling into an orgasm.

He pulled back.

She cried out at the loss.

"By the God An, you're so *fruking* gorgeous," he groaned, fingering her swollen folds. "Give me your hand."

Wrapping his strong fingers around her wrist, he pulled it from her breast and brought it between her thighs.

"Show me, Lisa," he growled. "I want to know how you pleasure yourself."

Lisa took in a shaky breath at his stern command. Shock and eagerness warred as he pressed her fingers into the wet heat between her thighs. She'd never been put in this position before. None of her previous lovers had ever cared what ramped up her sexual cravings. Especially after she'd already found her release. "What?"

"I yearn to know the best way to pleasure you." He swiped his tongue over his bottom lip and pushed away from her.

The sight of his magnificent naked body with his jutting erection was the perfect display of male dominance.

"Show me what you like. Then I'll give you what we both need."

Yes, please.

With tentative fingers, she obeyed. Circling her clit, she then rubbed over it, before running her fingers down the slick slit. She parted her nether lips and watched as his eyes were trained on her every movement. Gaining confidence, she rubbed over the entrance to her body before pushing a finger inside. She whimpered. Her mouth watered at the sight of his fingers easing over the thick flesh of his wide cock as he fisted it.

With a lowered, leering gaze, he stroked himself.

He was teasing her. The rat bastard had to know what he was doing to her. Well, two could play that game. She teased back.

Lisa pumped her fingers inside, massaging her clit. Groaning, she watched each rounded stroke Abalim made over his hard erection. She pulled her fingers out. Her juices glistened on her fingertips. She held her hand out to offer him the treat.

"By the nine galaxies, Lisa." He blanketed his torso over hers.

She sighed as his weight settled on her, bringing in his musky, tantalizing scent with each breath she took.

When his full lips parted, she slid her fingers inside the heat of his mouth.

When she pulled her fingers out, he pushed the head of his erection through her parted folds in one successful stroke, stretching her.

It'd been a long time since Lisa had a lover, and him burrowing into her was almost more than she could handle. "Abalim, oh my God, you feel so good." She lifted herself to her elbows, parting her thighs. "Yes, that's it." Eager for him, she wanted him hard and fast. Deep and strong.

He pressed into her, and his hard muscular thighs pushed her legs wider, holding her open.

Lisa watched his impressive girth slide into her, inch by glorious inch. He'd pull out, and she'd catch a brief glimpse of his dick's glistening dark skin before he flexed his hips to make it disappear back into her.

With each stroke, electricity blazed inside her. Erotic pleasure scraped over every nerve ending and left a trail of heat behind. Her sex drew tight with the need to release with each stroke he made inside her. Inch by glorious inch, her tender flesh throbbed. Gripping his shoulders, she hung on for dear life. After each thrust, a glittering vortex of pleasure ramped up, so intense she was terrified it'd steal her soul.

Lisa had written many love scenes in her career, but she'd never personally enjoyed the fantasies she committed to paper. What she and Abalim experienced went far beyond anything she dreamed of for her romances. Her imagination was a source of pride, but this was far beyond anything she could ever dream up.

"Ah, my inkheart." His hips jerked and bucked, filling her with the last inches of his steel cock.

He grabbed the globes of her ass and lifted her, keeping them joined on the soft bed of leaves and linen. The action caused him to rest deeper inside. Lifting her legs through the crooks of his arms, he circled his hips, hitting her pleasure center with each bump.

Lisa's inner core flexed, her womb clenching hard. Broken cries escaped her lips as Abalim moved in earnest. Slow at first, the easy strokes building the smoldering need inside her. Like a fire being coaxed into existence with each breath by a master. The burn started at her toes and all too soon soared to the tip of her head. She writhed, staring at him in dazed ecstasy as his movements became harder. Faster. More intent.

His expression twisted until it turned into a taut, savage line of lust. Peering through his thick lashes, his dark eyes glistened with an intense need. A rivulet of sweat beaded down the side of his temple.

He made love to her with heavy, hard strokes. Impaling her with a rapture destined to fill her senses until nothing else was real.

"Abalim!" Lisa cried, struggling beneath him. She ached. She yearned. She couldn't take much more. It was beyond heat, beyond the volcanic thrill of a roaring fire. It transcended mere fulfillment.

Torn apart by the need ripping through her, the upcoming exhilaration building inside her expanded with each plunge of his unyielding cock.

"Abalim! Abalim, please." She gripped him tighter, and her orgasm neared. Its force warned her of the oncoming destructive nature about to explode.

"That's it, my inkheart, my everlasting love." He groaned. "Hold me tight. Don't let go."

He released her legs, blanketing her with the heat of his wide chest, keeping his hands beneath her to hold her in place.

She wanted more and wrapped her legs around his hips, linking her ankles together. Good thing she did that. The man took her hard. Hard and fast, with enough force that when his hips pounded into hers, flesh slapped loudly against flesh. Then one last devastating push from him made Lisa shatter. She screamed his name when ecstasy detonated deep inside her. Arching under him, she tightened her legs around his trim hips as tremors of rapture consumed her. He spilled his hot seed inside her, and minor eruptions caused her womb to convulse in response.

As Abalim held her, he whispered her name against her neck. His body shuddered and jerked through his own release.

Wrapped in his warmth and their shared cocooned of pleasure, Lisa savored a sense of completion for the first time in her life.

Chapter Nine

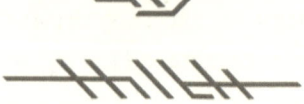

A slight pinch on his cheek yanked Abalim out of a sound sleep.

"What the...?"

"Mister Abalim, sir."

He stilled at the anxious tone in JR15's voice.

"You and Ms. Lisa need to get up and put your suits back on. There are several Lumarians headed this way. And I don't think they're very happy."

The small droid shivered as he trotted off the side of Abalim's face and rested on the bed of leaves next to his head.

Abalim blinked, trying to focus on his companion. "Is it still night?" He pushed himself up on his hands and looked over his shoulder at the draping vines at the opening to the hut. It was still pitch black outside.

"What's going on?"

Lisa's groggy voice made him smile. He sat up and watched her do the same.

She scratched the side of her head, making her short blonde hair stick up.

"I'm not sure, but JR15 says a group of Lumarians are on their way here." He got off the nest, putting his hand on his lower back, and stretched. It was amazing how comfortable that bed was. "We've got to put our suits back on before they get here."

She yawned and stretched her hands over her head.

He stopped and stared as her naked breasts rose and fell with her movements. Images of their lovemaking mere hours ago made his breath catch and his blood pool south. He dropped his suit he'd picked up off the floor reached out to grab her.

"Oh, no you don't, mister." She gave him a mischievous chuckle. "You touch me, and we'll forget all about those aliens headed this way. Then they'd find themselves watching something I'm sure will make them lose their shizzle."

He groaned when she bent and picked up her own suit. Damn woman would test the patience of the gods themselves.

He sat on the nest and put his foot into the leg of the suit. "Can you tell what they want, JR15?"

"I'm not sure, Mister Abalim, sir. It's hard to tell 'cause they're all talking together. But I can tell you they don't look very happy."

After putting his other foot in the suit, Abalim stood and finished dressing. With the flat of his hand, he sealed the garment closed at the nape of his neck. The small droid scuttled up the wall next to Abalim's head and leaped, landing on his partner's shoulder.

Once the droid settled he glanced at Lisa and frowned.

The woman struggled with closing the suit to activate it. She tugged at the top, but nothing happened.

Now he heard the angry murmurs from outside getting closer.

JR15 squealed and scuttled up the nape of his neck.

He rushed to Lisa's side. "Here, let me." With a flat palm, he pressed the side of the opening to make it close.

Just as the binds morphed together, the hanging vines over the door were shoved apart.

"Are they here?" Nyvira stomped in with Tharion right next to her. "Have you seen them?"

Abalim faced the Lumarians with his arms crossed. "Is who here? And why would you think they were?" He stood in front of Lisa in an automatic protective move.

"What's happened?"

His female was no simpering youngling who hid behind him.

She walked around him with ease, stood next to him, and clasped her hands in front of her.

"We have traitors in our village that threaten the lives of everyone at Aroonshire." Tharion stomped a foot and waved his hands. "If we don't stop them, all will be lost!"

Wow, drama queen much?

For the first time, Abalim heard Lisa's telepathic thoughts. He coughed into his fist to hide his bark of laughter. He didn't need to startle her, so he avoided responding to her in kind. It'd be better if they practiced her newfound abilities in private. He cleared his throat. "What do you mean, traitors?" He glanced at Lisa, who raised an eyebrow at him.

Nyvira held an illuminating pole and waved it around the small room as if she was looking for someone hiding in the dark. "Maelani and Dravik have gathered a small group of like-minded allies we suspect are trying to take the elders away. To prevent us from offering them in the Ritual of Renewal tonight."

"Council Leader." It was the guard Xalun who had stood sentry at the eldest tree earlier. "The elders' hut is secure."

"Are they all safely inside?" Tharion demanded.

Xalun gave a slight bow. "Yes, Council Leader. All are accounted for."

Nyvira closed her bright eyes and breathed a sigh. "Thank the god Echovara." She put a hand over her heart. "We are saved by his mercy." She flicked a thumb up the illumination pole and it dimmed. "We apologize for the intrusion. But I'm sure you can understand our fear of letting anything happen that would disrupt the ritual."

Lisa stepped closer to the female Lumarian. "Wait, I don't understand something. Why would you think they were in here with us?" She flicked a hand at the small room. "It's not like we can hide anyone here. Not to mention we hardly know them."

"That's because I overheard them say they had help from visitors from the outside." Xalun offered. His hand gripped the javelin he held and lowered his eyes. "And you are the last foreigners we needed to check on."

"Captain Xalun, make sure all of your troops are guarding the elders. This is no time to relax."

The guard gave a slight bow and left.

Nyvira put a hand over heart and addressed Abalim. "It is hours before sunrise. Please take this time to continue your rest so you can be fresh for the celebration later." She crooked a finger at Tharion. "Come, my bonded one. We need to prepare so we don't incur Echovara's wrath."

Tharion nodded. "Just so."

With that last statement, he left, following his female through the hanging vines.

"Well." Lisa snorted. "That was fun."

"JR15, are they out of earshot?" Abalim murmured in a low voice.

"Yes, Mister Abalim, sir."

Abalim nodded. He gave Lisa a mischievous smirk. "Ready to sneak around and find out what Maelani and Dravik are up to?"

"Ha!" She bumped him with her shoulder and grinned. "Who says you have to be a psychic to read my mind!"

***

Lisa couldn't believe how wide-awake she was despite so little sleep. Her face heated. Not to mention the sensual gymnastics she and Abalim had shared before she fell into blissful oblivion. But look at her now, sneaking around an alien village as if she were a heroine in one of her romance novels. Adrenaline rushed through her. Yeah, following the drop-dead handsome, muscular hero into the darkest night to uncover the vilest villain's plot...

"Stop here."

Abalim's deep masculine voice jerked her out of her daydream. Damn, she was doing it again. She tended to blank out at the worst moments as part of a plot revealed itself. Most of the time it didn't matter because she was in her office at home, immersed in her creations. Too bad over the years it gotten so bad it started to take over her life. That was one of the main reasons she'd joined the alien exchange to live the kind of life she'd only written or read about.

"We're here."

Abalim squatted and put out his arm as if she was dumb enough to keep on walking. Okay, maybe with her head in the clouds, she was. But still. She hunkered down next to him.

"JR15," he whispered to the bot on his shoulder. "Can you tell me how many are guarding the hut?"

"Oh yes, Mister Abalim, sir." His spider shaped robot quivered his bulbous butt. "There are ten guards surrounding the domicile."

Abalim looked over his shoulder at her. "Open your senses and tell me what you feel."

What? It was time for psychic lessons? Lisa gave him a narrow-eyed stare before giving in and closing her eyes. A wave of emotional sensations wrapped around her. There was excitement, fear, and a huge heaping of giddy lust from the guard, Xalun, as he daydreamed of Maelani. Ewww, she could've done without that last part. She mentally shook herself and put a block on her spidey-sense so she didn't get overwhelmed by everyone's emotions.

"I'm not sure how helpful that was." She gripped his firm upper arm to keep herself steady. "All I got was a jumble of emotions that I have no idea who they're from." She nodded toward Xalun. "Except for that one. All he can think about is Maelani."

Abalim's smile lit up his dark eyes as he searched her face. "That's very good. First chance we get, I'll teach you how to separate the emotions so you can pinpoint which ones you want to focus on. That way you'll have the ability to determine who's friend or foe."

Friend or foe. Sometimes he talked like an old codger. Lisa giggled. "Well..." she intoned. "Spill. Tell me what you know." Tit for tat. Time for the man to share the good stuff.

Abalim pointed to the guards wandering around the hut. "The guards you see are determined to keep the elders inside safe. What's important to us is they're not militarily trained in any way. Most of them are farmers or merchants." He stood and pulled her with him behind the nearest large tree. He peeked around it and pointed to the hut. "But I'm sensing something completely different inside." He frowned. "Those people are terrified."

"I don't blame them." Lisa studied the hut in the dim light of the full moon and the lit poles placed around the small one-story building. "I mean, even though these people grew up believing they might end up as part of the Ritual of Renewal, I doubt they thought for a minute they'd be in a group instead of doing this alone."

Abalim humphed. "JR15, would you do another sweep to make sure there isn't anyone else around?"

"Analyzing, Mister Abalim, sir."

"Why are you making him do that?" Lisa tugged on her ear and studied his intense expression. "You're not going to do what I think you are, are you?" Who said she needed psychic powers?

He grinned at her. "Probably." He turned and studied the small building. "We've got to get inside. Something just doesn't feel right."

"Mister Abalim, sir, no change in who is inside or outside the building."

"Thank you, JR15."

"What doesn't feel right? Do you mean in there or just everything in general?" Lisa let her senses go free. There... he was right. Something was off. Like an underlying plot percolating she wasn't aware of until she focused on it.

Abalim glanced at her and shrugged. "If I'm honest, everything." He circled the air with his forefinger. "Not just in the village and the ritual they're planning on performing later, but the whole situation the Xeltrians put us in. Why are we really here in the small village getting ready to watch them terminate their elders? Are we supposed to stop them or encourage them? And have you noticed the surrounding landscape? How every hour we're here, the plants appear to be dying?" He gestured to the leaves and bark of the tree they hid behind.

For the first time, Lisa studied the bark she stood next to. It had black patches that matched the ends of the leaves. She was no botanist, but it didn't look very healthy.

"And what about Saphira and her crew? Was it necessary to freeze them in stasis on their ship while we gallivant around here? Why not put them in a holding cell on Qorath?" He turned to study the hut and guards again. "There is definitely something else going on in there and here." He clenched his hands into fists. "When I think I've figured some of it out, something else happens."

Well, soaring space dung. The man was right. The last time she felt like this was when she'd walked in on the middle of a movie and never saw the trailer. She scrutinized her surroundings. Now the taste of unease she experienced was stronger. "What do you think we should do?"

His sigh rumbled from deep within his chest. "First, let's see what's happening inside that hut. I want to know how those elders feel about going through the ritual. Are they there willingly, or were they forced? If they're eager to do this, then why is everyone afraid? And why guard people who want to be a part it? I'm convinced someone or something changed how things are done here."

"Like what?"

Abalim scratched the side of his square jaw. "Like why are there some Lumarians going against the norms and insisting on seeing their mother before the ritual when they were never denied before? If everyone is happy about the ritual, why are they now going against generational traditions? I'd like to get close to Maelani and Dravik and find out what they're really afraid of."

"Ah, you're going to read their minds." *Hmm*, yep, sounded like a plan. "Okay, I'm with you. Read the folks in the hut first. Then we'll go and look for Maelani and her brother." She eyed the guards circulating the small hut before glancing at Abalim.

Abalim's eyes narrowed on the small structure. "Yes, that's the plan."

"Okay, so how do we get in without alerting the whole village?"

Abalim turned to her with a radiant smile. "Why, through the front door."

Oh sure. Through the front door. Why didn't she think of that?

***

Biting her lower lip, Lisa followed Abalim out of the dense foliage and headed straight to the guarded elders' hut.

He had his hands clasped behind his back and strolled as if he didn't have a care in the world.

She was about to warn him one of the guards was headed their way when the male turned around and went back the way he came. Her mouth fell open as she watched the guard from the opposite direction do the same thing.

Her neck heated. Idiot. She was with a powerful psychic. No need to sneak around. All he had to do was block everybody else's vision with a flick of his finger. She eyed his clasped hands. Not that he did anything as dramatic as waving his hand around like Obi-Wan Kenobi using the Force.

"Mister Abalim, sir..." The little robot JR15 spoke in a low voice. "I think I should warn you..."

Abalim pushed open the hanging vines and entered the small building.

Lisa was right behind him and almost plowed into his backside when he stopped.

"... the others I sensed in here weren't just the elders." With a high-pitched squeal, the spider-shaped robot scurried back to his hiding place under Abalim's dreadlocks.

Lisa would've given anything if she could hide next to the little guy. Tharion's and Nyvira's smirks made her nervous as hell. Pinching at the base of her neck had to be the tip of one of the spears the guard behind her carried. She didn't move as a warm line of blood rolled down her back. Taking a deep breath, she put her trust in Abalim. If, for one minute, he thought their lives were in danger, he'd sic his psychic mojo on them. He had to be stalling to get info. Yeah, that's what he was doing.

"Ah, yes. Why am I not surprised you're one of the traitors?" Tharion crowed. He snapped his fingers and glanced at Nyvira. "I told you these foreigners were part of this. Let's sacrifice them with the rest. This will make this year's Ritual of Renewal the best in generations! It'll be sung about for centuries."

Lisa peeked at Abalim.

The guard leaned into the spear to the back of Abalim's neck with a gleeful grimace.

But with that long thick hair, she couldn't tell if blood was drawn or not.

"Yes, yes." Nyvira waved away her companion's excitement. "Take them..."

"May I ask a question first?"

Lisa admired Abalim's relaxed stance. With that nonchalant attitude, she loosened up and did her best to mimic him. Even with crossed arms.

Nyvira put her hands on her trim hips. "What?" She tapped a foot. "I don't have all day, you know."

"Why are you forcing the elders to participate?"

Tharion's mouth dropped open. "How dare you question us!"

Lisa winced at the high-pitched squeal from the guy's mouth.

"We would all die if the elders didn't join with the god Echovara!"

"Aren't you being a little dramatic?" Lisa rolled her eyes. "All would die." She snorted. "Really?"

"Look around you!" Nyvira gestured with both arms around her. "Everything around us is dying because skeptics like them refuse to give the holy one his due." She pointed to the roof of the hut.

Lisa squinted and took a closer look. The same black goo on the twigs and leaves in the hut matched the outside plants. Her nose twitched at the rancid smell coming from it.

"But with this offering of younger accolades, our merciful god will halt the spread of death from stalking us. We will save our village for years to come!" Nyvira's eyes gleamed with fanatical intent.

"I..."

Lisa never heard what Abalim was going to say. Something sizzled at the base of her neck and she passed out.

***

Head pounding, Abalim groaned and rolled onto his back. He put his arm over his eyes. By the God An, why did he let his brother talk him into trying some new type of liquor again? He swore the last time he did that he'd never let Arakiba manipulate him into doing something he'd regret in the morning. But when they found themselves seven thousand years into Earth's future as free men, some of the temptations of the modern world were hard to pass up.

But anything that robbed him of his senses' ability to protect himself went beyond trying new things. A feminine moan next to him jerked him out of his musings and brought him back to reality. "Lisa!"

Ignoring the thundering in his temples, he scooted to where she lay on the hard dirt floor. Her face was paler than normal, and her luscious mouth twisted in a grimace.

He pushed a lock of her hair out of her eyes with a light touch of his fingertips. He searched for her pulse at the side of her neck and breathed a sigh of relief when it was strong and steady. "Lisa, my inkheart. Are you all right?"

She moaned again, her eyes fluttering open.

Her shoulders relaxed, and he found himself the focus of her mesmerizing blue eyes.

"Did you get the license plate of the truck that hit us?" With the heel of her hands, she rubbed her eyes. "Holy God, I haven't felt like this since my college days."

Abalim wasn't sure what college had to do with the pain in her head, but now wasn't the time to discover what she meant. "Never mind that." He helped her to sit up. "How do you feel?"

She snorted. "I'll live." Her clear sapphire eyes focused on him again. "I may regret it, but I'll live." She looked over his shoulder. "Where are we?"

In his hunched position, Abalim rested his elbow on his bent knee and studied their surroundings. It was then he noticed they weren't alone. Several younger Lumarians were sitting with some elders he'd never seen before. The only ones he recognized were Maelani and Dravik, who sat with an older Lumarian female. She embraced them under her arms and murmured soothing clicks and whistles while petting the tops of their heads.

"I believe we're prisoners in the elders' hut," he replied.

"What do you think they're going to do to us?" Lisa scratched the side of her head.

"Well, that's obvious." Dravik moved away from the female who had to be his mother and sneered. "They're going to sacrifice all of us tonight at the ritual."

His mother tweaked the tip of his pointed ear. "Dravik! There is no reason to think that's what will happen." She tried to pull him back to sit with her, but her son shrugged away and jumped up with his hands on his hips.

"Yes, we do, ma-mere. Nyvira made it clear she and Tharion believe our youth will give the village an advantage."

One of the young female Lumarians cried with gurgling sobs.

The elder female frowned. "They can't do that."

"Dravik's right!" Maelani joined her brother to face their mother. "We're all going to be sacrificed to Echovara tonight!" She flicked her wrist at the group, staring at her mother with wide, terrified eyes.

"Dravik, sit down!" Their mother's stern tone was firm. "I need you to calmly tell me what's going on."

The younger male Lumarian's mouth opened and closed as he narrowed his eyes at Maelani.

"Don't look at me!" His sister raised her palm in defense. "I think we owe it to ma-mere and the other elders to explain what happened after they were selected."

"Yeah," Lisa whispered to Abalim. "I can't wait to hear this."

He led her to one of the walls and sat. He leaned back and positioned her to sit in front of him, her back resting on his chest. He wrapped his arms around her waist, savoring her warmth as it seeped into him.

"Yes, please tell Alaria and the rest of us what happened once Council Leader Tharion confined us in here." An elderly Lumarian male spoke up. He had his arm around the sobbing young female next to him.

Maelani gave a respectful nod to him. "Yes, Elder Zylar." She started her narrative. "From what I understand from the past, it was common for family members to deliver food and comfort to the elders while they were in the elders' hut. Is that correct?"

The male gave a clipped nod. "Just so." He glanced around the room. "We've wondered why no one in our family came to visit."

"It's not that we didn't want to." Dravik picked up the story. "Whenever we tried, the guards kept us out and told us we weren't allowed to see or speak to you."

"Yeah, they chased us off with threats."

This came from one of the young female Lumarians snuggling under Zylar's arm.

"Chased off? Like criminals?" Zylar whistled and clicked with his bright eyes wide.

The male's disbelief and horror came through loud and clear to Abalim's psychic sense.

"For what reason did they give for that?"

Maelani's laugh was devoid of humor. "They told us it was treason to see or speak to you. And every time, we were threatened with exile."

A collective gasp went around the room.

"Exile?" Maelani's mother frowned with a sharp whistle. "They threatened you with exile?"

"That, and worse." Dravik put a hand on his mother's shoulder. "But Maelani and I found others who agreed with us that things with the Ritual have to change." The brightness in his eyes dimmed. "Too bad everyone who did that is stuck here with us now."

"Why do you think they don't want you to see or speak to the elders? Did you threaten to keep them from attending the ritual?" Abalim had to ask. It was a question that had bothered him for quite some time now.

"No, not at first. It wasn't until they told us we had to stay away did Dravik and I plan to take away ma-mere and anyone else who didn't want to be a part of the ritual." Maelani sat next to her mother and put her arm through her mother's, leaning her head against Alaria's shoulder. "That's what we were trying to do when the guards captured us."

Alaria snorted with a whistle. "Ever since Tharion and Nyvira took over the council, they have refused to let the selection process of the ritual happen as it had for generations. They were the ones who declared all elders had to take part, no exceptions. And I can only think of one explanation for this change." Her lips flattened with a flat whistle. "Power." She glanced at the other elders in the room. "Tharion and Nyvira have always acted like they were better than anyone else. It got worse when the council leaders perished in the last Ritual of Renewal. Since then, those two seized power and changed so many things in Aroonshire."

"If you could stop the ritual, would you?" Abalim twined his fingers through Lisa's. He wanted to hear how the group felt about the ancient tradition in their small village. It would be fruitless to intervene if these Lumarians weren't open to stopping it. As the old saying went, it didn't take a majority to make rebellion, it only took a few determined leaders.

Dravik snorted with loud clicks. "Anyone with half a brain would know the ritual hasn't been working lately." He pointed to the blackened and gray roof of the small hut. "Everything around us is disintegrating faster than ever before. It used to be we only conducted the ritual every other generation. But ever since that last ritual provided no relief, those two declared we have no choice but to sacrifice as many as we can." He glanced at his sister and the other younger ones in the room. "Even those of us in childbearing years."

"That is so," Maelani chimed in. "And who knows if it'll work or not? The rot is spreading faster and deeper. Everyone is terrified it won't help, no matter what we do."

"That is so. Our village is dying." The elder Zylar's announcement caused more in the small crowd to weep. "We don't know if our sacrifice will help at all. If all the plants and animals die, so will we." He gave a deep garbled whistle. "We tried to convince Tharion and Nyvira to search for a different way, but they refuse to even consider it." He swung his hand in the air as if to emphasize his point. "There has to be a different way to appease Echovara!"

Alaria's bright eyes dimmed with a tinge of yellow.

Abalim's mouth soured when a sense of her sorrow swamped through him.

"To answer your question"—she stated—"yes, we should do everything in our power to stop the ritual. It may be the only way to save our people."

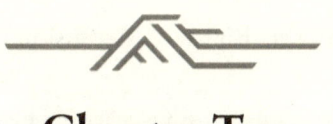

Chapter Ten

With nothing else to say, the group sat on the floor and leaned against the hut wall. Most of the Lumarians' postures were slumped in defeat while Maelani and Dravik spoke in low tones with their mother.

Abalim meant to ask JR15 to do some recon work outside the hut, but the vines over the entrance were whisked open with a dramatic swirl.

In walked Tharion and Nyvira with a group of guards behind them, pointing spears at those in the hut.

"Get up!" Tharion commanded with a flourish of his open hand. "Echovara will no longer be denied!"

The bewildered expressions on the captive Lumarians' faces probably matched Abalim's.

"It's not dusk yet!" Maelani exclaimed, standing. She grasped her mother's hand and pulled her close.

Abalim held Lisa's hand as they stood with the group.

Nyvira tilted her chin up with a regal sneer crossing her thin mouth. "Since we are offering such a large group, we have to start now."

Sniffles and moans from the captives lessened and were replaced by growls and loud clicks that rebounded in the small space.

"We demand the Right of Ascension." Dravik stepped forward.

"Denied." Nyvira gave him a scathing glare. She humphed and spun around with her head high.

With a sneer, Tharion followed. "Bring them." He glanced over his shoulder. "If they resist, blast them unconscious and carry them."

"Everyone must follow so no one gets hurt." Abalim put a hand on Maelani's shoulder. "I promise we'll figure something out."

Maelani's dull eyes simmered brighter before she nodded. She turned and whispered to Dravik, who whispered in a stern tone for the group to cooperate.

A few grumbles, but everyone fell in line and walked out of the hut.

The guards kept a tight ring around them.

Abalim squinted when they went from the dim hut interior to the bright sunshine. Even though it was filtered through the leaves of the gigantic trees, it was easy to see the sun had traveled down the skyline on its journey to end the day.

After blinking to clear his watering eyes, it dawned on him how quiet it was.

The normal sounds of people taking care of their daily business were muted. As were the sounds of insects and normal background noise of animals.

A line of Lumarians created a humanoid corridor that started from the elders' hut to the Ritual of Renewal tree at the end. Their bright pupilless eyes were shimmered in dull yellow while others were a blazing red. Some eyes were narrowed in anger or widened in shock.

Or, vice versa. No telling with aliens.

To avoid getting slammed by unwanted emotions, he braced his psionic abilities to block everyone. Except for Lisa. He carefully joined his mind with hers. Ugh, he was hit by her inability to control what she sensed, which threatened to overwhelm her.

My inkheart. He made sure his mental voice was soothing and nonthreatening.

She tripped.

He gripped her elbow to keep her steady. *Keep walking. I'll help you control the emotions you're drowning in.*

Her smile lit up her face. *Thank you,* she mentally replied, her shoulders drooping as if tension was released. Biting her lower lip, she glanced at the quiet Lumarians they passed. *Most of them don't want to see us sacrificed at the tree. Only a handful do.*

Unfortunately, it only takes a handful to intimidate the many.

A bright light from the tree caught his attention.

"NO!" Maelani screamed, with one of her hands extended. She burst into a run before any of the guards could stop her.

Her escape created mass confusion. The Lumarian corridor broke up as most of them ran behind her.

In the scramble, the guards were shoved aside and lost control of the prisoners.

"What's going on?" Lisa exclaimed as they ran to catch up with Maelani and Dravik in front of the massive ritual tree.

Abalim skidded to a stop and grabbed Lisa's arm to hold her in place. His eyes widened as he witnessed three Lumarians from their group along with Alarea, all handcuffed to the tree, disappear in a wave of shimmering sparkles.

"Oh, my god!" Lisa exclaimed with her fingers covering her mouth. "It looks like they've been transported." She gripped his forearm in a strong grasp. "Maybe they aren't being killed at all!"

He glanced at her with his brows furrowed and a frown. "Transported?" He'd never heard that word before. "What's that? I don't understand what you mean."

"Mister Abalim, sir." JR15 crawled out of his hiding place to talk on while riding on Abalim's shoulder. "It's a type of teleportation machine that is a subspace device capable of instantaneously sending an object or person from one location to another."

He sent an incredulous stare first at his bot friend and then at Lisa. "Really?" He studied the image of the last of the young Lumarians disappearing. If anyone asked him, he'd swear the tree absorbed them instead of them being sent somewhere else.

The crowd surrounded the tree with angry fists pumping in the air. The air filled with their shouts, whistles, and clicks.

At once a group of Lumarians turned their back on the crowd, held hands and began to sing.

We call to thee, Echovara

Ancient and mighty.
Accept our humble offerings,
Our souls
Our trust
In the name of our survival,
We sing our sacred chant to thee.

The wide bark of the tree moved and rippled until an image of an out-of-focus elder Lumarian became clear.

The crowd of Lumarians wailed in whistles and clicks, then they dropped to their knees with their foreheads on the forest floor. "Echovara!"

The resounding roar from the group was deafening. The group sang their god's name in perfect harmony. Filled with anguish, hope, and excitement.

Ignoring that he and Lisa were the only ones standing, Abalim narrowed his eyes at the image. "JR15, inspect the image and tell me about it."

"At once, Mister Abalim, sir." The bot wiggled his bulbous belly. "As I'm sure you suspect, Mister Abalim, sir. It is a hologram generated from the tree."

Abalim humphed. Nothing but smoke and mirrors.

"Mister Abalim, sir?"

JR15's quiet voice was hard to hear over the chanting of the crowd.

"I think you should know I am able to verify that the Lumarians who disappeared have not been killed. Miss Lisa is correct in saying they were transported."

"Are you able to determine where they are?"

"I am still analyzing that information. But I can verify they are not in the village."

Lisa reached over and grabbed Abalim's forearm. "What's he saying?" She nodded at the spybot on his shoulder.

Abalim crossed his arms and leaned closer so she could hear him better. "He's telling me you're right." He nodded at the large tree with its holographic face of an elder male Lumarian looking down at the crowd with condescending glee.

"The Lumarians they just 'sacrificed' were teleported somewhere else." He gave her a mischievous grin. "Want to be next?"

***

Lisa thought experiencing a transporter was great in theory, but the idea of her molecules scrambled and reassembled somewhere else made the hair on the back of her neck rise. She glanced at Abalim, who studied the scary face on the tree. Maybe he saw something she didn't. Besides, it was hard to think through the loud chanting of the Lumarians. She couldn't even tell if the creepy tree was saying anything because the face looked like it was stuck. The same expression twitched over and over like it was trapped in a loop.

"Are you sure we'd be safe if we did?" She tapped her finger on her lower lip. "I mean, look at it! I swear the damn thing is broken."

Abalim leaned his head and whispered something to his spider shaped robot.

She couldn't hear what he said, but when he lifted his eyes, his expression was eager.

"JR15 has analyzed the last transportation and verified I'd have no trouble controlling it if it didn't reassemble us correctly."

Lisa scrunched her nose. "What in the world makes you think you can control something like that?" She pointed to the tree over the backs of the bowing Lumarians.

"I'm not just a pretty face that only reads minds, you know." He gave her a mischievous smile and shrugged. "It isn't much different from teleporting." He clasped her hand and led her to the glowing tree. "Come on. I have an idea."

Wow, this was a whole new side of Abalim she'd never seen before. He acted like a giddy kid impatient to play with a new toy.

They weaved and stepped over the Lumarians bowing in front of the tree.

As she got closer, it became clear the tree was saying something. It sounded like it was trying to say its name, but got stuck in the middle. Over and over. "Jeez, that's annoying," she muttered under her breath. A sharp poke at the back of her neck made her wince. Well, crap. Not again.

"Look what we have here," Nyvira crooned in her ear. "Isn't this nice? You've brought yourselves close enough to Echovara so you can join him in eternity."

The pinch dug harder into her skin as a rivulet of warm blood trickled down the back of her neck. Lisa was so sick of this happening to her. All she wanted to do was turn around and punch Nyvira in the face. Yeah, that'd teach her.

"Just a couple more steps."

The hard grip on Lisa's upper arms didn't give her any leeway. She was dragged to a worn area in the rough bark in the shape of a Lumarian. She gasped as she was turned around and shoved hard enough into the trunk to lose her breath. Her head thumped against the unyielding bark, and she saw stars. Instinct had her trying to rub the back of her aching head, but that was a no-can-do with her arms bound wide and flat against the tree. Her legs were spread-eagle, and the bindings were so tight her ass smushed against the rough surface.

"Hey, bitch!" Lisa tugged and strained, trying to remove herself from the unyielding bindings. Like struggling ever worked. "Let me go. I didn't agree to be part of your stupid ritual."

"Put him next to her." Tharion demanded, ignoring her. "And make sure he's bound good and tight. We don't want him to get loose."

Lisa gasped as she watched an unconscious Abalim dragged next to her while two Lumarian guards propped him up with his back to the tree.

Bindings shot out from the tree and wrapped around his neck, arms and upper legs to hold him in place.

She tried in vain to see if his little spider-shaped robot was okay, but he was either hiding deep into Abalim's hair or he had somehow fallen off.

"Now put them next to her." Nyvira commanded, pointing a finger at the other side of Lisa.

Lisa's eyes widened when she saw Maelani, Dravik, and Zylar approaching the tree.

Several guards followed close behind with pointed laser spears. The one guard, Xalun, jumped ahead and faced the other soldiers in front of Maelani as if to stop them from taking her. He was quickly subdued and forced to the tree with the others. All were bound to the scratchy bark like she and Abalim were.

"You all have the rare and honored privilege of becoming one with the mighty and glorious Echovara!"

Nyvira's sneer made Lisa's blood boil. What a sanctimonious twit.

"Fear not. Your sacrifice will not be in vain. Once you join with him, you'll be giving life to all of Aroonshire for generations to come!"

With a dramatic flair, she took the crystal pendant around her neck and placed the iridescent gem in a divot on a small, raised platform.

A blinding light shot from the dais, making Lisa squeeze her eyes shut. She tilted her head to the side, trying to escape the painful glare piercing through her closed lids.

So much for us being in control. The thought crossed her mind before her world crashed, coating her in darkness.

***

As Abalim clawed his way back to consciousness, an accompanying orchestra of agony threatened to overwhelm him. It was a fight to open his eyes. Once he got them open, he couldn't see clearly. With a grimace, he narrowed them until an eerie, dimly lit cavern came into focus.

The walls were adorned with glistening stalactites, with the faint sound of dripping water echoing.

It took a shaky effort to sit up. Pressing a palm against his chest, he struggled with his fragmented memories to piece together where he was. A brief memory of being torn apart by a transporter made him grunt. Now the dull ache in his head throbbed in time with his racing heartbeat.

Lisa! Where was Lisa?

A feminine moan sounded next to him. Ignoring his burning muscles, he pulled her off the dank and dirty floor and cradled her on his lap. With a gentle touch, he brushed her short blonde hair out of her eyes. "Lisa? Are you okay?"

He opened his senses and gave her a psychic scan. The mental block he'd taught her was fragmented, giving him full access to her memories and feelings. She was just as disjointed as he was. Good thing her aches were disappearing like his were.

Her eyes fluttered open, and her sapphire eyes met his. She rubbed the side of her head with the palm of her hand. "I'm so sick of being knocked unconscious and then waking up feeling like this. Let's not do that again, 'kay?" She looked around the cavern and gave a deep sigh. "Well, hell. Where are we this time?"

An image at the center of the room caused Abalim's eyes to widen.

There, looming like an ancient sentinel, was a colossal, round machine that defied the cave's natural formations. Its massive metallic surface shimmered with an otherworldly glow, casting eerie shadows that danced along the craggy cave walls. A soft, pulsating hum emanated from it, vibrating within the rocky chamber.

He couldn't help but marvel at the intricate web of gears and cogs, all interlocked in a mesmerizing, symmetrical pattern.

That's where the answers had to be.

Speaking of finding answers, he tore his gaze away from the machine to find out how the small bot was. "JR15? You still with me?"

"Yes, Mister Abalim, sir." The small bot scuttled down his neck and rested on the end of his shoulder. "I appear to be in maximum working order."

Abalim bowed his head as the sharp tension in his shoulders melted away. "I'm so glad you weren't hurt."

"Are we the only ones here?" Lisa's eyes searched his face with pursed lips. "What happened to the Lumarians who were tied to the tree with us?"

Abalim frowned. "That's a good question." He glanced at her beautiful face. "You well enough to stand?"

With a sultry smile, she wrapped her arms around his neck. "First things first."

Before he had a chance to ask her what she meant, she pressed her plump lips against his. He opened his mouth and returned her caress, allowing his tongue to stroke hers with abandon. The drugging action made his head spin as all thought centered on where they joined. Placing his palms on the side of her head, he tilted her to gain further access. It wasn't until JR15 gave a little squeak did he remember where they were.

He broke the kiss and placed his forehead on hers. "Woman, don't start things we can't finish."

Her pink tongue peeked between her lips as she licked them.

His groin tightened, becoming a steel monster that demanded release.

Lisa gave a little wiggle, rubbing against his straining member. "Sorry." She shrugged with a sheepish grin.

Damn woman didn't look like she was sorry.

"Couldn't help myself." She jumped off his lap and held out her hand to him. "Come on, hunky man. Let's find out what happened to the Lumarians." She pointed to the large machine. "Think they're over there with that thing?"

Abalim didn't need her help to stand, but he wasn't about to pass up the chance to touch her. Clasping his hand in hers, he stood and gathered her in his arms for a quick hug. With a slight smile, he let her go and glanced at his AI companion on his shoulder. "JR15, can you scan this room and see if you can find where the Lumarians are?"

The little bot's silver-and-green body wiggled. "Already done, Mister Abalim, sir. Behind those mirrors along the walls are chambers filled with the bodies of the Lumarians."

Lisa gasped with her fingers covering her mouth. "Are they all dead?"

JR15 shook his small, bulbous head. "No, Ms. Lisa, ma'am. Not all. I have analyzed the ones who came here with us. They are thankfully still alive. But I cannot determine how long that condition will last."

Opening his palm, Abalim created a spinning sphere of light to help them see. "Which way, JR15?"

"To the left. They are lined up against that far wall."

"Dang." Lisa nodded at the light in his hand. "That's all kinds of handy. Bet you don't have to worry about running out of batteries."

Abalim gave her a mischievous smile. "What's better is I can make it do this." He tossed the sphere into the air. It hovered and gave a light soft enough to guide them.

"Well, soaring space dung! That's about the coolest thing I've ever seen." Her laugh was infectious.

He chuckled with her as he struggled to tamp down the urge to puff out his chest and strut like a pompous moron.

Holding hands, they cautiously ventured deeper into the cave. In the background was the odd rhythmic hum of the massive machine. With the help of his lighted sphere, they reach the side wall that resembled a hall of mirrors as far as the eye could see. When Abalim looked closer, behind each panel was a Lumarian cocooned in a state of deep slumber.

Inside, an internal low light reflected against the cave wall, creating a translucent radiance around the sleeping forms, giving them an almost divine radiance.

"Oh my God, Maelani!" Lisa cried and ran to one of the pods. The young Lumarian inside looked like she was asleep. Her bright eyes were closed and her mouth slightly open. "Do you think she's okay?" Lisa had her hands on the pod and looked over her shoulder at JR15 for the answer.

"Yes, Miss Lisa, ma'am. She is for now." He turned his little, round eyes to her. "But I'm afraid the elder Lumarians are having their energy drained. I am not certain how long it will be before they expire."

Lisa gasped.

"Can you determine what is causing that?" Abalim glanced at the large machine across the room. If his suspicions were correct...

"I cannot be sure, but I believe it's not only the personal energy from the Lumarians that is the target."

Abalim turned to his small companion. "What else is being targeted?"

"Look at that!" Lisa pointed to the floor where a long, thin tube glowed from one of the tubes to the large machine.

For the first time, Abalim noticed the thing was pulsating with a brighter light.

"Miss Lisa, ma'am, is correct." JR15 nodded. "As far as I can ascertain, the machine is searching for a specific item the Lumarian might be wearing. Unfortunately, their life force is drained as a byproduct of that search."

Lisa's lips pressed together. "Well, since we don't know what it wants, how 'bout we kick that piece of shit out of their stasis pods?" When it didn't move after giving it a swift kick, she tightened her hands into fists. "Okay, time for something else. Think there's an ax around here somewhere? I'd love to chop me some firewood." She glanced around as if an ax were handy in this dank, empty place.

Abalim put a hand on Lisa's tense shoulder and gave her a gentle squeeze. "Hold on, my inkheart." He nodded to the machine. "We can't be sure what would happen to them if we did that. Let's have JR15 analyze it closer."

"Yes, yes, Ms. Lisa, ma'am." The little bot nodded his head vigorously. "I will interface with the machine to see the best way to dislodge it from the Lumarians."

Lisa frowned and crossed her arms.

The action lifted her breasts nicely.

"You make it sound so easy." She glanced his way. "Think he can communicate with an alien machine?"

Abalim gave her a wide smile, doing his best to keep focused on her eyes and not some other tempting part of her anatomy. "Well...if he can't, then we'll find that ax so you can chop away to your heart's content."

***

L isa bit her bottom lip and glanced at the prone Lumarians. They didn't look like they were suffering, but she knew better. Their silent screams echoed in her mind courtesy of her new psychic powers.

Damned psychic crap. Why did she ever think it'd be an awesome thing to have? She clenched her jaw as she internally fought to stop from rushing over and yanking the suffering Lumarians out of the coffin-like death traps. She glared at Abalim and his little friend.

Abalim responded by touching her shoulder. With feather-like whispers, his mental tendrils coated her agitated mind and showed her how to block the agony from the captive Lumarians.

As relief swept through her, she squeezed his hand and gave him a grateful smile. "Yeah, that's much better, thank you." She sighed and threw her shoulders back. "Okay, let's see what we can find out."

His dark gaze studied her for a moment before he returned the smile. He grasped her hand and lifted it, then gave her knuckles a brief kiss.

Watching Abalim's full lips caress her skin made Lisa's breath catch as sensitive nerves came alive. Ooh, look at him. The man was a master at diverting her attention to more pleasant things. Things that didn't have to do with the dumb situation they were in. Just like one of her heroines, she was fast losing her heart to a dangerous charmer in the middle of their adventure. Yeah, but who said that was a bad thing?

She followed Abalim to the massive machine. The closer they got, the more Lisa fought the urge to run away. That sucker was huge. She'd never seen anything like it before. Circular with a pearly illumination at its back, like a streetlight's globe tilted, so the light shone around its back edge. Pulsating lights rolled around the outer edges, first bright and then dim. Like the pulse of a giant struggling to hang onto life.

Lisa looked at the small silver-and-green spider bot on Abalim's shoulder. "You think you can somehow communicate with that?" Talk about David vs Goliath...

The little bot bobbed his head. "Yes, Miss Lisa, ma'am." Semitransparent wings spread out of his back. Delicate like a lady bug with an iridescent sheen, the little guy rose from Abalim's shoulder and headed to the machine.

"Analyze first, JR15. Don't come in direct contact with it just yet," Abalim warned him.

"No sir, I mean yes, Mister Abalim, sir." The little spider whizzed toward the dull center of the machine.

Lisa gripped Abalim's forearm. "I hope he doesn't get hurt."

Abalim covered her hand with his. The warmth of his touch settled her shivers.

"Make a quick sweep around the machine," he told JR15. "Then come back and recommend what options are open for us on what to do next."

With a quick whistle, the bot zoomed around the machine. It didn't take long for JR15 to buzz back. With his wings flapping in silent mode, he faced Abalim. "Mister Abalim, sir, I believe I can activate the main communication. You wish me to do so?"

"Only if you deem it's safe." Abalim replied.

"Oh, yes, Mister Abalim, sir. It is quite safe. I will be right back."

The little guy zoomed back to the machine and hovered above the dull center.

Lisa couldn't tell what the little bot did, but the middle of the machine lit up and the ring surrounding it turned.

A piercing sound, sharp and shrill, pierced through the air.

Lisa covered her ears and squeezed her eyes shut as an excruciating pain sliced through her.

Then the rusted machine sputtered to life, and a high-pitched whine settled into a cacophony of creaks and groans echoing through the large chamber.

Daring to open her eyes, she pulled her hands away from her ears. What she saw made her jump.

A ghostly figure of a robed, elderly Lumarian male stood with his hands folded in front of him. He sported a nonthreatening warm smile.

Lookie here... Yoda anyone?

"Welcome, good citizens! We are so grateful you have finally answered our call." He gave a slight bow before waving to the machine behind him. "While we appreciate the bounty you keep sending us, we fear they are not what is needed to continue. For us to resume our life-giving directives, you must replace the Lumicor crystal!"

"Lumicor crystal?" Abalim stepped closer to the holographic image of the elderly Lumarian wobbling in and out of focus. "What is that?"

JR15 buzzed to his shoulder and settled, folding his wings under his dorsal storage.

"Why, it is the very source of life for the citizens of Aroonshire. Without it, we will cease to exist." He tilted his head and pursed his lips. "Surely, you, as the caretakers, are aware of this. Are you not?"

Lisa put a lock of her hair behind her ear. "Caretakers?" She glanced at Abalim, who stood with arms crossed and his forefinger tapping his lower lip. "Of what?" she asked.

"Of our glorious selves, my children." The elderly male chuckled. "After all, you created us to take care of you after we landed on this planet eons ago. Why, without us, everything around you would die in the toxic atmosphere. All the plants and animals would perish, along with the Lumarian people."

Abalim cocked his head. "And just who is this *us* you're talking about?"

"My child, do you not know who we are? We are Echovara!"

Chapter Eleven

Abalim studied the hologram. Looked like the Lumarians created this machine to produce some type of biosphere for them to live in eons ago. Only now the technology to maintain it was long gone. All that was left were legends and traditions spoken by this image without knowing the full truth.

"Are you telling us your power source is in danger of being depleted without this crystal?"

The male widened his arms as if to include the massive machine behind him. "Yes, yes! We have been waiting for far too long for you to come and provide us with the Lumicor we so desperately need."

Lisa crossed her arms. "If you need this Lumicor so much—" She thrust her forefinger at the prone Lumarians in their pods against the cave wall. "—why are you killing your people?"

The wispy form of the elder wrung his hands. "What choice do we have? When the caretakers stopped coming to see to our needs, we had the elderly brought here. We asked each one of them to provide us with the crystal, but none knew what we were talking about!" He hung his head. "We admit it got to the point we scared them so much we had no choice but to put them to sleep the minute they arrived. It is to our great sorrow that their life force has kept us going. Even as we speak, that is becoming useless. Especially since they cannot give us enough energy to grow more crystals." His bright eyes filled as large rolls of clear liquid that rolled down his sunken cheeks. "Our only solace has been the hope that our caretakers didn't abandon us and would return to correct that which went wrong."

Abalim narrowed his eyes at the image. Since it wasn't an organic being, he couldn't psychically connect with it. Good thing he had his AI companion to help. He glanced at the bot resting on his shoulder. "JR15? Do you think you can interface with the machine and see what you can learn about this crystal and where it needs to go?"

"Yes, of course, Mister Abalim, sir. I have already made a tentative connection. I'll be right back. I shouldn't be long." JR15's iridescent wings came out, and he fluttered back to the huge contraption.

"You will allow my small bot to examine where your power source is needed." Abalim stated to the machine. "In the meantime, display an example of what this crystal looks like."

The image bobbed his head. "Of course, caretaker." He held out his hand. On it, an oval-shaped clear iridescent crystal appeared, about the size of his fist. Abalim stepped closer to take a better look. If he wasn't mistaken, inside the rainbow of colors was the silhouette of a massive tree. Like the one that brought them here.

"Oh, wow. That's gorgeous!" Lisa exclaimed. She reached out as if to touch it, but pulled back with her fingers curling into a fist. "It kind of looks like the pendant Nyvira used to send us here."

Abalim nodded. "Yes, but that crystal was clear and didn't have this image in it." He pointed to the rotating crystal floating in Echovara's palm.

The hologram of the Lumarians' god frowned. "No, no, that won't do. It has to be exactly like this one! The etching of the tree tells us the crystal is at its full maturity."

"Well, all you gotta do is tell us where to get one, and we'll bring it back to you. Just point the way!" Lisa threw her hands in the air.

The hologram of the elderly Lumarian straightened and closed his fist, cutting off the spinning gem. "That is the responsibility of the caretakers, not us. You people had one directive, and you have failed at that small task." He pointed to the prone Lumarians in the stasis pod. "And that is the result of your incompetence."

"Damn, harsh much?" Lisa groused under her breath.

JR15 flew back and landed on Abalim's shoulder. "Mister Abalim, sir?" The bot's tiny voice spoke softly. "After analyzing the power input valve on the machine, I may have detected where we can find the power source the hologram describes."

Abalim raised an eyebrow as he glanced at the small bot who looked back with his round head tilted. "Really? Is it near?"

JR15 stood and rubbed his back legs together.

That seemed to be a sign he was nervous about what he said next.

"I can sense the same energy signal through that stasis pod." He pointed a tiny foreleg at the empty coffin-shaped mirror next to Maelani.

"It's in there?" Lisa's mouth fell open.

"No, Miss Lisa, ma'am." JR15 shook his green and silver head. "It is in the room behind it."

"That is not allowed!" The image of the Lumarian male grew. "It is forbidden to access the chamber of the gods!" His voice thundered, causing the ground to shake and loose dirt and rocks to fall from the ceiling.

No time to waste. "Hang on, JR15!" Abalim grabbed Lisa's hand and raced to the empty pod. "Come on, let's go."

"HALT! You are not allowed!" The booming hologram expanded until his face filled the room. "You must not go into the banned zone!"

The room shook, causing more debris to fall from the ceiling. Rocks the size of fists rained down.

Putting his free hand up, Abalim created a bubble of protection around them.

"Abominations! How dare you invade this sacred temple!" If a computer-generated hologram could go completely insane with rage, this one did. His incalculable anger shone through with his spitting mouth and bared teeth that matched his flaring nostrils. That and his high-pitched scream said it all.

Somehow, when Abalim created the protective bubble around them, it interrupted the hologram of them being Lumarians. Now their true selves were exposed for all to see. And neither of them had a chance to look anything like the fluid forms of a Lumarian.

While the pod had only been a couple of feet away, it took forever to get there. Maintaining the protective dome, Abalim searched the enclosed mirror-pod for a way to open it. He ran his fingers across the top and the sides. "Are you sure this is where we have to go?" Peering into the clear top, all he saw was the bed where a body would lie. "I don't see anything..."

JR15 flew off his shoulder and landed on the top right corner of the case. A slim rod from the back of his neck slid out and plunged into the pod. With a click, the clear top rolled back and at the same time, the bedding swung away and exposed an opening.

"I WILL STOP YOU!"

Abalim gaped over his shoulder. The hologram turned into a widened mouth, exposing double rows of sharp fangs with lines of black blood dripping down to the tips. The raining dirt and rocks above them increased with each shake of the ground.

"Quick, go in!" Abalim didn't wait for Lisa to take the initiative. He shoved her inside as JR15 zoomed in right behind her. He made it through before the bedding door slammed close. Grabbing Lisa into a tight hug, he squeezed his eyes shut and struggled to catch his breath. "Are you okay? I didn't hurt you, did I?"

She gripped his shirt with clenched fists. "No, no. I-I'm fine." Her voice was muffled, since her face was mashed against his chest.

She pulled back, and he opened his eyes.

Her clear-blue orbs searched his face. "Are you okay?"

He brushed his hand over the side of her head, smoothing her flyaway blonde hair away from her face. "I'm good." He took in a deep breath and watched JR15 hovering over his face. "You okay, my friend?"

JR15 wobbled up and down in flight. "Yes, Mister Abalim, sir. If it's all right with you, I'm going back to my place on your shoulder."

Abalim smiled at the bot. "Of course." JR15 zipped to land on his shoulder before scuttling to the nape of his neck.

"Where are we?" Lisa asked.

Good question. Keeping his arms around her, he turned them so they could see where they ended up.

***

L isa took a step back and put a hand over her heart to settle the vertigo making her dizzy. Before her was an endless, dimly lit corridor made of some kind of metal. Illuminating the hallway, an embedded light of rich deep red gave it an eerie vibe. If she didn't know better, she'd swear she was in a large submarine during a red alert.

"Where is that signal for the crystal, JR15?" Abalim's voice was calm and smooth.

She gripped his forearm, desperate to feel his firm muscles under her fingers.

"This way, Mister Abalim sir." The bot scuttled from his hiding place and stopped at the edge of Abalim's shoulder. He spread his iridescent wings and buzzed ahead of them. He only went a short distance before he stopped in front of a closed metal windowless door. "The Lumicor signal is inside there."

The door looked impenetrable. No doorknob, no latch, or anything that could be used to open it.

"How are we going to get in?" Lisa asked as she ran her hand over the surface. Maybe she'd find something by touch. Like a way out of this creepy place.

"JR15?" Abalim addressed the hovering bot. "Any ideas?"

The little guy's head bobbed. "I can try to infiltrate the system..."

The bot was interrupted by the door sliding up.

"... or we can just go in."

Keeping her grip on Abalim's solid arm, Lisa peeked inside. The small space had hardly enough room for the still figure on a metal slab. She narrowed her eyes. Was that the crystal man Rerqel showed them before? The last time she saw him, he was out of control and screaming death threats at them. Now he laid on the table with eyes closed. Relaxed in a way that only someone in a deep sleep could be.

"Is that the, what did you call him? A crystal something?" She let go of Abalim's arm and ventured in. She checked around, but no one else was in the bare room.

"He is called a Krystalii." Abalim's forehead crinkled between his dark brows. "I wonder how he got here." His full mouth thinned as he went still and his eyes unfocused.

"We brought him here while your worked through your trial."

Lisa jumped when Rerqel the Xeltrian appeared at the head of the table where the Krystalii lay. "Holy crap!" She exclaimed with a hand at her throat. Her heart beat a mile a minute. "Warn a person next time."

"We have determined that this creature is your key to solving the Lumarian dilemma." The willowy alien raised his forefinger to point at the prone emerald crystal form of the Krystalii. "End his life by taking his heart That's a perfect replacement crystal needed to save the Lumarians."

"What? Are you telling us we've got to kill him?" Lisa gasped.

Rerqel opened his arms as if to encompass the room. "We are not telling you to do anything. What you decide to do is up to you." He disappeared.

"I can't believe he'd even suggested such a thing!" Lisa crossed her arms and tapped her foot. "We can't go around killing one person to save another." She glanced at Abalim. "Right?"

When he didn't answer, she turned and studied him. Dang, the guy looked like he was zoned out. She tapped a finger on her bottom lip. Maybe she should try to peek into him mentally and see what he was doing. Lisa calmed her mind. It shouldn't be too hard to psychically connect with him. With a tentative touch, she slid in.

***

The dimly lit underground chamber was bathed in an eerie green glow as Lisa stood in front of Abalim.

She blinked. What... were they saying? She glanced around and became transfixed at the Krystalii, the enigmatic alien creature lying on a thick rock slab.

The crystalline body pulsed with an otherworldly light, casting intricate patterns of shimmering reflections on the smooth metal walls. When did it start doing that?

Lisa clutched her fists, her heart pounding as she glared at Abalim. "You can't seriously be considering doing what that crazy Rerqel suggested, can you? How is killing this guy going to help the Lumarians?

Abalim's dark eyes locked onto the Krystalii. His mouth tightened. "The Lumarians are on the brink of extinction. If we don't do something to help them, their entire civilization will be wiped out. How can we stand by and let that happen when there's a way to save them?"

Lisa took in a deep breath to stop from saying something she'd regret. "Are you telling me you think we should kill him? Then what? Hack him up and rip his heart out?"

Abalim's brow furrowed, his voice tense. "Don't you see, Lisa? This Krystalii came here to take over our galaxy." He shuddered. "I know what it's like to live under the rule of a dictatorial regime. And I swore if I could stop it, I'd never let that happen to anyone else." He widened his stance with crossed arms. "You don't have to do anything." His full lips tightened. "I'll take care of it."

Lisa ground her back teeth. How could he stand there and callously say he'd end the life of a sentient being? She had to sniffle back the unexpected tears. He wasn't listening to anything she said. How could he not take her opinion to heart? "Listen, Abalim." She placed her hand on his hard-as-steel forearm, fighting to keep the touch light and not shake some sense into him like she dying to do. "We've got to think of something else. I'm sure we can find another Lumicor crystal somewhere." She snapped her fingers. "How 'bout asking Saphira and her crew? They've been around the galaxy a time or two. They might know where we can find one."

Abalim took a step back, away from her hold. "Lisa, I wish we could, but we don't have time for that." He waved a hand around the small room. "Even if we could find a way back to *The Galactic Serpent*, we don't have enough time to leave Qorath and search for one. Didn't you see how fast Aroonshire is fading? Not only that, Maelani and Dravik are dying as we speak. Their life force is being sucked out of them, and I doubt they'll last much longer. He tilted his chin high. "I'm telling you, if we don't act now, it'll be too late."

Lisa put more distance between them. "So, that's it? You're not willing to try to find another solution? You'll just go around killing someone 'cause you think you have the right to?"

Abalim stood straight. "I'm not a murderer," he insisted. "But this creature came here planning on killing everyone in our galaxy. And to do that, he wants to take every human woman hostage and turn them into incubators for their young. That something you want them to do? Are you willing to let these things torture and kill other woman when you have a chance to stop it here and now?" He stomped to her and grabbed her upper arms with a tight grip. "Lisa, it's about doing what's right. Not only for us, but think about the innocents throughout the galaxy that will suffer if we don't act now. It's our moral duty to try."

Lisa shook her head, her eyes glistening with unshed tears. "Nothing is ever that black and white. Once we go down that slippery slope, we'll end up just as bad as those we fight against. There's got to be another way to do both."

She wiped a tear leaking out of her eye. She knew what it was like to be the one "sacrificed" for the good of others. When her parents died, her aunt and uncle couldn't take on her younger brother and her, so they put her in the foster system. She went willingly, thinking it would help her brother so he wouldn't be torn from their family. And she'd naively thought her family would visit her occasionally to check up on her. But she never saw them again. Which was hard on a ten-year-old.

Shoving her deep-seated emotions down the dark well in her mind, she blinked to clear her eyesight and rubbed her sweaty palms down her thighs. "Please tell me that how I feel about this counts for something."

Abalim recoiled as if she'd slapped him. "Of course, how you feel means everything. But this isn't about choosing between you and the Lumarians. It's about trying to save those we can."

Lisa's voice cracked, her righteous anger turning into despair. "It's hard to believe we can't find a way to work on this together, Abalim. I thought we had something special, something that transcended time and space. But now, you're willing to throw it all away, believing that stupid Xeltrian. How do you know if we can even trust what he's telling us?"

Abalim gathered her close, his indrawn breath shaky. "Lisa, I'm not throwing anything away. I'm trying to do something meaningful, something that would make a difference in the universe. I thought you, of all people, would understand that."

Lisa breathed in his spicy scent, leaning against his firm pecs. "I don't know, Abalim. Maybe I'm just an oblivious idiot who thinks someone like you would want to build a life with someone like me."

Abalim slid a palm down at the back of her head, his voice pleading. "Don't talk like that, Lisa. You and I share something I never thought I'd find to fill my empty life. Please understand, I can't turn my back on the Lumarians. I would've given anything for someone to step in for me and my brothers when we were slaves. The only thing we were good for back then were experiments and death. So if there's a chance I can help save these people from the same kind of fate, I'm going to do everything in my power to do so."

Steeling herself, Lisa pushed away to face him. Her heart filled with a mixture of love and heartbreak. "And I can't stand by and watch you commit murder." She gave him a tentative smile and rubbed the soft fabric covering the hills and valleys of his muscular chest. "I'd like to think of you as my hero, Abalim. But I can't support you taking this irreversible path."

Her words hung heavily in the chamber. The echo created a palpable tension between them. She gripped his forearms and searched the depth of his dark eyes. While his expression softened, his conviction was clear to see.

In the background, the prone Krystalii shimmered, casting a haunting glow as she and Abalim stood at a painful crossroads. The weight of their impossible division slid an impenetrable wedge between them.

***

Abalim jerked when a painful pinch pierced his neck. "Ow!" he exclaimed, slapping his hand over the offended area.

"So sorry, Mister Abalim, sir." The tinny voice of JR15 stated. "But you've been in a trance for quite a while now. I just wanted to make sure you were okay."

He blinked and took in his surroundings. He and Lisa were still in the cave with the prone Krystalii on the rock slab. Lisa was immobile in his arms while the Xeltrian Rerqel stood at the head of the table with his hands clasped in front of him.

Ablalim narrowed his eyes. He knew a Dreamwalk when he experienced one. "Why did you do that?" He directed the question to the willowy alien. Obviously, the alien hadn't gone anywhere.

"We wanted to see how you and your female experienced life-altering decisions." His shoulders twisted back-and-forth.

Abalim got the impression it was the alien's way of shrugging.

"We find it interesting that while you two disagree on this key issue, you were both open to listening to each other. Even if you hadn't reached a unified decision."

Lisa struggled in his arms.

He loosened his hold.

She spun around and faced their sanctimonious jailer. "You're right. We don't agree." She gripped the forearm he had wrapped around her shoulders. "The only thing we decided was we both want the impossible. A way to save the Lumarians without killing somebody to do it."

"If I may interrupt—" A broken cough came from the figure on the table. "—I believe I have a solution that might solve everything." The Krystalii coughed again, louder and deeper this time. He put his hand up to cover his mouth, but puffs of pulverized crystals spewed between his fingers. He coughed again.

Abalim pulled Lisa closer. With a tight grip, he tamped down the panic closing his throat and glared at the prone creature on the stone table. He didn't trust the calm demeanor from someone who'd been frantic the last time he'd seen them. Peering closer, his eyes widened. Were the crystals on his body deteriorating? Parts of him appeared to be broken and cracked, ready to fall off.

"What's wrong with you?" Lisa whispered. She moved as if to get closer, but Abalim held her back.

Remember, he has strong psychic abilities, he whispered in her mind. *You don't know if he's sending us an illusion or not. Don't let him touch you. It could be a ruse so he could grab you and disappear.*

"I will not harm your female," the Krystalii stated with a grimace. "My mission to obtain the Xeltrians as an ally is over before it began." Another deep cough. "I miscalculated, and my time in this dimension has run out. With my last remaining life force, my only wish is to help you thwart the Krystalii horde."

Abalim sent out a whisper of a psychic tendril to the alien. Not enough to draw attention, but enough to get a hint of his sincerity. He latched onto the outskirts of the alien's consciousness and wormed his way inside. There, a hint that the underlying part of his brain had once been locked down by some outside force.

In an instant, Abalim saw into the heart of the Krystalii. He'd lived his life held in hard captivity by their leader, who kept a solid block on the part of his brain that housed free will. Coerced into serving his master for thousands of millennia, this creature was forced to be a part of a regime that eliminated thousands of species. But deep inside, the creature before him suffered with each atrocity he involuntarily committed.

"What's your name?" Abalim asked the crystal figure in a gentle tone.

The Krystalii's sunken green eyes fixated on him. "I am called Aollu."

"What is wrong with you, Aollu?" Lisa asked, her tone equally soft.

Aollu glanced at her before fixating back on Abalim. "I believe there is something about this dimension that accelerates our life cycles. Even though I am relatively young for my species, I now am in the throes of advanced age. It is now my appointed time to return to the dust of my creation." He coughed into his hand. Not only did streams of crystallized dust whiff around, but now chunks of clear glass spewed out of his mouth.

Wheezing in a shallow breath, he never took his eyes off Abalim. "There is no need for you to hide your presence in my mind. The block put on me at creation has finally disintegrated." Another cough, this one dryer than the one before. "For the first time in my life, I am in control of my decisions." The smile crossing the dull emerald skin around his mouth cracked. A piece of his bottom lip broke off. "By my own free will, I wish to do something my lord and master would never have allowed me to do before." His eyes were steady but unfocused for a moment.

Abalim experienced the creature's dimming memories full of regret.

Aollu had led a lonely and isolated life, even with his consciousness buried deep within the hive mind of the Krystalii nation.

"I have shared with the Xeltrians a way to help halt the Krystalii invasion. And now, I would deem it an honor to give you a small part of myself to aid the Lumarians." A small solid, iridescent glass teardrop rolled out of the inner corner of his right eye. "I know doing this small thing won't erase the deaths

I caused to millions of sentient beings. But with my last breath, I hope to redeem my soul with the Omnipatron by doing this. I freely give you a part of myself that will allow the Lumarians to live."

He covered his chest with one of his hands. With a grimace, he let go a stuttered breath and pulled his hand away. He opened his clenched fist and raised it. In the center was a ragged emerald oval the size of a large man's palm. "Take it. Give this to the Lumarian Echovara. It will restore it to its former glory." He raised it higher. "I guarantee this will give them life for several millennia as well as provide them with the ability to grow life-crystals for the future when this one fades."

Abalim plucked the emerald from the Krystalii's corroding palm.

Lisa leaned over his hand and examined the stone with him. It was a beautiful gem with ribbons of various shades of green and black swirling within it.

"I swear a star is growing inside it," Lisa stated with reverence in her tone. She caressed the top with a forefinger. "I can't believe how gorgeous it is."

"Thank you, citizens." Aollu's voice came out raspy and harsh. "Saving the Lumarians will give me a divine purpose. I leave you now, to join the Omnipatron's everlasting source." The dim light in his emerald eyes faded as his final word quivered in the air. With a last rattled breath, his body disintegrated into a fine green powder.

Chapter Twelve

Lisa's eyes filled with tears she angrily wiped away. Look at her, feeling sorry for the creepy alien whose only agenda was to coerce the Xeltrians into conquering the galaxy with them. When Abalim put his arm around her shoulders, she leaned into his warmth.

Never be ashamed of having empathy for others, he admonished mentally. *It is our greatest strength.*

Yeah, but still. She pulled away and turned to face him. "Now, what?" She pointed to the emerald crystal in his hand. If she wasn't mistaken, the darn thing pulsated in the rhythm of a heartbeat.

Abalim's dark eyes lowered to look at the gem in his open hand. "Now we need to go back to Echovara and see if we can fix him."

Without a glance at the silent Xeltrian, they left the room with the Krystalii green dust floating lazily to the ground and headed back to the cave holding the Lumarians.

JR15 whizzed to the right corner of the closed door and inserted a small beam of light from the middle of his forehead. The door slid silently open.

Abalim motioned for Lisa to stand behind him against the wall as he peered inside. "JR, what do you think?" he asked the small droid hovering beside him. "Can you see if there's a place we can insert this into Echovara and save the Lumarians?"

The cute-as-a-button spybot nodded. Even in the low light, his metallic green-silver body shone with an attractive gleam. "Oh yes, Mister Abalim, sir. I most certainly can." He pointed a spindly foreleg at himself. "I have already downloaded its schematics. It will be easy enough to pinpoint exactly where it goes."

Lisa yanked on Abalim's sleeve. "That may be all well and good, but how in the world can we get back there without letting that stupid fake god kill us?" The image of the psychotic hologram chasing after them and causing massive earthquakes made her heart race. Last thing she wanted was to get squished in a cave on an alien planet.

Abalim's lips twisted in a grimace. "I doubt these suits generate the image of us being Lumarians anymore. Even if they did, the machine would probably see through it now." He glanced at the small bot. "JR15, since you've already got a readout on that machine, do you think you can fly in there and shut it down? Or at least pause it to give us enough time to replace the dead Lumicor crystal with the one Aollu gave us?"

"I will do my best, Mister Abalim, sir." With a hop and a flutter, he zoomed inside.

Lisa gave Abalim a sideways glance. "Poor thing. Always going off by himself." The little guy was so small it'd be easy for even a hologram to swat him away.

He nodded. "We'll keep an eye on him from this side of the doorway so Echovara won't notice us." He squeezed her hand. "Don't worry, I'll teleport him away before anything bad happens to him."

Lisa stepped around Abalim and peered into the room. "I sure hope so." She pointed her finger at the hologram image of the elderly Lumarian stomping around, waving his arms and muttering under his breath. "That thing has totally lost his cookies." She watched it stomp over to the stasis pod holding Maelani. "Soaring space dung! What's he doing?"

The hologram placed both hands on the side of the clear tube and threw his head back. The dim lighting inside the case darkened.

Lisa didn't think, just ran with her arms outstretched. "Stop it! You're killing her!"

"Lisa, don't!"

She ignored Abalim's terror-filled voice.

"Come back here!"

She didn't answer since she was allllmoooost there, close enough to push him away. Instead of shoving the jerk away from the pod, she ran right through him. Stumbling, she pinwheeled and turned around to regain her footing. "Asshole! What the hell?"

"ABOMINATION!" Echovara screamed, his voice booming throughout the chamber. "You are not allowed to defile these sacred halls."

A bolt of lightning out of nowhere hit her square in her chest, flinging her onto her back and making her slide several feet. She blinked at the raggedy ceiling and sucked in a painful squeeze of oxygen. *That freaking hurt.* She rubbed the bruised area between her breasts.

"Lisa!" Abalim rushed to her side and kneeled next to her. Grabbing one of her hands, he placed it on his wide chest.

With his other hand, he caressed the side of her face. "Are you all right?"

His welcome warmth calmed the nervous shivers racking her body. "What happened? Why aren't I dead?" She glanced over his shoulder and watched the hologram of Echovara stalk toward them. Her eyes widened, and she struggled to sit up. "Oh my God, he's coming!"

The hologram raised his arms. His screeching, booming voice caused the ground to shake, as rocks and debris crumbled and rained down.

"JR15! Pause the program now!" Abalim shouted and covered her body with his.

Abalim's strong shoulders wrapped around her and he tugged her close, protecting her from whatever Echovara threw at them. When she peeked around his shoulder, she watched the dust and rocks tumble and slide down the protective bubble he put around them.

"Yes..."

The high-pitched voice of the bot was hard to hear at first, but his ending words came through loud and clear. Abalim must have popped the protected bubble.

"Mister Abalim, sir. I have paused the machine." JR15's hovering body was at the side of Abalim's head. "I cannot confirm how long the hold will last, so you must hurry to replace the Lumicor crystal and reboot the machine."

Abalim tensed before pulling away from her.

She took in a deep breath. While she appreciated his protection, his weight had made it hard to breathe. "Is he gone?" When she had a chance to look around, she didn't see anything but the empty cave and the dimly lit glass pods against the craggy wall. The resounding silence was a welcome relief.

"For now." Abalim grimly said with a hand stretched toward her. "Let's go and see if the Krystalii's sacrifice works or not."

She nodded and took his hand to help her up. "Yeah, I'm with you. Let's get this done." She released his hand and brushed her hair out of her eyes.

"Follow me." JR15 buzzed and led them to the huge circular machine.

When JR15 reached the massive machine, he zoomed around the front to a small part on one of its sides. "This is where you need to place the crystal. See?" He used one of his pointy front legs to indicate an area close to the ground.

Lisa dropped to her knees to inspect the small indent holding a black crystal covered in dust and grime. Around the oval shape were faded engravings barely legible. "What does that say?" she asked JR15, pointing to the indistinct writing.

"Insert crystal here." The damn bot snickered.

"Huh." She smirked. "Simple instructions. Who knew?"

Abalim opened his palm where the pulsating emerald lay. Where in the hell did he keep that? Damn, later she'd ask him where he had it in his sinfully tight one-piece suit. She eyed his splendid physique lovingly displayed in the snug outfit that didn't leave much to the imagination. She clenched her hand into a fist to avoid reaching out to explore those tempting hills and valleys of his muscular form.

Later, my inkheart. Then you can explore me to your heart's content.

Abalim's amused retort caressed in her mind. She smiled and shivered in response. *I'll hold you to it.*

"All right, let's do this," Abalim stated. He held the pulsating green gem above the indent. The dimensions of the crystal and the pad weren't aligned, and his face contorted as if he was trying to decide how to place it so it didn't fall off.

He jerked and hissed as the crystal yanked out of his hold and floated in the air just above the indent.

"What happened?" Lisa gripped his forearm. "Did you do that?"

Abalim shook his head. "No. I think the machine grabbed it. Look."

The emerald twirled round and round. Faster, then faster until it became a swirling rainbow of various greens before zipping over and slamming into the indent. There it stayed snugly, as if it had been created for it.

"By the God An! I've never seen anything like that," Abalim whispered.

"Did it work?" Lisa asked. "What's supposed to happen now?"

"Ah, my friends!" An unfamiliar male voice spoke behind them. "You have done it!"

Lisa turned and faced the strange speaker. She gasped and took a step back.

It was Aollu, the green crystal Krystalii standing there hale and hearty with a wide smile and his fists on his trim hips.

***

A balim lowered his head and studied the Krystalii. He tried to psychically read the fellow's intent, but all he got was a blank slate. As if he wasn't there.

"Is he a good guy or a bad guy?" Lisa whispered through pinched lips.

"Come now, my friends!" The green crystals covering the alien reflected in the low light as he approached them. "I am utterly grateful to you for freeing me." He gestured to the massive round machine behind them. "As we speak, I am repairing that which has been neglected and restoring life to the Lumarians on the surface."

"But what about the Lumarians held there?" Abalim nodded to the stasis pods behind the alien. "That machine has been draining their life force and killing them."

The Krystalii's bark of laughter came as a surprise. Who knew the male had a such a strange sense of humor?

"That was the first thing I stopped when Echovara and I became one." He turned and approached the pod holding Maelani. "As of now, they are all safe and sound. I'm allowing them to rest and am giving them extra nutrients to replace that which they lost." His five-fingered crystal hand caressed the top of the glass case.

For the first time, Abalim realized the image wasn't a hologram. Had Aollu truly been reborn? "Why is it that you're in solid form?"

Aollu clasped his hands behind his back and turned to face them with a winsome smile. "When that machine was originally created, the representation of Echovara appeared in solid form as well." He waved a forefinger to encompass the cave. "As a matter of fact, the neglect is so extensive it will take me decades to put it back to its former glory."

"What do you intend to do with the Lumarians?" Lisa crossed her arms with a scowl.

Ah, trust his love to be suspicious. Not that he blamed her, given the memory of the first time they'd seen this creature when he was completely focused on destroying them.

"Honorable female, I assure you, you have no need to worry about them. They are my new purpose, and I will do everything within my power to make sure they live a happy life in a free-willed society." Aollu stood in front of Lisa and gave her a slight, respectful bow. He straightened and turned to Abalim. "I, however, need to ask a small favor from you."

Abalim's eyebrows rose. He couldn't imagine what the creature could possibly want. "You may ask."

"I wish to have limited services from your droid. I believe you call him JR15?"

JR15 squeaked on his shoulder, and his little body trembled.

"You have to be more specific about what kind of services you're talking about."

"I understand your concern." Aollu's calm reply loosened the tight knot in Abalim's chest. "There is a program that has to be rewritten in order for me to release these Lumarians from their stasis. It is a small code I'm not familiar with, and since he has already interfaced with the machine, I was hoping your droid might be able to put it back in working order."

"That's up to JR15, if he feels it's safe to do that." He glanced at his small green-and-silver companion on his shoulder. At least the little guy had stopped shivering. "JR15? Is this something you want to do?"

"Oh yes, Mister Abalim, sir."

If Abalim didn't know any better, he'd swear the bot was grinning. The little guy did love a challenge.

"I know exactly what area he is talking about. It won't take me long." JR15 poked Abalim's neck with a pointy foreleg. "It will give me a chance to double-check the intention of the Krystalii as well. Don't worry, I'll be right back." JR15's iridescent wings came out, and he leaped off Abalim's shoulder and flew back to the machine until his small body disappeared.

"Be careful!" Lisa put her hand next to her mouth and shouted after JR15. She dropped her arm and gave Abalim a sheepish sideways glance.

He placed his hand on her shoulder to comfort her. "Believe me, JR15 would never put himself in a situation he didn't feel he had complete control over."

"Excellent, excellent!" Aollu clapped. "With his assistance, we'll have these Lumarians released hale and hearty in no time. Until then, I believe you need to connect with the Xeltrians again, don't you?"

The mischievous smile curling his lips gave Abalim pause.

"You act like you know something we don't." Lisa's scowl deepened. "And why do I get the feeling we're not going to like it?"

The Krystalii gave a slight shrug. "I cannot say how you will react to this information, but I do know it is something you should be aware of." He waved his hand and gestured for them to follow him. "Come with me, and I'll show you what I can."

He led them to the opening of the hallway they'd come through before.

When Lisa glanced at him, Abalim frowned, but gave her an encouraging nod.

Aollu stopped at the entrance. The endless corridor hadn't changed. "Do you wonder what is behind those other doors?"

Lisa bit her bottom lip. "Not really?" Her glance at Abalim told him she was as puzzled as he was. "Why?"

"These are portals the Xeltrians created to house thousands of species in what I believe you call a *zoo*." Aollu pointed to the nearest door but didn't make any attempt to go into the hallway to show them. "I believe you would be most interested in that one."

"Are you coming with us?" Lisa asked.

Aollu shook his head. "No, I'm afraid I have to stay here within these walls." He twirled his forefinger to encompass the craggy cave. "I will disappear forever if I leave this sanctuary." He chuckled. "And after regaining a new lease on life, I'm loath to give it up so soon."

JR15 zipped back and landed on Abalim's shoulder. "All is good, Mister Abalim, sir." He wiggled his small body as his iridescent wings folded inside his back. "And I have verified the Lumarians in the cases here are receiving the nutrients they need to recover."

"Will they be okay?" Lisa gripped Abalim's upper arm.

The small bot nodded. "Yes, Ms. Lisa, ma'am. None of them have suffered any lasting complications. But they have to stay in their pods and rest for a while." He waved a foreleg at Aollu. "The machine is now programmed to let them out at the appropriate time."

Lisa eyed the Krystalii. "Won't you scare the crap out of them when they wake up and see you?"

Aollu's booming laugh made Abalim smile.

"I would never do that to them! I will look like this whenever I appear before them." His form quivered, then morphed into an image of a young male Lumarian with his arms widespread. "My natural form holds when I'm in the cavern by myself. But when I go to the surface, I'll appear to them as a hologram. When I do that, I'll retrain them to take care of themselves and show them the best way to appoint someone to maintain the machine itself." He reverted to his normal crystalline self.

"You'd better replace the two power-hungry jerks that call themselves the council as soon as you can." Lisa nodded to the pods. "They planned on sending more people to be killed to terrify the village into obeying their every whim."

"You don't say." Aollu rubbed his chin with his forefinger and thumb. "After escaping a maniacal dictator, I'll not allow that to happen to the Lumarians." He crossed his bulky, muscular crystal arms. "Trust me, I'm not going to let them suffer like that."

Abalim glanced at his bot companion.

JR15 nodded in answer to his unasked question. "I am positive he will do as he says, Mister Abalim, sir. The Lumarians are in good hands. No need to worry."

"All right." Abalim faced the Krystalii. "It seems you have everything in order here." He tilted his head toward the open door leading to the endless hallway. "You were about to tell us something?"

"Oh yes, that's right." Aollu gestured at the corridor. "See those doors? They are portals to various enclosures housing a plethora of species that were facing extinction at one time." He nodded to the cave behind them. "This, too, is one of their compounds. You are not on a separate planet, but have remained on Qorath."

"So that's what you meant when you said zoo?" Lisa's voice cracked at the last word.

"What's a zoo?" Abalim whispered to JR15.

"It's an establishment that maintains a collection of wild animals, typically in a park, for study, conservation, or to display them to the public."

Abalim's chest tightened. How could he have been so blind to where they were? And what did that mean about the Xeltrians' purpose in all this? Had he and Lisa become pawns in a ridiculous distraction game to prevent them from coming up with a way to protect them from the Krystalii?

"What about the Xeltrians?" Abalim addressed Aollu with his arms crossed. "Are they willing to work with your people?"

The ridge above the crystal man's eyes raised. "No." He rubbed his chin again. "At least not as far as I know. If I understand your purpose here correctly, the Xeltrians hadn't decided about their involvement with my people." When he smiled, his clear blocky teeth were easy to see. "While I gave up my psychic abilities when I merged with Echovara here—" He thumbed toward the massive circular machine. "—I can tell you've impressed them. I wouldn't be surprised if they end up working with you."

Lisa cleared her throat. "And just how would you feel about that?"

"Ah, little female. It is my hope that when Lord Baelon finds his way here, he will encounter such as you and realize his campaign is fruitless, like I have." He gestured to the sleeping Lumarians in their crystal coffins. "Even if my people somehow find me and insist I go back with them, I'm unable to leave here." He waved a hand around the cave. "I'm happy and content that my life continues here, with them. And I wouldn't have it any other way. Rest assured, I shared with Rerqel various ways to defeat Lord Baelon, so my people never enter this dimension." He crossed his arms over his chest with a slight bow. "Now, my new friends, it is time for you to discover your own purpose. And we all know it is not here." He opened a palm to indicate the doorway to the endless corridor. "May the Sacred Spirit of all, the Omnipatron, guide and bless you on your endeavor."

Now there was an exit line if Abalim ever heard one. He returned the formal bow with one of his own, one arm crossing over his heart. "If you have need of our services, don't hesitate to reach out." He had no doubt if Aollu decided he needed them, he'd find a way to do so.

"Just so," Aollu replied. "As you humans like to say, good luck." His smile was warm. "But I don't think you'll need it."

***

Giving Aollu one last look after that cryptic promise, Lisa followed behind Abalim. Dang, once again, they faced the endless corridor. Well, hell. She didn't like it any better the second time around. The place had a damp, musty odor that made her nose wrinkle. "What are we supposed to do now?"

"I guess Aollu thought we'd find a way back to the Xeltrians through here." The sound of his fingers scratching his bristled jaw echoed in the spacious hallway. "I'm not sure how we're going to do that." He gestured to the never-ending row of doors. "What are we supposed to do? Open each one?"

Now that was an odd thing for him to say. "Can't you just use your psychic mojo and see if you can feel where we should go?" She tried using her own newfound psionic abilities, but all she got was a headache for her efforts.

He gave her a sheepish smile. "I would if it was that easy. But the only thing I'm getting is blank space. I suspect the Xeltrians purposefully put a psychic blocker down this corridor so none of the species could communicate with each other if they had the ability to do so." He glanced at the ever-present silver-and-green spider-bot on his shoulder. "What about you, JR15? Can you analyze anything..."

"Mister Abalim, sir, I do believe our new friends are headed this way." The little droid squeaked and scurried back to his favorite hiding place underneath Abalim's long, dark dreadlocks.

"Friends?" Lisa stood her hands on her hips and peered at the subdued light filtering down the hallway. She couldn't see anything, but the sound of raised voices and running feet echoed toward her. She took a step back. "Whoa, sounds like somebody's headed this way. And boy, are they in a hurry."

Abalim's warm palm covered her hand. "It's going to be okay. It's just Saphira and her crew. I recognize their mental signatures." He grunted. "I can't believe they're here. The last time I saw them, they were frozen in stasis on their ship."

Lisa eyebrows shot up as she glanced at him. "Oh really? How in the world did they get here then?"

"Good question." He answered with the side of his mouth curled in a slight grin.

Her eyes widened as the group barreled toward them, blasters drawn. Complete with snarls and rumbling growls. What she didn't expect was the leader skidding to a halt just before them, raising a pistol, and aiming at the middle of Abalim's forehead.

"By *Ichor's Holdings*, boy! Did you do that to us?" the female snapped, her brilliant emerald-green eyes narrowed. "Put us in stasis?"

Talk about imposing! Lisa had no idea who this.... this female person thought she was. And she definitely wasn't human. Her skin tone was a rich coral color that looked amazing with her one-piece leather battle suit in butterscotch yellow. Talk about intimidating. Lisa's eyes narrowed. Taking in the female's otherworldly beauty made her mouth dry. No one should look that good, pissed off as she was.

"Now, why would I do that?"

At Abalim's calm answer, Lisa's hands gripped into fists. Damn man seemed awfully chummy with the pretty alien with the silky metallic-gold hair.

"You humans are known for reneging on your allies if it suits you." The woman's blaster hadn't moved. The muzzle was a mere centimeter from the middle of Abalim's forehead. "Why were we held hostage on our ship?"

"The Xeltrians did that, not me." Abalim widened his arms. "I'd much rather you monitored the situation than be paralyzed where you couldn't help me if I needed it." He cocked his head. "If the Xeltrians didn't let you go, how did you get free?"

She lowered the blaster and pursed her lips.

Her perfect, full upper and lower lips. The type of mouth that would tear Angelina Jolie's title of the Queen of Hollywood Lips away. Lisa suspected the rich, darkened color of those stupid lips was natural.

Now the blaster pointed at her.

"Is this the human female you were looking for?"

She crossed her arms. "My name is Lisa." She raised an eyebrow and her mouth tightened. "And you are?"

After a quick up-and-down perusal, the condescending smirk on the female's face made the back of Lisa's neck heat. Okay, the bitch and she were going to have words.

"I am Captain Saphira of the *Galactic Serpent*." The woman's smile widened as she put the blaster into a holster at her hip. "And this is my crew." She nodded to the people behind her.

Lisa tore her gaze away from Saphira and checked out the others. While the small group looked a lot like Saphira with their coral-colored skin, there was one little guy who had to be a completely different species.

He was a wiry scamp of a thing that couldn't be more than three feet tall. It was impossible to see most of his body since he was in a cape made of different colored patches, and kept a hood over his head. The only thing visible was his scaly face, mottled with shades of green-yellow. What stood out were his orange-red bulbous eyes.

For some reason, he gave her the impression that not much got by him. She attempted to open her psychic eye to check him out, just to see if he was dangerous or not. What she got back was confusing. She didn't get the impression of menace, but what came through was a sense of subterfuge. As she studied him, his eyes widened, as if claiming his innocence. Like she was dumb enough to believe that crap.

He clicked and whistled with a smirk.

Freakin' alien better not be laughing at her.

"Saphira, I'm glad to see you are all okay. But how did you get free?" Abalim asked in a firm tone.

"I'm not without my own resources." With her hand on one hip, she pulled out a necklace from her cleavage.

A teardrop gem dangled at the end of the thin metal necklace. It twirled in the dim light of the hallway, and at first, it was hard to tell what it was made of. Its sheen changed from light to dark and back again in the low deceiving light. It winked with an inner silver glow and looked like the Lumicor crystal the Lumarians used to power Echovara.

Darn thing was really pretty. She wanted one.

"This is my Soile crystal." Saphira twirled the gem, creating a swirling, soft inner light. "This is a rare jewel that circumvents any type of mental control that is put on me." She shrugged. "Once I was freed from the mental paralysis, it was easy enough to do the same for my crew." She narrowed her green eyes at Abalim. "I told you we came here to find our missing people." She waved a hand to encompass the long corridor and its endless doors. "Since we've been on this planet, Aera has emotionally connected with her daughter Eeveas." She pointed to the door next to Abalim. "And we believe she's in there."

"We've got to get in there now!" One of the females behind Saphira grabbed her, her pulsating orange eyes swimming with tears. "I sense she's in pain." She warbled a cry when she sucked in her lower lip after the last word.

"Are you sure she's in there, Aera?" Saphira patted the older woman's hand.

"Yes! Yes! I know she's in there. I can feel she has begun her birth pains!" Aera's brick-red ponytail bounced with each emphatic nod. "I have to be there with her!"

Lisa crossed her arms and studied the door. "How are we supposed to get in?" As far as she could tell, there weren't any knobs or buttons to make it open.

"Allow me."

Lisa jumped at the melodious male voice behind her. She turned and stepped back.

It was Rerqel. Of course it was Rerqel. Who else would it be?

***

The Xeltrian had to have teleported since Abalim didn't sense him until he spoke. He frowned. Damn alien sneaking up on him was irritating as hell.

"Why were you holding Captain Saphira and her crew hostage?" Abalim asked. "As a matter of fact, why are you holding all of these species hostage?"

The gangly alien spread his arms wide. "How else are we to learn about them?" Rerqel sauntered closer to the group. "I can assure you, none of them were harmed."

"Not harmed!" Aera stomped to the taller alien with clenched fists. "You have my daughter here, and she is pregnant with her first child!" She shook one of those fists at him. "How dare you take her away from her family when she needs us the most?" She pulled her arm back as if getting ready to slug him.

One of Saphira's security guards, Aesel, if Abalim wasn't mistaken, clamped a hard hold around her wrist before she let her arm fly.

When Aera looked back at him, he shook his head and gathered her into a comforting embrace.

The older Crichian stood stiffly, but kept her clenched fists over her stomach and gave the Xeltrian a hard glare.

Rerqel straightened as if insulted. His almost nonexistent mouth pursed in a frown. "I'll have you know that most of these species would be extinct now if not for us. We have taken them from planets that were dying, either by their own hands or by natural disasters, and gave them a new home. I assure you, none are the wiser. Take the Lumarians, for example. Their planet Nexoros was in the throes of destruction due to their warlike ways. They let their technology get away from them, and if it wasn't for us, they would've all died eons ago. We brought them here so they could live. Is that not a worthy cause?"

"Our species isn't on the brink of destruction." Saphira countered with a firm tone. "You had no right to kidnap any of our citizens."

Rerqel's forehead wrinkled. "Are you certain about that? The entire galaxy is on the brink of collapse with the oncoming invasion of the Krystalii. Would you not want your species to continue if we can ensure your people continue to exist?"

"What? You think sneaking around and stealing people from their families and homes is better than offering them a way to work with you?" Lisa snorted. "That doesn't seem like a very advanced directive to me."

Abalim took in a deep, satisfying breath. His woman had no fear of defending those she felt were wronged. A swirling, fluttery pang in his belly tightened. His woman? Did he really think of her like that? He glanced at her standing next to him.

She'd pulled her wheat-colored hair behind her ears, leaving the messy strands to fly free around her shoulders. Her fiery dark-blue eyes sparkled as she glowered at the Xeltrian. Someone looking at Lisa for the first time might not recognize what a unique beauty she was.

Here was a person who held the universe in awe at its endless possibilities for romance and connection. Her look on life, her passion for what was right and wrong, guided every move she made.

By the God An, he wanted to spend the rest of his life uncovering every facet of her personality. But what did he have to offer her? An ex-slave who was lost in this new era? Someone who still had to discover who he was. How could he weigh her down with half a man? The only thing he could offer was to protect her from others taking advantage of her. Maybe she, in turn, would show him how to live life to the fullest as a free man.

He turned to Rerqel. "Let's focus on one thing at a time, shall we? Why don't you let us reunite these folks with their people? We've sensed this female's daughter is in pain and is desperate for her mother." He put his arm around Lisa's shoulders. *I promise we'll talk to them later about this. But right now, let's focus on getting inside that room so they can calm everybody down.* He spoke to her on their telepathic path and sent a tendril of calm.

Fine. She replied in like manner. *But I think this ass needs to learn he can't treat people like some kind of science experiment all the time.*

Rerqel didn't move a muscle, but the solid door dissolved away, revealing a normal-sized entryway. "Agreed. You may enter."

When Lisa made a move to go in, he gripped her in place. *Let Saphira and her crew go in first,* he mentally suggested.

The two of them followed the Crichian and paused at the doorway.

His eyes widened as Saphira and her crew's emotions exploded with fear and awe.

"Is that the city of Islezaa?" Yve cried. "How is that possible?"

"What is this horror?" Saphira spun on Rerqel. "Did you somehow rip our entire capital city from Crichi and bring it here?"

Keeping his arm around Lisa, Abalim maneuvered them to have a better view. What he saw took his breath away.

They stood on a hilltop overlooking a sprawling valley. The sky above was a kaleidoscopic tapestry of multiple moons with nearby planets visible in the skyline, even in daylight. Their surfaces were tinged in shades of teal and lavender. Cosmic dust clouds refracted the sunlight, casting otherworldly rainbows in the sky. It looked like an ever-changing abstract painting.

The ground emanated a soft, ambient glow. Vegetation in rows that would make any farmer proud gathered in clusters, with leaves a mesmerizing mix of metallic colors. Here and there were bodies of water that shimmered like gems, the rippling water reflecting the dynamic sky above.

But the city itself was the crowning glory of the scene. Islezaa glowed with an ethereal opalescence, as if lit inside by magic. Sculptural skyscrapers rose in spirals and arches adorned with patterns reminiscent of the natural flora around it that shifted in hues in a choreographed dance of light. Floating platforms hovered like dragonflies throughout the buildings, connected by shimmering energy bridges rippling as if made of liquid glass. It was a celestial ballet of technology and natural beauty.

"Holy soaring space dung!" Lisa cried, gripping his hand draped over her shoulder. "Have you seen anything so freaking gorgeous in your life?"

He couldn't help it. "Only you, my inkheart. Only you."

Chapter Thirteen

Okay, that's it. Whenever the man opened his mouth and spouted such romantic mush, Lisa melted into a puddle of goo. Well... she'd show him. With a languorous ease, she swept her eyes over him, sending him a sultry, lingering promise. An unspoken invitation to ignite a fire no words could convey.

Abalim's Adam's apple bobbed as he gulped. His languid eyes half-draped like velvet curtains hiding deep secrets. He took her hand in his and brought it up to his full lips and gave her a lingering kiss. "I cannot wait until we are alone again."

"That makes two of us," she whispered, leaning forward, offering her mouth to his.

Before they could make contact, Saphira interrupted them. "Are you coming or not?"

Lisa grimaced and glanced away. She sucked her lower lip, aching to have Abalim cover it with his. With a sigh, she watched the other aliens enter the portal. They hurried toward the city in the distance.

"I don't think so," Abalim replied.

Lisa swung her attention back to him.

He looked at Rerqel. "He and I have a few things to work out first."

The Xeltrian gave a slight nod.

"If it's all right with you"—he addressed Saphira—"we'll meet you back on the *Galactic Serpent* when you're finished here."

Saphira's vibrant-green eyes narrowed. "That's fine with me." She glanced at JR15 on his shoulder. "Remember, keep your little friend out of my systems."

"Yes, ma'am." Abalim's answer came with a sincere small smile. "Your wish will be honored."

Saphira snorted. "See that it is." She glanced over her shoulder as if to check on her crew members before turning her attention back to them. "Shall I have the ship transport you up?"

"That won't be necessary," Rerqel interjected. "I will ensure their safe return." He waved his spindly fingers. "You may go."

Wow, Lisa thought. *Spoken like the arrogant jerk he is.*

I suspect it's natural for him. Abalim spoke to her on their private psychic channel.

Saphira gave the other alien a long look before she nodded and followed her friends.

Lisa watched the pretty captain trot away before facing Rerqel and Abalim. "What now? Are we going to the ship you talked about?"

Abalim crossed his arms and widened his stance as he faced the Xeltrian. "Can we go somewhere more comfortable than this?" He tilted his chin to indicate the endless corridor.

Lisa swore Rerqel's thin lips lifted in a wavering attempt of a smile.

"Of course."

His last word echoed in her head as the surroundings changed. Instead of the dim light of the hallway, she now stood in a strange-looking room. If she didn't know any better, she'd believe she was on the bridge of the *Enterprise* of Star Trek mixed with something completely different.

Bioluminescent panels pulsated with a soothing rhythm, illuminating the room in a kaleidoscope of soft, glowing colors. What might be control stations rose from the floor in ergonomic, glassy sculptures. In the center, something that had to be a command console hovered without any visible support. Its surface was a dynamic mosaic of shifting symbols and projections of star maps.

The ceiling arched into a translucent dome, giving her a panoramic view of the orbiting planet.

"Are you okay?" Abalim put his large hands on her shoulders.

Lisa took in a deep breath and nodded. The air was charged with a subtle, sweet fragrance mixed with an unknown flora. Quite like the air coming from the portal to Islezaa. "I'm great." She gestured to the room. "Hey, did he just sneak us aboard the spaceship you talked about?"

"Yes, Ms. Lisa, ma'am," JR15 answered from his perch on Abalim's shoulder. "This is Captain Saphira's ship, the *Galactic Serpent*."

"Interesting place for you to take us to." Abalim's dark eyes narrowed on the alien. "Care to tell us why we're here and not somewhere on Qorath?"

"It is more expedited this way," the willowy Xeltrian replied. "You see, I will be going with you to the Chancellor's

Palace. I wish to coordinate the resistance to the Krystalii with the galactic government."

Lisa gasped and put her fingers over her lips. "You mean you're going to help us?" She glanced at Abalim. "That's a good thing, isn't it?"

"What made you decide that?" Abalim's stiff posture made it clear he didn't trust what the alien told them.

"We were impressed when you worked together without having any sort of history with each other. You respected each other's vastly different upbringings. And when you went into the Lumarian village, you did not try to force the villagers into doing what you believed would be the right thing. You worked with them to help them discover a better alternative. Even if the alternative went against their traditions."

Rerqel glided to the rounded display showcasing his rotating planet. He appeared to be studying it before he turned around to face them. He clasped his spindly fingers together and tilted his head. "But most of all, you were able to work with the Krystalii called Aollu, even after he threatened you. Both of you went out of your way with him while ensuring his actions would not harm the Lumarians. This shows an ability to decide what is best for all involved rather than your own small, petty concerns."

Lisa's lips thinned. Damn. He just insulted them with praise. "So, what now?" She asked, crossing her arms.

Rerqel once again focused on the display of Qorath. "For the first time in several millennia, we cannot foresee the future." His voice retained the sound of multiple people talking, as if they all spoke in one voice. "The only thing clear to us is I must go with you. Only then will we have a chance to halt the dimensional invasion from the Krystalii." His large eyes blinked sideways as his pasty skin darkened. "We are ashamed to admit their capabilities far outweigh ours."

Wow. That must've taken some heavy-duty balls to admit that. From the moment she'd met the Xeltians, they acted godlike, as if nothing could touch them. It was kind of scary they felt as vulnerable as anyone else.

"We are very grateful for your support." Abalim put an arm around Lisa's shoulders and pulled her close. "Is there anything you need from us before Saphira and her crew come back?"

"No." The sound of his reply came out wispy. "I will await here for the crew to return and discuss my intentions with them at that time." This tiny mouth once again curled into a slight grin. "If they are resistant due to the way we took their fellow Crichians, I may need your assistance to ensure my continued health."

"Yeah, imagine that. The nerve of some people getting a little testy when you go around kidnapping and threatening their family." Lisa snorted. "I think when this is all over, I'd appreciate it if we could revisit that little zoo you've got going on."

Rerqel stood frozen, his unblinking black eyes staring at her.

She stiffed so she wouldn't squirm under his scrutiny.

Abalim squeezed her shoulder. "Something to consider much later," he said. "But for now, Lisa and I are going to find something to eat and retire until we leave." Abalim gave a slight nod. "If you have need of us, just send me a mental query and I will respond." He tugged her close. "Hang on." He whispered in her ear before the scene changed in an instant.

***

Instead of standing on the alien bridge, Abalim teleported him and Lisa to the room he'd been given to sleep in aboard the *Galactic Serpent*. It wasn't much to look at. Just a small, windowless room lit by soft blue-green light reflected against the black metal walls. The only furniture in the room was a single bed jutting from the wall without any visible means of support hovering over the floor. On top of the bed was a pile of blankets made of plush, patterned materials and a few fluffy pillows.

Lisa pulled away and glanced over her shoulder. "Where are we?"

Her cute little nose scrunched.

"I teleported us to the room they let me use on the *Galactic Serpent*." He couldn't resist caressing the back of her head to feel her silky blonde strands. "I thought while we waited for Saphira and her crew to come back, we would take this time for ourselves."

She stepped back and held onto his forearms with her head tilted. "You're just going to leave Rerqel on the bridge all by himself? Do you think that's a good idea?"

He nodded. "Good point. JR15? If I teleported you back to the bridge, would you keep an eye on our Xeltrian guest and let me know if he does anything suspicious?"

"I will, Mister Abalim, sir!" The butt of his green and silver body wiggled as if excited. "And I will let you know when the Crichians come back."

"Have you linked back with the *Galactic Serpent*s communications?" Saphira may have told him that JR15 couldn't access the ship's systems, but she didn't say anything about him not accessing their transmissions going in or out of the ship. Not to mention any interesting internal talk.

"I never closed the channel I have with the ship, Mister Abalim, sir," JR15 replied.

Abalim grunted. He should've known that was something his little droid would do. "That's good. Listen, I want you to contact your father and update him on what's going on here. If you have to, use the communications on the ship's systems to give you a boost." He held his hand out.

JR15 scuttled from his shoulder and settled on his palm. "Yes, Mister Abalim, sir. I can't wait to tell him everything we've done!"

Abalim brought the bot closer to his face. "I'll set you on the communication panel there on the bridge. Keep yourself out of sight and try to make sure Rerqel doesn't know you're watching him. If you have any trouble, don't hesitate to come back here right away. Okay?"

"I'm quite sure I won't have any trouble." JR15 gave a little dance.

Abalim gave his companion one last look before sending him back to the bridge. With a sigh, he lowered his hand. Not for the first time, he wished he had some type of psychic connection with his droid friend. He didn't like sending the small bot to places where it might not be safe for him.

"There he goes again," Lisa stated in a soft voice, with a gentle touch on his elbow.

He gave her a reassuring smile. "I don't think Rerqel would do anything to hurt him." He gave a small chuckle. "Besides, that Xeltrian is psychically strong enough that he could do anything he wanted to us. It's not like a small droid could stop him."

"Well, that's a comforting thought." Lisa hummed and glanced at the messy bed he'd left behind.

Her sarcasm made him grin. Putting his forefinger under her chin, he brought her face around.

She gazed at him with steady bright-blue eyes.

"I admit, I selfishly brought you here to be with you. But first—" He nodded to the opposite wall from the bed. "—there's a food replicator here we can use. I don't know about you, but I'm famished." He drew her close to whisper seductively in her ear. "We're going to need our strength for later." His smile widened when she shivered.

"Hmm, later, eh?" She pulled back, gifting him a seductive smile of her own.

Her sensuous tone sent chills down his spine. As if his hands had a will of their own, he splayed his fingers wide across her satiny throat. His other hand rested on the gentle swell of her breasts. Touching her made it hard to breathe, hard to think of anything but how he reacted when touching her soft, fragrant skin.

"Yes, later," he whispered at the corner of her mouth. Her warmth ramped up his anticipation and his breath caught, trapped. To save himself, he swooped in and seized her lips. Her mouth was hot, an open invitation for his possession. Food became the furthest thing from his mind. The entire universe centered where they were joined. The lustful hunger rose out of nowhere, consuming him. It took away any sense he had and replaced it with savage need. Her moan filled his mouth with a need all her own.

Abalim broke off the kiss and latched his mouth onto her neck. He darted his tongue across her skin as he drew in her tantalizing scent. He then trailed featherlight licks over the front of her throat. When his mouth touched her chin, he peppered it with gentle nibbles. His body hardened in reaction, thickening against her. He returned to the base of her throat and swirled his lips and tongue over her pulse. At the same time, he palmed her breast through the malleable fabric of the alien suit she wore.

"Abalim." she whispered, gripping his thick, long hair.

The woman was every bit as possessive as he was. With a grunt, he lowered his mouth to the hard peak of her breast, allowing his tongue to replace his fingers. He laved her nipple over the fabric, coaxing the nubbin into a harder point, reveling in the heat of her skin as he filled his mouth and suckled.

When he moved his mouth from her breast, he gathered her in his arms and pulled her fully flush against him. Their heartbeats thundered in unison, strong and fast. He returned to the tempting skin of her neck and scraped his teeth back and forth over the pulse beating so frantically. Desire pounded through him, making him frantic to consummate their union. To show her how much she meant to him.

The sound of her stomach growling yanked him back to reality.

"Oh, my gosh!" Lisa put a hand over her stomach. "How embarrassing." She stepped back with a sheepish grin.

Abalim inhaled to slow his racing heart. Her musky perfume, along with their combined excitement, blanketed the air between them. He caressed her cheek with his thumb. "No, I'm grateful for the reprieve. I promised to feed you, and here

I'm letting myself get carried away." He took her hand and led her to the plush pile on the messy bed. "Sit here and I'll bring you something to eat." He raised her knuckles to plant a gentle kiss. "But I warn you. Once we're done, we'll explore other ways to give you gratification."

Her mischievous smile warmed his heart. "Gratification?" She chuckled. "I sure like the sound of that."

***

Never, Lisa decided as she ate with Abalim, ever had she'd enjoyed a meal as much as this one. Even if she couldn't identify half of what the man put into her mouth. He insisted he feed her from the picnic feast he created with the room's replicator. To make things comfier, he pulled a blanket from the bed and spread it on the floor, giving them a perfect place to lounge on while they ate.

When he spread the food before her, her mouth dropped open. My god, what a bounty! On one plate were delicate, spiral shaped canapes, glowing faintly with a blue hue that exuded a sweet, tangy aroma. On a plate beside it lay crispy ruby-red tendrils, crackling softly. Their spicy, smoky flavor reminded her of mouthwatering barbecued treats that coated her mouth with an exotic, slightly metallic aftertaste. It turned out one of her favorites came from a pile of fluffy, golden puffs. Displayed in a tantalizing pyramid, they emitted a cloud of savory steam that blanketed the air with hints of garlic and some unknown but intoxicating alien herb.

For dessert, nestled in a crystal bowl, were small, translucent orbs filled with a shimmering liquid. When Lisa put one in her mouth, a refreshing mix of mint and citrus left a burst of pleasant, cooling savory goodness behind.

But it was the easy and open conversation she and Abalim had that brought an added layer of decadent pleasure to the meal. Her earlier fears of them not being compatible melted away. Here was a man who had his own strong opinions and wasn't afraid of hers. Exactly the kind of relationship she'd always dreamed about. There was only one thing that she couldn't wait to clear up.

"I do have one question that's been bugging me since I met you." Lisa sat back and suckled one of the luscious dessert orbs.

"Oh?" Abalim's dark brows rose. "What's that?"

Her brain checked out at the sensual way he suckled his own dessert orb with his full lips. She almost lost her train of thought.

Almost.

"Um, you've been calling me inkheart since we met. What's up with that?" It was a weird thing for an ancient like him to use as an endearment.

Abalim's dark cheeks flushed as he chuckled and spread his hands wide. "Ok, here's where I confess how I let one of my nephews talk me into something."

Lisa smiled and settled back. This ought to be good.

"My nephew, Pete, is a bit of a harmless prankster. Reminds me of my brother Asmodel." He smirked and rubbed his earlobe. "Anyway, once things settled down from the invasion, he claimed it was his duty to indoctrinate my brothers and me into modern society." With his finger and thumb, he plucked another dessert orb and put it into his mouth.

For the first time there was a hesitancy in his obsidian gaze, something in the way his full lashes lowered quickly, then flicked up. After a few chews with his eyes unfocused, he swallowed and then brought his attention back to her.

"He warned us he was about to expose us to something that held mankind in a tight, unrelenting grip. No one was immune to its influence. While it was mostly viewed as a good thing, in the wrong hands, it could be twisted into coercing parts of the population into doing evil and harm against others."

Lisa frowned. What in the world was he talking about?

"With those dire warnings, he introduced us to movies."

She blinked. Movies? What the...

He chuckled. "And he promised the first movie would give us a historical glimpse into mankind and how they viewed life in general."

Her eyebrows raised. "Oh lordy. What movie did he show you?"

"Monty Python's *The Meaning of Life.*"

Lisa couldn't help it. She whooped with laughter. "Oh my God, my mother made me watch that ridiculous movie when I was a teenager! Please tell me that's not the only movie you've seen."

His smile was full of mirth. "No, but when that movie was over, Pete claimed we had to know how humans viewed aliens. So he played *Galaxy Quest.*" He laughed and grabbed another dessert ball, chewed, then spoke. "By the time that movie was over, we were terrified of being around humans. The prospect of becoming slaves again looked pretty good." He chuckled. "Thank the God An, his older brother Raiden put a stop to

Pete's teasing and explained how movies were supposed to be for entertainment and not "historical" vids like Pete claimed."

Abalim leaned back on one of his elbows and crossed his ankles. "Then Raiden went into detail about the human need for storytelling. And the fascinating people who created those tales and legends that have been handed down throughout the centuries."

She grinned and wrapped her arms around her bent knees. "That's a great story, but you haven't answered my question. Why do you call me inkheart?"

"Well, by then, the whole family joined us and declared we needed a movie-marathon night. When they asked us if we had any special interests, I told them I was fascinated by how these stories came about. That's when they explained the concept of people called authors and how they created these fantastic tales.

"I was so fascinated by the process of anyone creating an unknown reality, one of my nephew's wives, Julienne, insisted I watch a movie called *Inkheart*. I think she had a crush on the leading actor, but I found myself drawn to the drama of people who wrote stories from just their imagination, giving it a life of its own. Whenever possible, I devoured what I could about the variety of authors throughout the centuries."

"And then I met you."

His intense gaze made her speechless.

"Here you were, someone who fabricated stories out of thin air and put them into worlds that didn't exist. You gave them a solid foundation for all the trials and tribulations to work through." Abalim chuckled. "I confess, while on the *Galactic Serpent* headed here, I had JR15 download several of your novels to an eReader I created with the help of their replicator." He leaned closer to her. "I especially loved how you had the uncanny foresight to end your stories with a satisfying, happy ending."

As if he said something that startled him, Abalim jerked his head back and frowned, moving away from her. "Well, this has been nice, but as we know, real life has a way of inserting itself." He glanced over her shoulder before facing her again. He didn't look her in the eye. "Once we leave here, what are your plans?"

Lisa pressed her lips together. "What do you mean, what are my plans? The Krystalii must be stopped, and I'm gonna be a part of that!"

His smile was weak. "Yes, I understand that. But what happens afterward? I mean, what I'm asking, is since you didn't get a chance to attend the alien exchange program, do you plan to go back to it?"

Her mouth opened and closed like a cod fish as her thoughts raced. "Why in the world I be interested in going to that after meeting you?" Did she completely misunderstand what happened between them? How could the man not know what he meant to her? He was a freaking psychic, for God's sake! You'd think he'd not only see what he meant to her in her mind, but he'd feel what she did.

She bit her bottom lip to stop from spouting something stupid. For once, she opened her new psychic ability to sense what he was feeling. What came back shocked her. Anguish, anxiety, defeat, and sadness mixed with a healthy dose of fear.

He shrugged. "You know you don't have to still see me when we go back."

His monotone voice made her scowl. Okay, that was it. Meal over. If the big jerk hadn't figured out how she felt about him, it was time to prove it.

Keeping her eyes glued to his, she plucked away the food he held and threw it over her shoulder. Its soft landing on the blanket was ignored. Mesmerized by his intense, dark gaze, she gathered the strength needed to declare once and for all what she felt about him. "Listen here, mister. You and I belong together." She reached out and brushed one of his dreadlocks away from his striking features. "We share a deep connection that transcends the mere word *love*." She leaned into him and kissed the side of his mouth before whispering, "I dare you to tell me I'm wrong."

He shook his head, his eyes squeezed shut. "You—" He swallowed hard, and his Adam's apple bobbed. "You... I didn't want to presume..."

She kissed the other side of his full lips. Silly man. She'd make sure before they left this room that he'd have no doubts about them being together. At all. "I give you full permission to merge your mind with mine." His breath on her face was warm, inviting. The skin of his mouth was so soft, so persuasive, it made her heart leap. "I love you with every fiber of my being, Abalim. I am the keeper of your heart, as you are the keeper of mine. Join with me, know me, and leave all your doubts behind."

His lips crushed hers in a devouring, masterful stroke. His mouth was hot and male and exciting. Lisa circled his neck with her arms. Together, they entered a world of hunger and passion. She slid her hands over his suit to caress his well-defined muscles. She ached, and her body turned liquid and needy.

"Abalim." His name came out in a tortured whisper.

He gave her lower lip a gentle nibble. "Shall I give you all that I am, inkheart?" His hand shaped her breast, and his thumb teased her nipple into a hard peak. He leaned down until his mouth replaced his hand over the soft mound, hot and moist, sucking through the fabric of her suit.

Lisa arched and caught his hair to drag him closer. An insane fever rose inside her, a physical tsunami threatening to take over. Her knees went weak, and she cried out, afraid she'd shatter.

He licked along the valley between her breasts.

"Yes." She strangled a reply and surrendered. Just like that, the master became the servant.

"We have too many clothes on." His voice was husky.

When he spoke the last word, cool air caressed Lisa's body in all the places Abalim didn't cover. No time to marvel at the wondrous way he made them both naked. She wiggled her hips and kneaded his dark tresses with a whimper. The slick feel of his taut skin against hers ramped up the spinning sensation deep inside her womb. Unable to resist the urge, Lisa burrowed her hand between their groins and grasped his thick length, her fingertips memorizing the feel and shape of his heavy erection. With her touch strong and sure, she traced every inch of him as her fingers danced and played with him.

"Lisa." Her name came out somewhere between agony and ecstasy.

Releasing her hold, she pushed at his immobile chest, craving to taste the treat her hand explored. "Let me... I want..."

His dazed expression told her he wasn't listening. "Abalim... move!"

"No, my love. I will not last if your luscious lips touch me there. I need you too much. Now, like this." With gentle strength, he nudged her knees apart and settled his firm groin inside the cradle of hers. The heat of his steel as he entered her became everything. Inch by slow inch.

She shuddered with pleasure as he drove himself home.

He caught her hips in his large hands, gripped her tight, and surged inside, burying himself deep.

Lisa's body rippled with life, an oncoming cataclysm destined to send her into space. Never had she expected that what she held dear would narrow down to one man. To this one person who moved in perfect unison with her.

As his body drove into hers with long, hard surges, their minds merged. Like two halves becoming one.

His fingers wound in her hair while his hips rotated in a maddening rhythm, teasing her slick womanhood. The hood holding her clit unfurled as if it had a mind of its own. Each movement between them created a fire that burned and spread. Flames took over, and an intense heat roared in her ears. Hunger built, then swamped her with burgeoning energy until she was frantic.

Then, it was too much. Dark, endless joy rushed through her, squeezing low and bursting free. She screamed with the intensity of it as Abalim's body shuddered above and around her.

"Lisa." His groan rumbled seductively, deep in his chest. "My inkheart. I can't tell you how grateful I am we are together. I love you with everything I am." He rolled them so they faced one another on their sides. With a gentle smile, he brushed the wayward, damp strands of her hair away from her eyes.

His unwavering gaze bore into her, and her heart skipped a beat.

Abalim's sincere claim brought tears to her eyes. "Oh, Abalim. What I feel for you is beyond mere words." She concentrated on opening her mind, making sure he felt what she had a hard time putting into words. But she had to try. "I'm so in love with you, I can't imagine living my life without you."

She caressed one of his high cheekbones with her forefinger. His skin was warm to the touch, but firm. "You've captured me completely. I confess I'm addicted to your touch, your kiss, your voice. You're the only one who makes me feel this way. You are my life, and I'm yours."

He stilled. Keeping his dark gaze on her, he brought her hand to his mouth and gave it a soft kiss across her knuckles. "I have so much to learn about this new time I find myself in." He cocked his head. "Not to mention the strange creatures coming for us from another dimension. Are you sure you want to put up with someone who doesn't understand what's going on more often than not?"

She scoffed and shook her head. "You know more than anyone I've ever met in my life." She traced the soft mound of his bottom lip. "We'll face everything together and win." She leaned in and gave him a soft kiss. "No matter what."

His masculine grin made her insides quiver. With a deft move, he wrapped her in his arms and spun them until she was firmly under him once again.

She widened her legs to let him in. And he did, sliding inside her slick entrance as if she was made for him. She moaned in response.

"Yes," he murmured in her ear. "No matter what."

Epilogue

"**A**balim, wake the *fruk* up."

Abalim jerked and opened his eyes. Instead of snuggling with Lisa in his quarters aboard the *Galactic Serpent*, he found himself in a familiar room millions of parsecs away. It was his brother Adapa's man cave that he used whenever he generated a Dreamwalk.

Glancing around the tranquil, intimate room, he enjoyed the deep, rich wood aroma of the wall paneling and floors. The homey scent of the dark leather chairs and couch. Settling into the leather recliner across from Adapa, he glanced around. It was obvious he and his brother were alone.

"About time." Adapa grunted. "What were you, drugged or something?" The man sprawled on the couch across from Abalim. One hand was on the backrest while he held his favorite jug of dark ale with the other, with one ankle resting over his knee.

Abalim had no intention of explaining his exhaustion was due to the lovemaking marathon he'd indulged in with Lisa. Damn woman was as insatiable as he was. "Why are we alone?" He swiveled his head to make sure he didn't miss anybody. "Where are our brothers?"

Adapa narrowed his eyes and took a long drag of his drink before answering. "Don't worry, they're on their way. You're the last one I had to get in touch with." He straightened and put the stein holding his stout on the dark wood coffee table in front of him.

Taking a full breath, the aroma of the sharp creamy hops from the drink made Abalim grin in appreciation. He couldn't wait to get back to Earth to get the same drink in his hands.

"Things are happening faster than we thought possible." Adapa sat back, splaying both arms across the back of the couch and spreading his legs wide. "Your little friend, Lord Baelon, appeared around the planet Zerin and its moon, where the Chancellor's Palace is. They've responded with a full contingency of battleships. You've got to get back here now. Whether you found the human woman or not." He cocked his head. "So? Did you find her?"

Abalim leaned back in the comfortable cushion of the leather chair. "As a matter of fact, I have. Right now, we're waiting for the crew of the *Galactic Serpent* to return before we head back." He scratched the side of his bristled jaw. "But even if we left right now, we wouldn't arrive at Zerin for at least a month."

The hair on the back of his neck rose at the smirk creasing Adapa's mouth. He hated it when the damn ass knew something he didn't.

"Lucky for you, we've obtained new space-folding schematics from a friendly source and downloaded them into your JR unit. All you have to do is get your, ah, hosts to allow him to share it with them." He tapped fingers of one of his hands on the back of the couch. "Convince them it's a boon for them helping you get back to us so soon."

Abalim doubted Saphira would have any qualms about grabbing something like that.

"That is not needed."

A new voice next to Abalim made him jump. Son of a bitch! How in the hell did Rerqel sneak in here without him or his brother knowing?

"Who the *fruk* are you?" Adapa stood with slow and measured intent. The tendons in his neck bulged as his jaw clenched.

Abalim waved his hand for his brother to sit before he did something stupid. "Sit down, Adapa, before you embarrass yourself." He thumbed at the gangly alien standing between them. "This is Rerqel. A Xeltrian from the planet Qorath." He laced his fingers on his lap. "He's a powerful psychic in his own right. And has been our, ah, host for the last few days."

"And he is here why?" His brother scowled and thumped back onto the couch.

"I have no idea. Let's ask him." Abalim faced the Xeltrian. "Why are you here?"

"I am here to expedite our voyage to the planet Zerin." Rerqel's large eyes blinked sideways. "I believe that is what you were discussing, am I correct?"

"Condescending asshole, isn't he?" Adapa mused with a twinkle in his eye as he addressed Abalim.

Abalim snorted. "You have no idea."

"Time is of the essence, and it is best we coordinate our efforts before the Krystalii are ready to strike." Rerqel ignored their banter. "I fear if we don't join our defenses now, all efforts will be in vain."

"Didn't you tell me you couldn't get a clear premonition about the upcoming war with them?" Abalim frowned.

"That is so." Rerqel clasped his fingers together limply in front of him. "However, collectively we have ascertained how the Krystalii plan on overtaking this galaxy."

"Ah, brain over psychic visions. How original." Adapa smirked.

"This is no laughing matter, hybrid," the Xeltrian snapped.

Abalim's eyebrows rose at Rerqel's show of anger. Wow, the guy experienced fear. Now, wasn't that scary as hell?

Adapa's brows furrowed. "Care to share what you've come up with?"

"Agreed." Rerqel widened his arms as if to embrace them. "Listen closely. There isn't much time."

While Lisa and Abalim have found their Happily Ever After... the adventure continues in Book 2 - Asmodel

Also by Keri Kruspe

Watch for more at https://www.kerikruspe.com/.

About the Author

"Author of otherworldly romantic adventures"

A writer since the age of twelve, Keri Kruspe has always been fascinated with otherworldly stories that end with the dream of Happily Ever After.

A native Nevadan, Keri resides with her family in the wilds of Northwest Michigan where she enjoys the stark change in seasons and the pleasures each one brings. An avid reader, Keri loves an enjoyable bottle of red wine, a variety of delicious foods and watching action/adventure movies...usually at the same time. You can find her most days immersed in her fantasy world on her latest novel while foot tappin' to classic rock. When not absorbed in her writing, Keri works alongside her husband in building their dream home or discovering intelligent life in America in their RV.

Read more at https://www.kerikruspe.com/.